Good
Heavens

Good Heavens

A Novel

Margaret A. Graham

Fleming H. Revell
A Division of Baker Book House Co
Grand Rapids, Michigan 49516

Published by Fleming H. Revell
a division of Baker Book House Company
P.O. Box 6287, Grand Rapids, MI 49516-6287
www.bakerbooks.com

Printed in the United States of America

Library of Congress Cataloging-in-Publication Data
Graham, Margaret, 1924-
   Good heavens : a novel / Margaret A. Graham.
       p.   cm.
   ISBN 0-8007-5938-9 (pbk.)
   1. Housemothers—Fiction. 2. Young women—Fiction. I. Title.
   PS3557.R2157G66 2004
   813′.54—dc22   2003024362

Scripture is taken from the King James Version of the Bible.

For
Cindy VanSandt,
a gifted pianist who gives me
oceans of emotions.

Common sense is genius in homespun.

Alfred North Whitehead

1

Taking a job at the Priscilla Home was the farthest thing from my mind when Dr. Elsie asked me to consider it. Well, actually, she hardly *asked* me to consider it; she just as much as *told* me I was going. When I realized she was serious, I knew I had to set her straight before she railroaded me right out of South Carolina to the regions beyond.

"Dr. Elsie, have you forgot how old I am? The day has passed when I could say I'm pushing sixty from before or after the fact."

She just looked at me as much as to say, "So what?"

Now, I respect Dr. Elsie. She's done a lot for me personally as well as for the people in Live Oaks, and I'd do anything she asked of me—anything within reason, that is. This was out of the question. So I told her, "I'm retired, and right now I have got more on my plate than I can handle."

She sipped her ice tea and kept all her attention on the

birds at the feeder, so I added, "You know I have only went through the eighth grade."

I wasn't telling her anything she didn't already know, so nothing I said fazed her. I tried another tact. "Sounds like your board is scraping the bottom of the barrel to find somebody."

"No," she said. "There are other applicants."

"I can't imagine anybody asking for a job that means living way up there in the woods. . . . You say it's the job of resident manager? What kind of a job is that?"

"Fancy name for housemother."

"Housemother? Housemother to a bunch of women addicts?" I laughed. "The women in the Willing Workers Sunday school class are more than I can handle, much less women of the world. Besides, I have got no heart for born losers."

I don't think she was listening to a word I said. When she finished her tea, she got up to go, and I followed her out to the car. "It's nice of you to ask me, Dr. Elsie, but you understand . . ."

She started the engine and then looked back at me through them horned-rimmed glasses. "Esmeralda," she said, "you're the woman for the job. It's an opportunity you can't pass up." Before I could say a word, she let off the brake and was rolling down the driveway.

Opportunity? I thought. *Good heavens, it's an opportunity all right—an opportunity for disaster!*

As I watched her make the turn onto the street, it crossed my mind that maybe Dr. Elsie was losing her marbles. You know, people retire and the next thing you hear they're falling apart, and some of them wind up at the funny farm.

❧

I thought I had dismissed that "opportunity" from my mind, but at night I couldn't sleep for thinking about it. Priscilla Home was in North Carolina, high up in the hills, far away from everything and everybody except one or two summer people who had cottages up there. Now that she was retired, Dr. Elsie was one who lived up there year round. Soon after Beatrice and Carl got married, she retired, left Live Oaks, and moved with all her books to live in a little place she'd bought. As long as I had known Dr. Elsie, she'd been on the Priscilla Home board—she and Mabel Elmwood's husband. That stuffed shirt was on every board he could get his name on.

Beatrice had supported Priscilla Home ever since we were girls, and I had too, off and on. Beatrice was the best friend I ever had. We grew up together in Live Oaks, and when she had to move away to find work, we wrote to each other and talked on the phone. She was lonesome and awfully dependent on me, but all that changed. When she met Carl she became a different person. Soon as he sold his business and his house, they got married and started traveling all over the country in that RV he bought. It was hard to keep in touch. I missed her a lot, but getting married was the best thing that ever happened to Beatrice. Carl was one fine Christian man, even though he was sometimes corny. I knew he'd say I should take that job at Priscilla Home but, like Dr. Elsie, he didn't have a clue as to my responsibilities here.

Trouble with Dr. Elsie was that she had not got much common sense. Here I was a widow woman with a house to look after, a garden to make, and church work up to my ears. As if that was not enough, there was my neighbor, Mrs. Purdy, blind as a bat and dependent on me to keep her house in shape, get her groceries, and see to it she got some cooked meals. And there was Elijah, that dear man, who was still doing odd jobs for me and everybody else in town. Sooner or later he was likely to get down, and I'd be the only one to look after him.

No, there was no way I could pick up and leave Live Oaks, and that was that!

Trying to put Priscilla Home out of my mind, I kept busy working like a house afire, but while I was doing a load of wash, a thought did come to me: *What if this is something the Lord wants me to do?* Well, I shook my head and told myself that could not be, but come night-time, the possibility kept tumbling about in my head. Night after night I tumbled with it, tossing and turning until the wee hours.

Something Splurgeon wrote in that book I have got kept needling me. He said, "A clear conscience is a good pillow." I had to figure it might be my conscience bothering me; that, or else I was coming down with something. The bad part of it was that this was something I couldn't talk to anybody about, not even Pastor Osborne, for fear somebody would get me more confused than I was already. In our Willing Workers Sunday school class, the women can solve any and everybody's problem except their own, and they'd love to stick their nose in this business. Clara for sure; she's the president, and once she gets wind of a thing like this, she makes up her mind about it, gets the class to back her up, and wades right in to tell a body what they should do.

I did pray about this thing, but I told the Lord how ridiculous it was, a woman my age being asked to pull up stakes and take over a job she knew nothing about. I tell you the truth, for days I felt like I was walking around in a daze. The longer this went on, the more it got to be a live-in nightmare!

Then it happened. I looked out my window to see the Willing Workers arriving. At first I thought it might be Thelma, the Yankee from Chicago, behind the wheel, but it wasn't. It was Clara and Mabel Elmwood; before they even got out of the car, my blood pressure had shot up. Since I had not told a soul about this proposition, it didn't take a rocket scientist to know how they found out—Mabel's husband, Roger, is on the Priscilla Home board. Well, I'll tell you, I was ready for them. Before this was over I would put them in their place and tell them in no uncertain terms to keep their noses out of my business.

I brought them in the living room and set them on the divan. I was so mad I didn't offer them a drink or anything. "Well," I said, "I know you didn't come here to kill time. What's on your mind?"

Mabel looked at Clara, and Clara looked at Mabel. I don't like to be critical, but neither one of them was anything to look at. Clara always claimed she had an hourglass figure. Well, if she did, all the sand had sunk to the bottom. With her long neck, she put me in mind of an ostrich. And she had got just about as much sense as one of them silly birds. Mabel, on the other hand, would fit right in a carnival sideshow. Trying to fake the bloom of youth, she wore enough rouge to paint a barn and had taken to wearing eye makeup, which didn't do nothing but make people wonder if she was sick. And twice a week she went to the beauty parlor expecting miracles. One week she came out wearing false eyelashes! I could take her press-on nails, but false eyelashes on a woman with cataracts ripe for surgery was about the tackiest thing ever seen in Live Oaks.

"Well, speak up," I told them.

"You tell her," Clara said.

Mabel was holding my red velvet cushion up against her chest for comfort—or protection. "I'd rather you tell her, Clara."

Over the years I'd had to deal with these women, and all I have to say is, they have always been and always will be like Job's friends, miserable comforters, and I do mean *miserable.* They didn't know enough to come in out of the rain, but they thought wisdom would die with them.

Clara sat up straight, twisting her mouth the way she did when she was busting to let you know she knew something that was none of her business. "Esmeralda, first let me say this is a private meeting, and before we say anything, I want you to give me your word that this conversation will go no further."

"We haven't had it yet."

She didn't say anything right away, as she was having trouble with her upper plate. Well, if she'd pay the price for decent teeth, they wouldn't get loose like that. With her thumb she kept pressing until she got the plate in place and then waited to see if it was going to stay there. Satisfied that at least it would hold temporarily, she commenced again. "Do I have your word that you'll not let anyone know that Mabel and me have been here?"

"Why don't you want nobody to know?"

She looked to Mabel, but Mabel only hugged the pillow and gazed up at the ceiling.

"Well," Clara explained, "Mabel's husband is on the Priscilla Home board of directors—in fact, he's the president, and this is about that offer they made you."

"So that's it, is it? Well, let me tell you a thing or two—whatever it is you have to say here today will go right in one ear and out the other, so there's not a chance in the world anybody will hear it unless the devil has give them some kinda psychic power. Now, say what you have to say. I got work to do."

Clara stretched her neck about a yard long and lit in. "Esmeralda, I hope you are not considering that job at Priscilla Home."

They both leaned forward, peering at me, expecting me to up and tell them my thoughts on the subject. When they realized I wasn't going to give them that satisfaction, Clara lit in again. "Esmeralda, it would be the worst mistake of your life to go up there in those hills to work with those loose-living women who are at best sots! All you will hear up there is foul language and four letter words. Women like them are born losers, freeloaders, and—" she lowered her voice to a whisper, "some of them have got herpes and the like! You don't want to waste what time you have got left playing nursemaid to that trash, now do you? Don't the Bible say we should not cast our pearls before swine?"

I know I'd had a low opinion of women who couldn't hack it in this life, but I resented the way Clara was talking about them. I don't know what I expected her to say about me taking the job, but in a way she was saying what I wanted to hear. It was just the principle of the thing, them taking it upon themselves to advise me. I was a independent woman, and I had always made my own decisions without any help from the likes of them two.

"We love you, Esmeralda," Mabel was saying in that syrupy way she has got. "What would Willing Workers be like if you weren't here to help us?"

I hated it when Mabel whined.

Clara nudged her. "Tell Esmeralda what Roger said."

I thought Mabel was going to ruin my cushion, twisting it the way she was, so I gave her a frown that said "Knock it off." She lightened up on the cushion, patting it back into shape.

"Well," she said, "Roger says this job of resident manager would not be in your best interest, Esmeralda, and Roger ought to know, he's been on that board for years."

I couldn't have cared less what Roger Elmwood thought, and I must of showed it because Mabel started backing off. "Mind you, Esmeralda, it was not easy for us to come to you this way. It's just that we love you to pieces, and we don't want you to make a mistake we would all regret the rest of your life."

Clara was fooling with that upper plate again, but she was so anxious to say her piece that she took a chance and started in again. "Esmeralda, you can't pay any attention to Dr. Elsie. To hear her tell it, Priscilla Home is the only place in the world a female addict should go. But I tell you, there are plenty of places like AA where women caught up in the bondage of drugs can find a support group. That's what they need, a support group. Somebody from mental health was on TV the other day talking about addicts, and he said the country has plenty of rehab places where they can find the help they need if they want it, and their insurance pays for the treatment. The people who work in them places have training and experience. Now don't get touchy with me, Esmeralda, but I ask you, what training and experience have you got that fits you for that job?"

"Would you all like a glass of ice tea?" I asked.

I went in the kitchen, and while I was making the tea, I mulled over what they had said. Even though I didn't want to admit it, Clara had a point. I didn't have any training for that job. Of course, I already knew that and had no reason to give Clara credit for bringing it to my attention.

I served them the tea with oatmeal cookies and said I'd rather not talk any more about going to Priscilla Home. I asked Mabel how she was feeling, because I knew that would change the subject. You ask Mabel how she feels, and you get an organ recital.

❧

After they left, I went outside to feed the birds. I guess my mind was made up; I was ready to call Dr. Elsie and tell her I couldn't take the job. But I didn't want to do it right away and give them two Willing Workers the satisfaction of thinking they'd influenced my decision. *I'll wait a day or two,* I thought.

I didn't really feel good about giving up what Dr. Elsie called an "opportunity." But it was true; I didn't have any experience with alcohol and drugs, much less training in how to deal with people who did. Now if the job didn't involve contact with the women, just running the house, I could handle that. But, no, if you live in the same house with them, you can't get around having to deal with them. I hated to disappoint Dr. Elsie, but one of those other applicants were bound to be better qualified for the job than me.

I don't know why, but the whole thing made me feel blue.

I wished I knew how to call Beatrice, just for old times' sake, but I had no idea where she and Carl were—still out west somewhere. I wished I could just go back to living the way it was before Beatrice got married. With her gone, I really didn't have a close friend except Elijah. And Elijah was a friend for other kinds of problems, not this kind. Besides, he was too busy doing odd jobs for all the white people in town.

Well, I couldn't wait any longer to get this thing settled. I went to the phone to call Dr. Elsie and was just about to lift the receiver when the phone rang. Speak of the devil, and he will appear—it was Beatrice! She was just bubbling over, excited about seeing Carlsbad Caverns and telling me all about the bats flying out of the caverns at night to catch insects.

She had not run down when I interrupted her to tell

her about them offering me the job at Priscilla Home. Upon my word, she got as sober as a judge. After hearing me out, I heard her say, "Carl, I want you to hear this."

"No, Beatrice, don't bother him," I said. "I think I've made up my mind. I don't have the training or the experience to be housemother up there."

"What do you mean?"

"Just what I said."

"Wait just one minute, Esmeralda," she said with that edge in her voice, which meant she absolutely disagreed. "Have you prayed about it?"

"Well, sure."

"I mean, have you prayed it through? Do you know positively what the Lord's will is?"

"Well, I—"

"You really don't know what his will is, do you?"

"Now listen here, Beatrice, the Lord don't send us a bolt out of the blue to tell us what to do. He gives us common sense—circumstances—things like that to keep us on track. Don't you think he has give me sound judgment?"

"Sometimes, yes, but this is too important for you to pass up without knowing for sure what he wants to do with you."

"That's easy for you to say."

"Esmeralda, I've got to get off the line. Carl says tell you . . . What's that, Carl? . . . He says tell you don't take no wooden nickels. Now, I'll tell Carl what's going on, and you know we'll be praying for you."

Wooden nickels—I couldn't remember when last I'd heard that expression. *Carl needs to move his self out*

17

of the twentieth century and into this millennium. And I'd just as soon Beatrice not tell him my business, but how can I tell her not to?

I know I was feeling cross, but it was just because I was more confused than ever.

I sat on the porch for a while. It was cool out there, so I went back inside. I went in the kitchen to fix a bite to eat—opened the refrigerator door and stood there looking to see what looked good. Nothing did. I wasn't hungry.

Finally, I just plopped down in my recliner and let go. "Just show me, Lord!" I said and opened my Bible where the bookmark was. Nothing I read spoke to me, and my mind just kept rambling, going over again all the troubling things I could imagine. *What if I did take a job like that, what would I do with my house? Rent it? Renters don't take care of a place.* I couldn't just go off and leave it. I dared not sell it; it was the only security I had for my old age. No, I could not leave my house.

I leaned forward to lay the Bible on the end table, but the recliner popped up and the Bible fell on the floor. *I got to get Elijah to do something about this chair,* I told myself. Everything I kept filed in the pages of my Bible had fell out, and as I was gathering up all them little keepsakes, my eyes fell on a little scrap of paper with the lines of a poem on it. It was a poem I planned to frame and hang in my kitchen but had never got around to doing it. I read the words again:

> Only one life, 'twill soon be past;
> Only what's done for Christ will last.

I sat back down to ponder about that. So far as I could tell, I was living by those words. I tried to do everything, not just church work, for the Lord's glory. But the more I thought about it, the more I felt, well, unsettled, you might call it. I fingered that scrap of paper and asked the Lord if he was trying to tell me something.

Well, I was soon to find out. Without much faith that anything was going to happen, I spread my old King James on my lap, and it opened right at Isaiah 6. That's the chapter where Isaiah has a vision of the Lord in the temple and he overhears the Lord asking, "Whom shall I send and who will go for us?" Isaiah told the Lord, "Here am I, send me."

I tell you the truth, my heart commenced to pitter-patter. I can't tell you how many times I had read that chapter before—and heard many a sermon on it—but never in my life had it shot an arrow straight to my heart! At my age, was I supposed to tell the Lord, "Here am I, send me"?

I read on until I finished that chapter, but I didn't remember a word I'd read. All I could think about was that question: "Whom shall I send and who will go for us?"

Well, I was in no frame of mind to answer the way Isaiah did.

Somebody was at the door, so I got up and answered it. It was the postman with postage due on a letter. I had to find my pocketbook and dig in that bottomless pit for the four cents to give him. By the time I did that and put on my glasses, I saw it was a letter from Percy Poteat. I was fit to be tied. That no-count, good-for-nothing moocher—just like him not to put enough stamps on a letter to send it all the way.

I opened it and read what he had to say. Said he had got married in Oregon to a widow with grown kids, and that he and his new wife were riding his motorcycle back east. Said he wanted to show off his bride to the people in Live Oaks and could they stay at my house a few days.

The nerve of that guy! The last time I'd seen him, I'd sent him packing so he wouldn't break up Beatrice and Carl. For some reason, all her life long, Beatrice had been crazy about Percy Poteat. Then she met Carl. They were about to be married when Percy showed up on his Harley-Davidson. He had run through at least three wives and was looking for another. I tell you, all he wanted with Beatrice was a good cook and housekeeper. I knew I had to put a stop to that, so I did.

When Beatrice found out, she shamed me pretty bad about sending him packing—not because Percy was any threat to the way she felt about Carl, but because she was concerned for Percy's soul. Carl had been talking to him about the Lord, and they had both been praying for him, but before they got anywhere with Percy, I had caused him to hit the road.

Well, I'd never felt good about that. I knew Jesus died for him same as me, but at the time I wasn't thinking about Percy being lost—I just wanted him to *get* lost! I figured it would ease my conscience if I agreed to let him and this new wife freeload here at my house for a day or two. To my credit, whenever I thought about Percy, which was only once in a blue moon, I did pray for him.

I put the letter away and plugged in the vacuum cleaner. If there is anything I'm allergic to, it's a vacuum cleaner, but I was in no mood to sit around chewing the cud about the Priscilla Home offer. I would get the house all cleaned up, and then maybe I could relax and pray.

Far into the night I was working like there was no tomorrow, finding more things to do than the law allows, but that question the Lord was asking was worse than a fishbone stuck in my craw. I couldn't get rid of it. I tried to tell myself that it was just a coincidence that the Bible fell open at that chapter, but it didn't do any good.

After I'd done everything I could think to do, the ironing, the mopping, and cleaning out the utility room, I climbed up on a chair and washed off the top of the refrigerator. That was always the last thing that ever got done at my house, since the top of the fridge is the last thing anybody will ever see, unless it's Clara when she stretches her neck. Like I always say, housekeeping is something you do that nobody notices unless you don't do it.

I put all the cleaning rags in the washer and turned it on, heard the clock strike 2:00 A.M., and stood there thinking. With that question "Whom shall I send?" hammering away in my head, I decided that this thing was not going away until I got something settled once and for all. I plopped down in the recliner.

Of course, I was wore to a frazzle, so I just told the Lord I would appreciate if he would make it perfectly plain to me what he had in mind for me, and I'd do it.

"I'm here if you want to send me," I told him, but I can't say my heart was in it. I would have to be absolutely sure before I made a move, so I asked for a sign. "By chance you want me to take that job," I said, "for starters, what say you tell me what to do with this house?"

What I am about to tell you is hard to believe; it knocked me out of my tree! The very next day, about noon, Pastor Osborne drove up in the driveway. When he opened the door and pulled the seat forward so the two little boys could pile out the backseat, I went around to the passenger side and lifted Angelica out. I shook my head; that little car was not fit for a family. All three of the kids made a beeline to the backyard to see Elijah, who was working in my garden. They loved that man to death.

The pastor sat on the glider while I went inside to fix him a glass of tea. It made me mad the way the deacons were dillydallying about giving Pastor Osborne a raise. Now that he had taken on three children, the church was not paying him enough to keep body and soul together, much less buy a decent car.

I brought the tea on a tray with one of my fried apple pies and set it down. "Pastor Osborne, when my ship comes in, I'm going to buy you a four-door. You need a four-door."

"Well," he said, "we could sure use one, but Betty and I are content with what we have. In fact, we've never been happier, Esmeralda. All those years we waited and thought we'd never have children, and then the Lord gives us three. It's one of those answers that's 'exceedingly abundantly above' all we asked for or imagined."

We talked about the mission trip the young people were going on and about Boris Krantz, who seemed to be working out good as youth director. He told me Boris was helping Horace, the sheriff's son, who wanted to be baptized. If my guess was right, Lucy Mangrum, the Spanish teacher, had her cap set for Boris. Well, she was a fine girl, and he'd be lucky to get her.

We could hear the children squealing, having a good time.

"I reckon Betty has her hands full now," I said.

"Loves every minute of it. She's had to throw away a lot and stuff every nook and cranny in the house to make room for the children and us, but she loved every minute of it."

"How's it working out?"

"Fine. The boys and Angelica have bunk beds in the other bedroom. It's a small room so it's crowded in there. As the children get bigger, it won't be long before we'll have to do something. We thought when the time comes, we would ask our landlord if he would build another room onto the house. I talked to Elmer down at the hardware store about how much an addition like that would cost, and he said if the landlord laid out that kind of money he'd go up on the rent. Elmer said we'd be better off to look for a three-bedroom house if we can afford it. Maybe we will, sometime."

My mouth dropped open. "A three-bedroom house?"

He nodded. "That is, when the time comes. Betty and I are already praying about it."

Without giving it another thought, I knew what I had to do. I asked him, "How'd you like to have my house?"

He laughed. "Yeah, right!"

He thought I was joking.

❧

Before I left town, it was all settled. I put my furniture in storage, and the Osbornes planned on moving into my house the following week. They would pay me the same rent they'd been paying for that little cracker box house, and I had their first month's rent in my pocketbook. The Willing Workers agreed to look after Mrs. Purdy, and Horace said he'd see to it Elijah didn't lack for anything. Of course, Horace had caught that HIV virus from Maria, so the chances were he wouldn't outlive Elijah. But I figured we'd cross that bridge when we came to it. The good news was that Horace had made a turnaround and was living for the Lord.

❧

Well, I couldn't believe I was actually on my way to North Carolina in my old Chevy loaded with all of my stuff, as well as clothes, sheets, towels, pillows—anything the Willing Workers thought we could use at Priscilla Home. I felt about as happy as I did the day Bud and me got married. Of course, that day, we thought we had a future, that we'd have children and grow old together. When he stepped on that mine in Vietnam and come home so wounded he was not his self, our dreams was over and done with.

I didn't cotton to the idea of leaving Bud back there

in the cemetery, but before I left, I went up there and told him good-bye and that I'd be back. I knew he'd want me to go.

If I'd had good sense, I would've been scared about what lay ahead, but right then I was making good time around the curves and up the hills, singing God's praises at the top of my lungs.

2

It wasn't easy finding Priscilla Home. The last ten miles were on a dirt road, the Old Turnpike, which twisted and turned, worming its way up the mountain. It was about as wide as a narrow-gauge railroad track, one you wouldn't want to meet a car on, much less a pickup truck with a hillbilly behind the wheel. The mountain laurel was budding on both sides of the road, and the overhanging limbs formed a green leafy arch decorated with a dusting of snow. For April, the weather was cold, with a sky holding on to winter.

When I finally saw the sign THE PRISCILLA HOME, I heaved a sigh of relief and turned in at the drive. Set among a forest of giant trees was a big white house with a lawn set off with a rock wall all around. On the porch were a dozen or so women sitting in the rockers or on the steps, bundled up against the cold, most of them smoking. I tooted the horn, but no one waved. The drive went around to the back of the house, and seeing the door to the first floor, I pulled up there and stopped. By the time I got out of the car, a young woman was coming out. *Must be the director,* I thought. Looked to be around thirty. Not much to look at, although she wasn't making the most of what she did have. I'm no fashion plate myself, but I try to look decent. She had on jeans and a Carolina sweatshirt, which was okay, but her hair was a mess and she needed some makeup.

"Good afternoon," she said. "You must be the new resident manager."

"That's right."

"I'm Ursula Sloan," she said. "Director of Priscilla Home."

By then the women had come through the house and were spilling out the back door. Most of them were young, and I knew they must have been curious about me, but their faces didn't show it. They all had the same hangdog look about them.

"The ladies will bring in your accoutrements."

I didn't have a clue about *accoutrements,* but the women were ready to help me unload the car. "Most of this stuff is for the home," I told them and proceeded to separate boxes and bags from my stuff.

Many hands made short work of unloading the Chevy. The director told the women to take my things upstairs to the second floor and put the rest on the third floor. "You can put your car in the garage next to mine," she told me. I looked at a long van parked next the dumpster. "We don't have room for the van in there," she explained. "That's my apartment above the garage."

Ursula waited while I parked the Chevy, and then I followed her inside. We entered a first floor room full of chairs and tables with a fireplace and mantel. "This is the day room," she told me, "and adjoining this room is the craft room, laundry room, and a downstairs bedroom with bath for visitors. Your quarters are on the second floor."

This Ursula talked fast like a Yankee, so I knew she wasn't from North Carolina. I followed her up the steps, and at the head of the stairs on the left was the kitchen, where a couple of women were cooking something in a big pot. We turned right onto a short hall beside the staircase leading to the third floor. One box of my stuff was at the end of the hall before one door, and Ursula was fumbling with keys to open another door labeled "office." The hall led into a parlor, and while she was trying to unlock the office, I stepped into the parlor to take a look-see.

That parlor was downright posh with couches, chairs, tables, and lamps—even had a baby grand piano in there. The hardwood floors and solid wood paneling made the room look like a picture out of one of them home decorating magazines.

In back of the parlor was a small sitting room with a fireplace dividing the parlor from the dining room. I couldn't get over all that wood in those rooms—the floors and walls with those wide windowsills—you just don't see real wood with its natural grain nowadays. On the far side of the dining room, the front door opened onto the porch, the porch I saw coming down the driveway, and another door on the right led into the kitchen.

Ursula found me and led me through the kitchen back into the little hallway. I spoke to the two cooks, and they nodded back at me. In the office Ursula proceeded to tell me, "Your room and bath has one door that opens onto the hall and another that opens into the office. We keep the office secured because the medicine cabinet is in here, and the phone. The ladies are only allowed to use the phone on weekends."

As we entered my quarters, I poked my head in the bathroom and saw it looked okay—lots of cabinet space. It was a corner room with windows on two sides overlooking the backyard. Except for the one box outside the door, the girls had placed my things in neat stacks, leaving me walking space in between. The room was furnished with a bed, lamps, an easy chair, and a television on a table. Living in one room would take some getting used to, but having the run of the whole house would help me make do.

"The ladies have the third floor," Ursula was saying. "Each room has twin beds, a desk, and a closet. There are a couple of community bathrooms. After dinner you may go up there if you like."

"When's supper? I'm starved."

She hesitated, and her glasses slipped down on her nose. With her finger on the bridge, she righted them and spoke in a tight kind of voice. "As soon as it's prepared. You'll want to freshen up, so I'll leave you for now. They'll ring a bell for dinner."

After I had been to the bathroom, I unpacked a few things and was groping around in the closet for hangers when I heard the bell. I ran a comb through my hair, threw on some face powder, and took a look-see in the mirror. I figured I would pass.

Ursula seated me at a round table with herself and four of the women. After the blessing, everyone filed into the kitchen to be served. I tell you, everybody was morgue quiet. The cooks standing on the other side of the counter before that large pot dished out boiled corn, two roasting ears onto each plate. That was all! No butter, no bread, no tea—nothing! I must have looked shocked, because Ursula explained, "Corn is the only thing we have left in the freezer."

When we had all received our two ears of corn, we sat down. I introduced myself, but it was like pulling eye teeth to get the women to tell me their names and where they came from. The woman next to me was middle-aged or older and so thin a puff of wind could blow her away. The rings on her fingers were so loose I didn't see how she kept them from falling off. Said her name was Lenora Barrineau. Said she came from Manhattan. That's in New York City. For a woman her age, her graying hair was too long, and it did nothing to help that vacant look in her eyes. The hair dragged her face down, if you know what I mean. Handling the corn with those long, thin fingers and mincing each bite made me guess she had been raised fancy.

Across from me sat a woman wearing an old hunting jacket that seemed to be as much a part of her as her skin. Hers was a face you don't see anywhere but in the backwoods, because it was a face left over from the Great Depression. She could've been forty years old or a hundred—age don't count living a hardscrabble life. She gave her name as Dora something or other, from

Tennessee, and she seemed to be all by herself—apart from the others.

Ursula introduced the other two women, Linda and Portia, who were roommates. She didn't name their hometowns; the way they'd been living they probably didn't have hometowns anymore. They were young—too young to be in a place like this, but I guessed years didn't count when you had got a tattoo like Portia's crawling up your neck telling the world to imagine where you'd been and what you'd been up to. Them two could teach me things I didn't want to know. Linda wore a baseball cap turned backwards on her head, which was something I wouldn't put up with if I was in charge, not at the table. She was stocky, had a gold bead through her nose, and five or six earrings in each ear.

Why everyone was so quiet was hard to understand. I tried to get a conversation going by telling them about my trip up the mountain. When that didn't work, I tried telling the story about Mrs. Purdy's cat being lost for five days—how I finally found Flossie Ann in a dresser drawer. That story usually made people laugh and ask questions, but not this bunch. The small girl—the one with the tattoos—looked like she shivered, and Linda, the girl beside her, said, "Portia hates cats. Don't you, Portia?" She got no answer.

Frankly, I was glad when that meal, if you can call it that, was over. We carried our plates back to the kitchen, and I asked Ursula, "What's the schedule for this evening?"

"This evening? I am multitasking."

I guess that meant she was busy. "And the women?"

"They can take care of themselves."

Already they had filed out onto the porch and were lighting up again. I went back to my room to unpack some more. I was beginning to think that things were not as they should be at Priscilla Home. *First thing tomorrow morning,* I told myself, *I'm going into Rockville to see what I can do about this food business.*

After I finished unpacking, I slipped in the kitchen and checked out what foodstuffs they had and made a list of things they needed, which was just about everything.

Early the next morning I was driving into town on the Old Turnpike, which was so foggy I had to run my wipers and creep along. All the way into Rockville I prayed the Lord would show me how he was going to provide for us, because I was sure he was going to do just that. In my wallet I had the money Pastor Osborne had paid me for his first month's rent, so I had that to spend. Before I left Live Oaks I had intended to save every penny he sent me until I had enough to buy him a decent car, but it looked like the Lord had something else in mind, at least for this first month's rent.

I figured the place to begin was a supermarket, and I found one without any trouble. It didn't take long to load two shopping carts full of staples—flour, meal, sugar, cooking oil, rice, grits, oatmeal, coffee, tea, dry milk, dried beans, peanut butter, and some seasonings. I paid for that, stashed it in the car, and went back in the store for some cheese, milk, and eggs. Then I headed for the produce department.

In the back of the store, I found the produce manager ripping green leaves from the outside of cabbages. They do that to make the produce look fresher than it really is when they put it on the counter and sprinkle water on it. Well, I couldn't let the manager get away with that.

You'd think I was the Queen of Sheba the way I talked to that man. "Mister, don't you know you are throwing away the best part of them cabbages? All the vitamins and minerals are in those outer leaves that have soaked up the sun."

"Hey, if you think so much of those leaves, you can have 'em. Here's a sack; help yourself."

As fast as he peeled off the leaves I stuffed them in that bag, and before you knew it, I needed more bags. It made the fellow curious that I was taking so much. "You got a big family? Having company?" he asked.

"No," I told him. "It's for Priscilla Home."

Right away he lightened up, said he'd heard of that place. "That Old Turnpike is a washboard of a road, ain't it?" he said, and I agreed.

Seeing he had several shelves of vegetables he was going to have to offer at discount, I asked him, "What's the best price you can give me on the whole lot?"

"Hey, I just work here," he said. "I'll have to ask the boss." He stopped what he was doing and disappeared behind swinging doors.

In about five minutes he reappeared with the store manager in tow. By then I had made up my mind the limit I would pay.

"She wants a price on all o' this stuff," the produce man explained.

Both men surveyed the shelves, and then the store manager said, "Lady, if you can use this stuff, you're welcome to it. You'll be doing us a favor to take it off our hands—save us having to rewrap and reprice it."

He turned to go back through the swinging doors, so I called after him, "How much?" But he was gone.

"There's no charge," the produce man told me. "Here, I'll help you bag it."

I can't tell you how happy I was as I left that store. I still had money left and was beginning to feel like that woman in the Bible with the pot of oil that didn't give out.

There was a meat market up a ways from the store, so after I'd stashed the vegetables in the backseat, I drove up there. In the worse way I wanted some red meat for those sad-looking women.

A round-faced man in a white apron and cap was leaning on the meat case and spoke to me as I came in the door. Before I buy, I always check a meat counter to see if it's clean, and his was. There were hams, roasts, steaks, sausages, pork chops, chickens, and hamburger meat all neatly displayed in trays. I decided my best bargain would be the hamburger. It being Monday, I knew the meat he had was probably left over from Saturday, and he'd favor a quick sale of hamburger. So I pointed at the price posted and told him, "I can use all you got of that ground beef if the price is right."

He rolled open the sliding door of the cabinet, pulled out the pan of hamburger, threw a paper on the scales, and dumped the meat on. "I'll weigh it," he said and leaned his head back to read the numbers bobbing on that little glass tube. He was taking so long I figured he was trying to decide on what he would charge me. Finally he announced, "Eight pounds, four ounces."

"So, what's your best price?" I asked.

He didn't answer; he just asked me if I was going to put it in my freezer.

"No," I said. "It's for Priscilla Home, and after a meal or two there'll be nothing left."

"Priscilla Home?" He turned to look at me. "How many wimmin you got up there now?"

"About a dozen, I guess. I just came yesterday."

"You a patient up there?"

"No, I'm the new housemother."

He started wrapping the meat. "Hold on," I said. "You didn't give me the price."

"Two dollars," he said, wrapping twine around the package.

"Did I hear you right? Two dollars?"

"That's right."

"That's giving it away!" I didn't want to take advantage of the man.

He placed the meat on the counter. "I ain't a-losin' a penny, because as my granny used to say, 'Give and it'll be give back.' She was one good woman, and she'd roll over in her grave if I didn't do what I'm a-doin' for them pore wimmin."

"Well, since you put it that way, I reckon we don't want your granny rolling over in her grave, now do we?"

As I was rummaging through my bottomless pit for my

wallet, the butcher leaned his arms on the counter and looked out the window. "You know," he said, "there's somebody you ought to meet. Name's Mary—runs the donut shop."

I found my wallet and paid him two dollar bills. He rang it up and handed me the meat. "Can you manage it?"

"I got it," I said, then thanked him and asked if they had a day-old bread store in town.

"Sure have. It's right down this street next to the video store. You can't miss it."

I was almost out the door when he called after me. "Do you know where the donut shop is?"

Of course, I didn't. I shook my head.

"Well, it's on the other side of Main Street." He came out from behind the counter to point the way. "Go down here to the foot of the hill and hang a left. There's some roadwork a-goin' on down there—street's been flooded, but you can get around it. You'll go 'bout half a mile and see the post office on the right. Mary's shop is on that side street runs alongside the post office. You can't miss it."

I knew I wasn't interested in buying donuts, so I thanked him and was again about out the door when he added, "Every day when Mary closes shop, she throws away tons of those good donuts. You go down there at closing time, and she'll be glad to give you all the donuts you can use."

Now that was a different story. I thanked him again and said I'd be sure to check that out.

After I bought the bread, I went looking for the donut shop. I saw the post office but was in the wrong lane to make a turn. I tell you, I had a mischief of a time finding my way back. The streets in that town were something else! They twisted and turned and backtracked like you wouldn't believe. It looked like to make the streets they just paved over the trails the pioneers had made going across the mountains. Made me laugh; they probably done that on purpose to discourage tourists from settling in Rockville.

Mary and I hit it off right away. She was about my age, sixty-something-or-other. She said we could have all the donuts, Danish, and cream horns left over at the end of any day—that she had back trouble and it would be a help to have us unload all that stuff. I could not believe my ears!

❧

On the way home, I thought of a way we could give a little back for the donuts. On the days we came for the leftovers, I'd bring a couple of the Priscilla girls, and we'd help Mary clean up of an evening—wash those heavy trays and mop the floor.

Driving back up the mountain, my heart was so full I just kept singing and saying, "Thank you, Jesus! Thank you, Jesus!"

❧

By the time I got to Priscilla's it was nearly lunchtime. The girls swarmed around the car to help me unload.

Seeing all the groceries seemed to break the gloomy spell that hung over the place.

I asked them where Ursula was. One of the women, I think it was Linda, said Ursula was having a counseling session. I left it to the girls to take care of the groceries, and I climbed the stairs to my room.

I hadn't read the Bible all day, so I welcomed a little quiet time before the lunch bell rang. After I went to the bathroom, I plopped down in that easy chair. It didn't fit me like my old recliner, but I thought maybe in time it would. I got out my prayer list and opened the Bible at the bookmark.

I had hardly got started reading when Ursula called me into her office.

3

Ursula sat down behind her desk, looking very disturbed. "Esmeralda, by what means did you procure all these foodstuffs?"

"For the most part I paid for them."

Those eyeglasses slipped down on her nose, and she peered at me over the top of them. "We can't do that here. We cannot spend our own funds to finance Priscilla Home."

"Why not? I can't ask the Lord to give us groceries when I have the money in my pocketbook to pay for them."

"That will not work here. There are always many needs at Priscilla Home, and you could spend every penny of your income and still not meet all the obligations."

She was so matter-of-fact, so sure of herself, I could see how easy we might lock horns. Ursula was a stringy woman and didn't fit in that big office chair. She tried leaning back in it but that didn't help. Then she started fooling with a paper clip, bending it out of shape. "When

I first came here as director, my father instructed me meticulously about how to bring Priscilla Home up to professional standard."

At her age, is her daddy still running her life? I wondered.

"My father is a learned man, and I respect his judgment," she was saying. "Fund-raising is the board's responsibility, he said, and he forbade me spending my money on needs here. That would lead to my financial ruin."

"Is the board doing the fund-raising?" I asked.

"No," she said, a bit put off by my asking. "It hasn't worked out that way." Leaning forward, shuffling a stack of papers, she appeared to be looking for something. "Here, this is what I'm looking for," she said as she handed me a Priscilla Home prayer letter. As I was reading it, she informed me, "This is a faith ministry. We depend on donations from our constituency and from grants given by foundations. That letter you have in your hand was mailed to our contributors two weeks ago. We should soon begin receiving contributions in the mail."

It was a prayer letter, all right—like so many of those letters I would get and have to throw in the trash because it took all I had to support my own church. "You send out letters?"

"Yes, we send out letters. That informs the public of our financial needs—"

"And you ask foundations for charity?"

"Yes, of course." She looked provoked. "That's the way all nonprofits are funded."

"Nonprofits?"

Annoyed, she threw the paper clip in the wastebasket and started toying with another one. "Yes, nonprofits like hospitals, research centers, and so forth. Any such organization can apply. I spend hours writing proposals for grants, and since I came here two years ago, we've received one, a grant of fifteen hundred dollars. I have eleven proposals in the mail and am in the process of writing six more."

The way this conversation was going made me uncomfortable. I didn't exactly know how to say what I wanted to, but I had to say something or I knew I'd regret it later. "Ursula . . . I don't think of Priscilla Home as just another nonprofit organization. It's a Christian ministry. To ask for money makes it look like the Lord can't take care of us."

Ursula sat bolt upright, her elbows on the desk and her fingers twisting that paper clip to beat the band. "Do you consider that my appealing to a foundation and writing letters to our constituency makes us mendicants?"

"I don't know what you mean."

"Mendicants are religious persons who live off alms. Do you consider that my appealing to foundations and sending letters to our contributors is begging?"

"What would you call it?"

The phone rang. She answered it and spoke briefly with somebody. As she was talking, I noticed the black circles under her eyes. *No wonder,* I thought, *she's probably up half the night writing them proposals to foundations.*

When she got off the line, there was an edge in her

voice. "Esmeralda, how do you propose we fund this ministry?"

"Just trust the Lord. Don't that seem like the most natural way?"

"Doesn't," she snapped.

"Well, whatever. It seems to me that if we can trust the Lord to save and keep our souls, we ought to be able to trust him to provide for his work."

Her face flushed. "Are you saying I don't trust the Lord?"

"No. I'm not your judge. I just think it's up to the Lord to keep Priscilla Home running as long as he sees fit, and when he's done with this place he will stop providing for it."

"According to that, Esmeralda, it appears the Lord is indeed finished with this ministry." Throwing the paper clip in the wastebasket, she reached in a desk drawer, pulled out a stack of papers, and slid them across to me.

They were all unpaid bills—all past due. Bills for electricity, propane, gasoline, hardware—I was shocked to see one in there from the meat market where I'd bought the hamburger meat. If I had known Priscilla Home owed that man money, I'd have never asked him for his best price. I thought of what a good man he must be not to have mentioned that bill to me.

"Esmeralda, we have forty-two dollars in our bank account. If we don't pay Mountain Power and Light this week, they're going to discontinue our electricity. What do you propose that we do, pray about it?"

If she wasn't sarcastic, she was close to it.

"Ursula," I said, "when I was young, things were nip and tuck for me. Through those years I learned that the Lord always provides if I trust him and if I don't waste what he gives me."

"Don't you think I have prayed?" she snapped. "I've prayed and I've done what I could to raise revenue, but Esmeralda, we are at our Rubicon! Yesterday I called the president of our board, Mr. Elmwood, to ask his permission to negotiate another bank loan. He approved, and tomorrow I'm going to the bank to borrow ten thousand dollars."

"A loan against the property?"

"What else? After we pay our creditors, we'll have about two thousand dollars left for future expenditures."

"How will you pay back the loan?"

"With monthly payments."

I didn't say anything. I was hard-pressed to know how to speak my mind without getting her riled up even more.

"You disapprove?" she asked, her dark eyes snapping. "Do you have a better plan?"

"You must think I fell off a turnip truck."

"A turnip truck? What are you talking about?"

"Never mind." I waved my hand in the air. "Ursula, I do have a better plan. What would you think if I went into town, met all these creditors, and asked for a bit more time?"

"Oh, we could never do that! Besides, a few more days' delay won't change things. What we owe is much more than we could expect to come in within such a short time."

I spoke softly so as not to offend her. "Splurgeon says, 'He pleases God best who trusts him most.'"

"Splurgeon?"

The bell rang for lunch, but we still sat there, not saying anything. The smell of fried onions drifted our way. I heard the screen door banging as the girls piled off the porch and came inside.

Finally Ursula broke the silence. "You would do that? You'd go into town and ask all those creditors to give us extensions?"

I nodded.

"What if they say no?"

"Then we'll cross that bridge when we come to it."

She shook her head disgustedly. "I perceive that your faith exceeds mine, Esmeralda."

"No, we all got a pinch of faith, and it only takes a pinch if we put it in the Lord."

Unconvinced and probably pitying me, she stood up and stacked her papers, muttering, "The mustard seed?" Not waiting for an answer, she said, "Very well, Esmeralda, you go into town and see what you can do. I'll delay asking for a loan until you report back to me."

After lunch, Ursula gave me the addresses of the creditors, and I wrote down the directions to each of the businesses. Then I took off down the Old Turnpike for Rockville. *This won't be easy,* I told myself and braced for whatever might happen.

❧

Asking for and getting extensions proved to be easier than I thought. There wasn't a creditor who did not graciously agree to give us ten more days to pay the bill. Last of all, I went to the meat center, dreading to face that butcher. After I apologized for bargaining with him about the hamburger, I asked if he could hold off on our bill for ten more days. "Miss Esmeralda, don't give it another thought," he said. "If you don't never pay that bill, that'll be okay with me. Like I told you, my granny would have it no other way. If she was alive, she'd like as not whup my butt if I made it hard on you folks."

"Well, now," I said, "we don't want your granny's ghost coming back and doing a thing like that, do we?" We laughed, and I said I'd see him in a few days.

By the time I finished with all that business, it was nearly 6:00, so I dropped by the donut shop, and Mary gave me scads of goodies to take home to the girls.

But you know, on my way home as I was waiting at a red light, it suddenly came over me just what I had done—I had taken on the responsibility for upwards of eight thousand dollars of debt! I had acted on the spur of the moment—didn't even pray about it—and just took for granted the Lord would bail us out. I slapped the steering wheel, mad at myself for having done such a thing without being sure it was the right thing to do. Maybe the Lord *was* through with Priscilla Home. That could very well be the case, because there didn't seem to be anything spiritual going on there, just counseling sessions. What we needed was a preacher—some good Bible teaching. *Oh, my! Lord, what have I done!*

As I was driving out of town, still stewing, I saw a flea market. It was closed, but it gave me an idea. Maybe we could find stuff at Priscilla Home that we could sell at the flea market. That might bring in a few dollars. A few dollars, yes, but we needed eight thousand! Unless hundreds of contributions came in from that prayer letter or one of those grants came through, there was nothing in sight that might bring in eight thousand dollars. I felt sure I had run ahead of the Lord and opened my big mouth without thinking it through. It wouldn't be the first time I'd done that.

Well, if I was wrong, it was too late to undo it. *Lord,* I prayed, *I'm sorry. Maybe you want to teach me a lesson . . .*

I was feeling down about the whole thing—mad at myself, really. Elijah had always said, "The Lord will make a way out of no way." To be sure, this was a "no way" situation, but under the circumstances I couldn't be sure the Lord would see fit to make a way for us.

The rocks and holes in the Old Turnpike were becoming familiar, and I knew that if this running back and forth to town kept up, it wouldn't be long before I could travel it with my eyes closed. Rain was beginning to fall—the way it does in the mountains—drizzling, teasing you into wondering if it's only going to be misty or if it's going to be real rain. Dampness just closes in on you. The heater in my car did nothing to help. Even so, I dreaded getting back to the home.

❧

When I rolled down the driveway, no one was outside on the porch smoking so I thought they must be eating supper.

I brought the donuts to the kitchen and saw that everybody was in the parlor. I ate a donut before going in to see what was going on.

"This is 'Group,'" Ursula told me, and three women on a couch made a place for me. They told me who they were. The three were as different as day and night—one was the daughter of missionaries; she was probably in her early twenties and pretty as a picture. I thought she said her name was Angela. The next girl was forty, I'd say, wore her hair straight back, tucked in with a comb, and wore fairly decent jeans and sweater. "I'm from Arkansas," she said. "I'm a cosmetologist." But before she could give me her name, Ursula asked her, "What is your drug of choice, Melba?"

Melba looked across the room to the other women. "Oh, I don't know," she said. "I never saw a drug I didn't like." That went around the room like a current, sparking snickers.

The girl on the end of the sofa was so thin I thought she might be sick. She had a real pretty face and blond hair but was so skinny that if she turned sideways a body couldn't see her. Ursula spoke for her. "Evelyn has three years of college and looks forward to an acting career."

I politely acknowledged the three on the couch and looked across at the other women, expecting to be introduced to them, but Ursula cut short the introductions. "You'll get to know the other ladies soon enough," she said, "but we must get down to business. Group is where we get together and share."

The girls were looking back at her, stiff as boards. "It helps us to open up if I prompt them," Ursula explained. "Tell us, Evelyn, what is your drug of choice?"

"Vodka," she said politely. "I like vodka."

I couldn't see the point of all this, but I guessed Ursula knew what she was doing. She seemed pleased that Evelyn was willing to say what her choice was; she continued asking the same question all around the room but didn't get another straight answer, so she changed the question. "Tell us, Dora, what is your definition of an honest person?"

As well as wearing that hunting jacket, Dora wore heavy boots and worn-out overalls. I had never heard her say a word before, but at length, she did answer. "A honest man runs good likker and sells at a fair price, and he don't move bound'ry marks to steal a neighbor's land."

The girls looked amused at that, and Linda laughed out loud, even though Dora hadn't meant it to be funny. Ursula nervously adjusted her glasses and, unsmiling, moved on. "Well, Linda, what is your definition of an honest person?"

Without answering the question, Linda turned the tables. "Miss Ursula, cut the crap. What you really want is for us to spill our guts, right?" She slid the baseball cap around and back again.

Ursula's face flushed.

"Well, I'll tell you my story. I was molested from the time I was four, been beat every day of my life, raped, and sent to thirteen different foster homes, seven rehabs. But when I was sent to the West Virginia Correctional Center, I had the time of my life. That is one great place! Good food, nice people, activities. 'Three hots and a cot,' we called it, but it was more'n that. I got my G.E.D., and I plan to go on to college and study criminal justice."

"Excellent. What you are telling us is, you suffered because of the ill treatment you received as a young person and you did something for which you were incarcerated. Perhaps you would like to tell us what you did that resulted in incarceration."

"It wasn't my fault. There was this doctor left his prescription pad in plain sight. He made it so easy I'd of been a fool not to take that pad. I must have wrote a hunnert or more prescriptions—not just for me but for all my friends." She was laughing. "Man, we had a twenty-four/seven party going great until I got busted."

Ursula looked pleased as punch that someone was opening up. "Linda, you made a bad choice stealing that prescription pad, didn't you? You made a bad choice, Linda, but you are not a bad person."

I'm telling you, Ursula said that with a straight face. I couldn't believe my ears!

Linda stopped laughing. "Hogwash! It wasn't me made a bad choice, it was that doctor. He had no right leaving that pad in plain sight. If I didn't pick it up, somebody else would have. That's the way it's always been for me—every trouble I ever had come from choices other people made, not me."

"Yes, perhaps, but when you were released from that correctional facility—"

"So, I broke probation. Reason that happened was because of the crowd I fell in with. They were the only friends I could find, and to be friends with them you had to go along, drinking, druggin', an' stealing, big time. I was the only one got caught. The judge wouldn't let me go back to West Virginia. He told me I had to go to another rehab, so I come here."

I didn't like what I was hearing. The other girls were enjoying all this talk, and I could well imagine how Linda would fill in the details of her rotten past when they were upstairs or out on the porch by themselves. I felt I had to put a stop to this if I could, so I spoke up. "It seems to me that airing our dirty underwear don't do nothing to glorify God—"

"Doesn't do *anything*," Ursula repeated, her face tight as a tick.

"Did I say something wrong?"

"'Don't do nothing' is a double negative," she informed me. The women were really enjoying this—seeing us at odds was probably the most fun they'd had in a long time.

"Whatever," I said and went on, confused and flustered. "We don't need to air all our troubles. Splurgeon says, 'He who talks much of his troubles to men is apt to fall into a way of saying too little of them to God.'"

Would you believe that Ursula corrected me again! "Don't you mean 'Spurgeon'?" she snapped. "Charles Haddon Spurgeon?"

"No," I said, confident that I was right. "His name is C. H. Splurgeon."

"C. H.? The C. H. stands for Charles Haddon, and his name is not *Splurgeon*," she insisted. "His name is Spurgeon."

The girls could hardly contain themselves—a few of them were trying to be nice, but the rest were practically rolling on the floor. I felt so foolish I could have run out of that room. I had never called Reverend Splurgeon anything but Splurgeon, and I was sure that was what everybody else called him. I told myself, *She must be thinking about somebody else.* Then again, she wasn't the kind to be wrong about anything.

Ursula turned her attention to Portia, who was sitting beside Linda. "Now, Portia, tell us about yourself."

But Portia hung her head and had nothing to say.

I sat there trying to figure out what I had done to provoke Ursula so bad. Maybe she was just having a bad day. If nothing else, our money problems were enough to stress her out.

We kept waiting for Portia to say something. That tattoo gave me the creeps. It twined around her neck like ivy. I'd seen tattoos before but nothing like that one.

Ursula tried again. "Portia, Linda said you hate cats. Why is it you hate cats?"

There was a long pause, and it didn't look like she was going to answer. Every eye was on that thin, narrow face, waiting for her to say something. When she did speak, her voice sounded dry as gravel. "I was locked in a closet with a dead cat for three days."

Shocked is hardly the word for it. Everybody in the room looked stunned. That is, everyone except Linda, who piped up, "I was locked in a motel room for a week and gang-raped by ten sheriff's deputies."

Even Lenora, the frail one with the empty eyes, stared at Portia and Linda in shocked disbelief.

We had hardly recovered when the bell rang and Group ended.

The women were quick to exit the room, dashing outside where they could smoke. I wanted to go in my room and close the door, but I knew Ursula wanted to hear how it went in town, so I followed her into the office. Obviously upset, she shut the door behind us.

"Esmeralda, your interruptions in Group are not helpful. They disrupt the program. Do you know how long it has taken me to get even this far with these ladies? They have such low self-esteem, they won't open up when we are one on one, but as you saw today, in Group they are less intimidated."

I didn't say it, but I thought to myself, *Why wouldn't they have "low self-esteem"? If you steal a prescription pad and write prescriptions for all your friends, how can you feel good about yourself?* As I saw it, this Linda felt proud of what she'd done, but I wasn't going to bring that up and challenge Ursula. Something was building up inside of her, and it wouldn't take much to make her explode.

"I instituted Group," she was saying, "to create an informal atmosphere among peers, which is a device that works well. Until they verbalize their feelings, I cannot diagnose and remedy their problems. You have certainly truncated the process, Esmeralda, and such interference will not be tolerated."

Where I come from, younger people respect older people like me. Imagine her dressing me down like that. I had to bite my tongue. Of course, I'm not the kind that stays speechless for long. "Ursula, if these girls—"

"Ladies," she snapped. Her stringy body was twitching with nerves, and she was going to town on another paper clip.

Ladies? I thought. *Ladies don't wear tattoos and do such things as I'm hearing here.* But I didn't say what I was thinking.

I could stay quiet in ten languages if only I knowed ten. I did put in my two cents' worth, though. "Well, if these ladies have low self-esteem, in most cases it's their own fault. If I had done the things Linda done, I'd be ashamed to show my face."

"That's hardly the point. I would appreciate it if you would leave analysis to me. I have my master's in psychology and am well qualified to assess and rectify whatever we have here."

"I'm sure you can, Ursula, and I don't mean to get in your way. It's just that I don't think there's much good comes out of wallowing around in the muck and mire of a miserable past when we could be looking to the future—you know, looking to what Jesus can do for us."

"That is a simplistic view. My heart's desire is to see these ladies come to know the Lord, but it is absolutely necessary to assiduously address the insidious circumstances that have entrapped them. Once we resolve the problems that led them into addictions, then we can lead them to Christ. My practice is based on biblical principles, Esmeralda. I know what I'm doing!"

She had reached the boiling point, so I didn't say anything, just waited for her to cool down. We sat in silence. Finally she said, "Well, what's your report?"

I told her all the creditors were willing to give us ten days more, and I asked her if any money had come in.

"Not a thing." She started scanning the receipt ledger.

"We can depend on getting fifty dollars from a church in Rock Hill, but they are irregular in sending it. . . . Dr. Elsie sends us a hundred dollars a month, but it must have slipped her mind now that she's in Vermont taking care of her terminally ill sister. . . . There is a Mrs. Hirsch whose daughter was helped at Priscilla Home. The daughter lived a Christian life for a year or two after leaving here, but then she was killed in an automobile accident. Her mother used to send us ten dollars a month from her social security check, but she hasn't sent us anything in several months."

"The widow's mite," I remarked.

She closed the book. "Just how many widow's mites will it take?"

"I don't know," I said, and even though I wasn't sure what God had in mind, I told her, "but I believe God can make a way out of no way."

"Don't you think I believe that, too?"

"Of course, you do, Ursula. And you believe in putting feet to our prayers. So do I. I passed a flea market in town, and I got to thinking we might find things here to sell down there."

"There's not much left. The former housemother went through everything and sold it to the thrift store."

"That piano—does anybody play it?"

"No. Lenora Barrineau played piano in nightclubs, but she won't play here. That piano is in very bad condition."

"Then we don't need it?"

"Not in its present condition."

"Then what would you think of placing an ad in the Rockville paper and offering it for sale?"

"We might as well. An ad will cost every penny of what we have in the account, so we should ask at least a hundred dollars for it."

"Let's ask five hundred. We can always come down."

Ursula leaned her elbows on the desk with her face in her hands and sighed. "Esmeralda, there will be no end to this financial burden. Even if we were to get all these bills paid, we'll always be up against money problems."

"So you're saying we ought to plan ahead?"

"Plan ahead? With what?"

"First off, we have got to look for ways to economize—turning off lights, not running the washing machine or dishwasher unless they're filled. Trying to make fewer trips into town, that kind of stuff. And you know that level ground next to the road? That patch catches morning sun, and I think we can make a garden there—grow our own vegetables."

"That ground has never been plowed."

"I know, but we should be able to find somebody who has a tractor who'll plow it for us."

"And what will you pay him with?"

"I don't know. We'll just have to take one step at a time."

The phone was ringing; she answered it and then covered the speaker with her hand. "It's Mr. Elmwood."

I left to give them privacy and went to my room.

4

I have never been one to wear my feelings on my elbows, but Ursula correcting me in front of the women got to me. Every day she found something I said that didn't set well with her. If it wasn't a verb out of place, it was a dangling participle, whatever that was. Ursula could write a book about dangling participles.

After I had closed the door to my room and was getting ready for bed, I could hear Ursula talking on the phone to Elmwood. I'm not one to eavesdrop, but I did hear her say something about somebody "grating on her nerves." That had to be me. That hurt. I'd had many a disagreement with people, but nobody before ever said anything like that about me. At least not that I could hear. And it cut me to the quick. That woman made me feel so stupid, so foolish, I couldn't stand it.

Even after I was in bed, she was still talking to Roger Elmwood. Then in a few minutes she was knocking on my door. "Esmeralda, Mr. Elmwood wants to talk to you."

"Just a minute," I said and got up. Throwing on my robe, I went in the office. Ursula had left and shut the door behind her.

I picked up the phone. "Roger?"

He jumped right in with what he had to say. "Esmeralda, there are a few things I need to talk to you about. You understand that as president of the board of directors I'm responsible to see that things run smoothly up there. There's a chain of command you may not be aware of, but you need to respect it. I know you mean well, but the Priscilla Home financial situation is best handled by the director and the board, not by you, the resident manager. Miss Ursula told you I authorized a bank loan to cover all the bills and enough to tide you over until there's a response to the prayer letter. Out of the goodness of her heart she went along with your asking our creditors for extensions; however, the board has always handled our shortfall professionally, by a bank loan."

As if that wasn't enough, he was not through. "Now this other thing, this business of your spending your own money to buy groceries disturbs me more than anything. Esmeralda, the board did not hire you to play God up there."

My blood pressure shot straight through the roof. "Roger Elmwood, I was led to believe that this is a faith ministry, and in my book, faith means trusting the Lord to provide. As for my spending my own money, let me remind you that before Jesus fed the multitudes he had the disciples bring him what they had. That's all I was doing—just giving the Lord my loaves and fishes."

Before he could say one word, I set him straight about

Ursula. "And as for me getting on Ursula's nerves, I'd like to go on record as saying that she gets on my nerves, too!"

He cleared his throat. "You listen to me, Esmeralda, it's up to you to make this thing work. If you two can't get along, one of you will have to go. I must warn you that the board is not only satisfied with Miss Ursula, we feel fortunate to have a director with a master's degree."

I felt like spitting in his eye! "Mr. Elmwood, the Lord brought me here, and it's here I'll be until the Lord tells me it's time to go!"

"I see," he said. "Oh yes, Mabel says to tell you hello."

"Have you finished?"

"Yes, I've finished."

"Then I'm hanging up," I said and slammed down the receiver. *The nerve of that big bag of wind!* I was so mad I could have spit gumdrops.

There was no use trying to sleep, so I sat in my chair and fumed. I was so hurt and so mad I couldn't help it; tears just spilled over. Splurgeon said, "Words often wound more than swords," and that's the truth if ever I heard it. You wouldn't believe the thoughts that went through my mind. I felt like packing up and leaving—getting out of the house before anybody else got up. Ursula was nothing but a snake in the grass—there was no way I could put up with that high-handed, know-it-all, walking dictionary! She couldn't speak a sentence but what she used them jawbreakers nobody could understand. She called herself a Christian, but there wasn't a woman in the house who would want to be a Christian if Ursula was the only example they ever saw.

Dr. Elsie has been on the board longer than Roger Elmwood, and she'd not stand for him dressing me down the way he did. I would have called her right then and there if she was not way up yonder in Vermont taking care of her sick sister.

It was about 3:00 in the morning before I wore myself out and figured I better get a grip before I had to face Ursula and the women at breakfast. I got out my old King James and opened it. If ever I needed a word from the Lord it was then and there.

My Bible was so full of stuff, and it was so marked up and falling apart, I had to handle it carefully. The way I found things in it was funny. I had a hard time remembering chapters and verses—references, you know—but I could remember what side of the page it was on and even where it was at, top or bottom. Most of the time I remembered the book a verse was in but not always. Still, I could usually find what I was looking for, and if I couldn't I had a concordance in back.

Like I said, I needed some word to help me get through the coming day, but I couldn't think of anything right off the bat, so I opened to the Psalms, which always seemed to say something to my soul. As I was thumbing through, there was this one page where the corner was torn and I was wondering if I shouldn't scotch tape it back together. That's not always a good idea, of course. Other pages I had mended that way didn't work too good. The tape got yellow and made the pages pucker. Smoothing out that corner, I saw verses I had underlined some time or other, so I read them. "Those who are planted in the house of the Lord shall flourish in the courts of our God. They shall still bring forth fruit in old age; they shall be fat and flourishing."

Good heavens, wasn't that exactly what I needed? "They shall still bring forth fruit in old age," he said. For a little while I just sat there, letting that balm in Gilead soothe my wounded soul. It cooled me down, I tell you, and I had to ask the Lord to forgive me for being so mad, for saying them things—well, maybe not just saying them but feeling the way I did. I wanted to promise the Lord that I'd love Ursula, but the wounds were too raw to make a promise like that.

I read on for a while and then climbed back in bed. I wasn't feeling very good about myself, about not having enough love to go around, none for Ursula and precious little for the women in the home. If I wanted any sleep at all, I had to get my mind off it.

As I repeated them verses to myself, something struck me funny and I had to smile. It was that last line about being "fat and flourishing." I was willing to claim the part about bringing forth fruit in old age, but as for the "fat and flourishing" part, that was something I could do without! I wished I could tell Beatrice that one—she'd get a kick out of it.

I slept an hour or two before the wake-up bell rang. I lay there a few minutes listening to the sounds coming from upstairs—feet padding around, toilets flushing, water running, hair dryers humming. At home I would have been up, had the coffee made, and been sitting in the recliner having my devotions by this time. The first couple hours of the day I spent that way—reading, praying, singing a hymn or two—but here in Priscilla Home there was so much commotion and so little free time, I couldn't settle down and feel alone with the Lord. I think that was a big part of the trouble. It looked like the only way I could get back on track was to get up earlier than everybody else, but for this morning the only time I had to pray was while I was dressing and fixing my face. Before I opened my bedroom door to face the world, I asked the Lord to set a watch before my big mouth.

At breakfast everyone was quiet, myself included, and after breakfast Ursula asked me to come in the office. Dreading what this might mean, I followed her, and we sat down across from each other.

"Esmeralda, what is your agenda for today?"

I answered with the first thing that popped in my head.

"We need a garden, so I thought I would try to find someone with a tractor who'll plow the ground for us."

I knew she thought this was foolish, so I was surprised when she said, "Very well. Perhaps you should take one of the ladies with you."

That wasn't necessary, but I wanted to be cooperative. "Okay," I said. "Which one?"

"How about Linda?"

I shook my head. "No, not Linda. She thinks she's the bell cow."

"The bell cow? Whatever do you mean?"

"Just that; she thinks she's the bell cow."

She still didn't understand but went on, "Well, I can never get a word out of Dora in the counseling session, so you might as well take her along. Try to get her to talk. If there's no breakthrough soon, there's no use in our keeping her here."

Dora and I headed out without a clue as to where to go, so we drove down the Old Turnpike. I wasn't going to have somebody in the car without talking, so I commenced by saying we'd have to pray the Lord would lead us to where we could find a tractor and a man to drive it. "You ever drove a tractor?" I asked.

"Nary a one," she answered, staring straight ahead. "Tractors ain't for hollers."

Whatever does she mean by that? But I wasn't about to let on that I didn't know. "You got any idea where we might find what we're looking for?" I asked.

"Follow the sun. It'll lead you to a valley."

That didn't make an ounce of sense either, but curious to find out, I took a chance. "A valley?" I repeated.

"Valleys is for big planting. Tractors come with big planting."

Now that made sense.

As we drove along we came to a break in the trees where a clearing stretched down a hillside. I didn't see any tractor, but a flock of wild turkeys was feeding along the edge. I stopped the car and eased out my door to watch. The turkeys had their heads held high and their feathers drawn in close, and even I could see they were on the alert. I counted an even dozen before a wild gobbler took off in flight forty feet above the ground, flying over our heads, going a good sixty miles an hour. With his head stretched forward, his feet stretched behind, he hardly flapped his wings. Gliding higher and higher, his bronze feathers shone in the sun until I lost him beyond the trees.

When I turned around to see where the flock was, they were out of sight.

Climbing back in the car, I said to Dora, "That was a sight to behold," and figuring wild turkeys were nothing new to her, I asked why that gobbler didn't flap his wings.

"He depends on his legs more'n his wings to fly," she told me.

"I guess people hunt wild turkeys?"

"There's coon hunters and people too lazy to work lays in the woods a-shootin' turkeys, pheasants, rabbits, squirrels, ground hogs, and the like. They'll skin a ground hog and make strings for their boots of its hide."

We rounded a curve and were in the deep woods again. It was chilly and dark enough for headlights. Dora mumbled, "There's woods spirits along about here."

I slowed down to a snail's pace. "Woods spirits?"

"Like as not."

Neither of us said anything, but my mind was running wild trying to imagine what she meant by woods spirits. I don't mind telling you, that road did look spooky. "What can they do to us?"

She was slow to answer, so I repeated the question.

Her voice was as raspy as a dying man's. "They've been known to send a pickup over a cliff."

I thought I better not press my luck by asking more questions, but I tell you right now, I was glad when we broke out of that overhanging thicket and saw sunlight again.

We had not gone far when Dora leaned over the dash and looked up at something. "See, lookit yonder atop that rise."

I looked but all I saw was a chimney where a house had been. "You mean that chimney?"

"See them trees all black and burnt? That house burnt to the ground, all right. . . . Fire be the devil's work. Where he burns he leaves his spirits to guard the place."

"That so?"

"Them what has sense about woods spirits don't go near a burnt-out place. Afore I had good sense, I oncet dared it by myself. Had to find out for myself if what they say be true."

She stopped, and I wanted her to go on talking. "And?" I asked.

"It was Widder MacIntosh's place burnt to the ground afore I was borned. What's left of the old place is the chimbley a-standin' stout against the gales for so many years nobody knows the count. I spent all the daylight hours up there a-roamin' 'round among them charred timbers black as Satan's soul. The widder ain't yet done with her place—her lilies be still a-bloomin' up there, pushed up from the ground atwixt them timbers.

"Oncet the wind commenced to pick up, and I could hear it singin' in that chimbley like it was glad I was there, I thought nothin' of plundering around about its foot, but I should have stayed shy of that. I found me a brick up there like as I never seen afore—thin and fluted both sides, four holes drilled through an' a-covered with green moss. Purtiest brick ever I seen. Most likely the widder kept it for a doorstop. When I brung it home, that's what I used it for, a doorstop. . . . Wisht a million times I had left it lay up thar next that chimbley where it belonged."

"Why?" I asked.

She would not answer.

We had gone past where we could see the chimney, but she was still worrying on it. I got the feeling there was much more to this than she was telling. "It's a boding thang to keep in mind—that old chimbley a-standin' up there all by its self so stout the devil hisself can't knock her down."

We were coming to what looked like a road on the left, and she told me to turn. "This here's a valley road."

It was hardly a road, more like a lane with two ruts running underside the mountain on the left and dropping down fifty feet or more on the right. Dora was holding on to the dashboard and leaning toward my side of the car like she was holding the Chevy away from that steep drop-off. When we got beyond some trees that were blocking the view, I could see a stream winding through a meadow below. Sun reflecting on the water made a yellow ribbon of it. Dora was right, this was a valley road.

We had hugged the mountain for less than half a mile when we saw a tar-paper shack clinging to a small patch of level land between the road and the embankment. There was a woodshed with cordwood stacked neatly, an area of mowed lawn, and a slope going up to the road with rhododendron and blueberry bushes.

What lay below the embankment on the far side of the shack, I could not see, but a pull-off place beside the woodshed was where I aimed the Chevy and stopped. "Maybe somebody here can tell us where we can find a tractor, Dora."

We got out of the car to see if anybody was around. Smoke was coming out the chimney, so I figured there must be somebody around. In back of the house and down the hill a piece was an outhouse with the door open. Not likely anybody would be in there with the door wide open—on the other hand, there might be, but I for one was not about to go look.

A porch on the front of the house was just big enough for a bench where somebody could sit and look out over the valley. Across the valley, alders and willows bordered the stream, and a flock of crows were flying overhead, cawing. I called out, "Anybody home?" Nobody answered and nobody stirred in the house. There wasn't a soul in sight, much less a tractor. I was ready to give up when I heard a horse snorting. Sounded like it was coming from below the embankment, so we went over to the edge to see. An apple tree clung to the side of that steep incline, and where the ground leveled out flat at the bottom, there was a fenced-in garden plot. At first the tree hid the horse hitched to a plow, but then I noticed it looked like somebody had just stopped plowing in the middle of a row.

All of a sudden, Dora scrambled down that bank like a billy goat, and then I saw what she saw. A man was lying on the ground apparently asleep or drunk or something. I slipped and slid my way down to find out what was what.

When I got down there, I saw he was older than me by some years, white as a sheet and holding his chest. "What's wrong, Dora?"

"A-hurtin' in his chest," she said.

Sweat was pouring off him, and Dora was trying to help him sit up. "Leave him lay, Dora." It looked to me like he was having a heart attack. "We got to get him to a doctor." I looked around to see if there was a way I could get the car down there, and I saw that the road did wind around the apple tree down to the level of the garden. "I'll bring the car around," I told Dora and got back up the bank on my hands and knees.

By the time I drove the car down there, Dora had the fellow on his feet. She opened the door, and together we managed to get him inside. "You get in the back, Dora."

She shook her head. "I'll wait here," she said, and I had no time to waste asking why.

On the way into town the man told me his name was Lester Teague; it was plain to see he was a mountain man, born and bred. His bib overalls looked to be as much a part of him as Dora's hunting coat was a part of her. Sick as he was, he didn't talk much. I figured he had to be at death's door to be letting me take him to the hospital.

When Lester started gasping for breath, I got scared we might not make it into town, so I speeded up. Once we left the turnpike and were on the paved road, I really pressed the pedal to the metal, gunned it up hills and whipped around curves with my tires squealing for mercy!

Well, we made it. They took Lester right away, gave him an EKG and so forth. We spent hours in the emergency room. Reminded me of the time I took Maria to the hospital, her sick unto death and me not knowing her name. She was Spanish, and the only name I could think of was Carmen Miranda, so when I checked her in, that's the name I used. I had to bluff our way in because she didn't have insurance or nothing.

Lying about who Maria was had cost me plenty! I should have known I wouldn't get away with that lie because never in my life have I ever got away with anything I done wrong. As soon as Maria died, it all came out, and the hospital started billing me for her treatment and those days she spent in that private room. At first I balked. Then I stalled. But in the end I had to admit it was my responsibility. I was glad for the job at Priscilla Home because the three hundred I got each month went right on that bill.

The doctor wanted to keep Lester overnight for observation, but the old man wouldn't hear of it. Lester hobbled over to the cashier, took out a roll of bills, and peeled off enough to pay his fee. Everybody's mouths dropped open. The doctor gave Lester some pills and told him to put one under his tongue when he had chest pains and to go to his personal physician for a checkup. The chances of Lester Teague having a "personal physician" was about as remote as me having a Cadillac. I could have told that little intern right then and there that Lester Teague would not be going to any doctor, but that was better left unsaid.

❦

On the way back to Lester's place, I had to stop for gas. Once I filled up I had four or five dollars left. Back in the car, I did the talking. I told Lester we were from Priscilla Home; he knew the place. Told him about the turkeys. Told him we were looking for a tractor. Asked him whose house was it that had burned. All he said was that it had burned the night of the big storm a few years back. "Lightning hit it."

By the time we got back to his house, Lester had stopped holding his chest. But before I let him get out of the car, I looked for Dora. I could hear something going on down by the garden and went to the edge of the bank to see. Lo and behold, she had finished the plowing and was watering the horse. Seeing me, she wrapped the reins around the plow handle and climbed up to where we were at.

Lester had got out of the car by himself and wouldn't let us help him get to the porch. Once we were on the porch, Lester sat on the bench and we sat on the railing. Through the screen door I could see inside the kitchen. There was a woodstove in there with a pot on it, a sink, a dishpan, a straight-back chair, and some things on a table covered with a dishcloth. It looked neat enough.

I wanted to wait to see if he was well enough before

we left him. He was breathing okay but he was still pale. I took him to be a man in his late seventies. He had a good face and was lean with a back that bent forward. Whit leather was no tougher looking than he was. I was wondering if there was somebody who might look in on him from time to time.

"You got any neighbors around here?" I asked.

"One or two."

"Where do they live?"

"Up the Boone Fork."

"How far?"

"Eight or ten crow-fly miles."

Hardly neighbors, I thought.

I looked at Dora to see if she had any idea about what we should do, but I couldn't read what she was thinking any more than I could read Lester's mind. *Two of a kind.*

"I see you have got grapevines growing on your fences," I said just to make conversation. "What kind are they?"

"Concord and Catawba." He shifted on the bench and leaned forward to show me which were which. "Them down yonder on that bottom fence be blue, and the ones a-goin' up t'other way be red. Come fall, bring some buckets and help yourselves."

"Thank you, we will," I said, pleased as punch at the prospect. With enough grapes we could make jelly and jam to last us a winter.

"Come summer there'll be blueberries," he was saying, "an' you can pick all you want o' them as well. Come afore the birds take over."

"You sure?"

"I got little use for 'em. Bring ever' bucket you got."

Lester's color was getting better, and I figured if we were going to leave, we better go. No doubt Ursula was already on her ear wondering what was keeping us. We'd just have to give up on finding a tractor until another day. "Well," I said, "I guess we have to be going. You sure you're going to be all right?"

"I'll be all right," he said.

"Promise me you won't do nothing for a day or two."

He didn't promise.

"Well, don't be foolish," I told him. "Take care of yourself."

I was already down the steps when he called after me, "Say you could use a tractor?"

"We could sure use one."

"Well, I ain't got no tractor . . . but if you've a mind to, you can borrey the horse I got and the plow."

I thanked him but said we were looking for a tractor and a man to drive it. I turned to Dora, but she had jumped off the porch and was bounding down the hill to where the horse was. *What in the world?*

I walked over to the edge of the bank to see what she was up to—she was unhitching the horse! "Now look here, Dora," I yelled. "We got no way to get that animal up the mountain!"

She wasn't listening. I looked back at Lester, hoping for help.

"She can ride him," he told me.

I tell you, I was flabbergasted! "Ride that horse all

the way up the mountain? We got no hay—nothing to feed him."

"You got grass, he's grass fed," Lester said.

I could not believe what was happening. Dora hitched the horse to the apple tree and was getting ready to load the plow in my Chevy. "Drive on down here," she told me.

If ever a body was floored, it was me! But I did as I was told; got the car down there, turned it around, and opened the trunk.

Dora and I got the plow and tackle half in and half out of the trunk, but the lid wouldn't close. That didn't bother Dora. She led the horse alongside the bank where it would be easier to mount up, steadied him, then threw her leg over his bare back and was astride him in less time than it takes to tell it.

I climbed back in the car and drove slowly around the apple tree and back onto the rutted road. With the trunk lid up, there was only a narrow space I could see through to the back. Dora was following right along behind.

Above Lester's yard, I leaned my head out the window and yelled down to him, "How long can we keep him?"

"Long as need be," I heard him say.

I thanked him, still shocked at what was happening, and put the car in gear. Dora flicked the reins, and we were on our way. I drove at a snail's pace and kept looking in the rear through that little gap to make sure Dora was coming along okay. Even bareback, she was riding as natural as if she and that horse were lifelong friends.

Once I was sure we were underway okay, I tried to

think of what I would tell Ursula. She might just make us turn around and take the horse and plow right back to Lester. Of course, I had to believe this was the Lord's way of helping us make a garden, but convincing Ursula of that would take all the gumption I had got.

As we were rounding those curves climbing back up the mountain, suddenly all this struck me so funny I started laughing historically! I could just see us riding up at Priscilla Home with all those girls sitting on the porch watching—wide-eyed and open-mouthed, probably wondering if they were having the D.T.s. This had to be about the funniest thing that had ever happened at Priscilla Home, and if this didn't make them laugh nothing ever would. At least we would give them some excitement.

But Ursula? Ursula would never see anything funny about this.

5

When we arrived back at Priscilla Home and the women saw Dora riding that horse in back of the Chevy, they came sailing off that porch like a flock of wild geese and followed us around to the back laughing their heads off. "Hey, Miss Ursula, lookee here!" Linda hollered. Ursula must have been in her office and not able to hear Linda.

"We didn't find a tractor," I told the girls, "but Dora here can plow with this horse, so we borrowed it for a few days. Here, can you help me get the plow out of the trunk?"

They were quick to get hold of both ends and heave it over the end of the trunk. Evelyn lifted out the tackling. Even though her meat and drink, vodka, had reduced her to skin and bones, she always jumped to do her share of the work, and that made me worry that she would do too much and get down sick.

Dora slid off the gelding and led him in back of the garage to where there was water. "He needs a rest," I explained. "Besides, Dora can't start plowing until we clear out the rocks in that patch."

"Not me!" Linda exclaimed.

"Yes, you," I replied. I told myself, *There's no way that big strong girl is going to shirk doing her part.* "And now's as good a time as any to get going on it."

"I didn't come here to do farm work," she argued.

"Neither did I," I told her, "but your stay at Priscilla Home is free, so it's little enough to ask you to help out wherever you're needed."

"That's right, Linda," Angela told her. "Every other rehab costs a lot of money, and since you don't have insurance, where do you think you could go? You ought to be glad there's a place like Priscilla Home."

"Aw, shut up!" Linda said as she picked up a hoe and followed along behind the other girls. They were headed for the place by the road where we planned to plant. Once they got started working, I went inside to face the music.

Ursula was on the phone, so I went in my bathroom to wash up. In a few minutes she called me. "Esmeralda, Dr. Elsie is on phone." Oh, I was glad to hear that; I was very anxious to talk to her. Ursula handed me the receiver and left the office.

"Dr. Elsie?"

Always to the point, Dr. Elsie answered, "Esmeralda, I called to tell Ursula my check is in the mail. We've been busy here, and I neglected to send it on time." She paused; I tensed up; more was coming. "Esmeralda, you can help that girl, Ursula. She's a newborn Christian, came to know the Lord her last year in grad school."

There! I knew it! Ursula had complained about me to Dr. Elsie. Smarting from that knife in my back, I listened, wanting nothing more than to give Dr. Elsie an earful about that snake in the grass. But Dr. Elsie was breezing along, giving me this song and dance about Ursula.

"Ursula was saved through one of those campus ministries, I forget which one, and I doubt she's had much nurturing."

I picked up on that "nurturing" business, and Dr. Elsie, who's about as plainspoken as a body can get, explained, "You'll have to wet nurse this one."

"On the 'sincere milk of the Word,' I suppose," I snapped, still smarting.

She caught my drift and pressed on making a case for Ursula. "Esmeralda, she's the only Christian in her family, and her parents were not in favor of her taking this job. They both teach in a university and from all I can tell, they're agnostics. They have ambitions for their only daughter and Priscilla Home is not one of them."

"How in tarnation am I supposed to teach that woman anything—she's so educated, so high and mighty—half the time I don't know what she's talking about!"

"You'll find a way," she said, as confident as always that I am some kind of wonder woman. "I have to go now," she said and hung up.

I stormed back in my room, furious and ready to pack my bags.

In a few minutes I heard Ursula come back in the office. When she called me in, she could see how mad I was. "Esmeralda, I can help you with anger management. There's a protocol—"

"Ursula, it strikes me that you, too, have a temper."

She ignored that remark. "Let's not quarrel," she said. "We have more to worry about than our personality conflicts. The mail came, and there was only one contribution. It's from the youth in your Apostolic Bible Church. They had a car wash and sent us the profit, thirty dollars. If they washed all the cars in South Carolina it wouldn't bring in what we owe. Esmeralda, we've waited long enough for a miracle. I've decided to do something."

"We still have a few days before we have to come up with the money. There's some reason we're having to wait."

"Chapter and verse, please."

It took me a few minutes to come up with something. "For starters, what about Mary and Martha?"

"Mary and Martha?"

"Right. After they sent word to Jesus that their brother was sick, they waited and nothing happened. Even after Jesus got the message, he stayed where he was two whole days before he left to go to them. His staying away like that and making them wait had a purpose. He was waiting so Lazarus would die and be buried because he wanted to raise him from the dead."

"So what's the point?"

"Ursula, there's always some good reason why we're made to wait."

"Maybe for you but not for me. Tomorrow I'm going to the bank, so don't plan to go anywhere. One of us has to be here at all times." She stood up. "Oh, by the way, did you get a tractor?"

"No," I said and left it at that.

"There's a letter here for you." She handed it to me as she was going out the door.

The letter was from Beatrice, and I took it in my room to read it. Feeling like a string of spaghetti left in the pot, I sat down and waited for what was sure to happen. The minute Ursula discovered that horse and plow, the fat would be in the fire. I tell you, this place was getting to me.

Well, I opened Beatrice's letter. As you know, Beatrice is my lifelong friend, and I missed her. That is, I missed having her look to me for every little thing. She had Carl now and didn't need me that way. Beatrice had changed more than any one person I had ever known. Sometimes now, instead of me telling her what was what, she told me—actually jerked a knot in me one time about Percy Poteat.

Beatrice's letter was all about the Grand Canyon and other places they had visited. I wasn't much interested in all of that. At the bottom of the letter were Bible references. She never did that before. *It must be Carl's influence,* I thought.

I heard a commotion outside under my window and got up to see, knowing full well what it was. Ursula was down there with several of the women all talking at once, excited about what must seem to her to be proof positive that I am a wacko. I didn't see Dora. The horse was alongside the garage eating grass.

Ursula was coming back inside, banging the door behind her. I braced myself and went back in the office to face this cyclone storming up the steps.

She burst in, her face red as a beet. "Esmeralda, what in the world have you done?"

"You mean the plow?"

"The horse!"

"It's for plowing the garden."

"I assumed as much. Whatever made you think I would put up with having an animal on this property?"

"I didn't give it the first thought," I said just to aggravate her. "There's no reason we can't make a good garden up here, raise our own vegetables and can stuff for the winter. Self-help is better'n begging."

She ignored that last dig. "Did you tell the ladies they would have to clear the ground of stones?"

"I did. A vegetable garden is not a rock garden."

"Don't you think I know that?" she snapped.

I was getting a kick out of nettling her. "Don't your books tell you work is good therapy?"

"Therapy or not, it's time for Group and they must all assemble in the day room!"

But she didn't ring the bell. She sat down and looked across at me, those dark eyes sparking. "From whom did you buy or rent that animal and plow?"

"It's borrowed. Lester Teague let us have it for nothing."

That took some of the wind out of her sails. I believed I was winning, but I'm not the kind to gloat.

"And pray tell, who is Lester Teague?"

"He's a mountain man lives below us on a side road." I went on to describe him.

"Sounds avuncular," she said. "Don't think you won't have to pay that man one way or another."

"Oh, we've already paid him."

"With what?"

So I told her the whole story. By the time I finished, she had calmed down; didn't say anything more about the horse, just started in on her kind of business. "Did Dora open up to you?"

"Well, I don't know if you'd call it opening up, but she did talk. Some of it made sense, some didn't."

"For instance?"

There was no way I was going to tell Ursula all the strange things Dora had said. I shrugged my shoulders and passed it off, saying, "Oh, this and that."

"Nothing of consequence?"

I shook my head.

For a few minutes neither of us spoke. Then she swiveled in her chair, started in on another paper clip, and began again. "I think you should know something of Dora's background. The sheriff and her sponsor brought her here under a court order. What led up to her arrest is a long story. Some years ago, Dora was driving under the influence with her three-year-old boy in a pickup truck when she sideswiped another vehicle. She was driving on a dirt road on the side bordering a steep incline. There had been heavy rain that night, and the edge of the road gave way under the truck sending it over that embankment."

Something about this seemed familiar, and as Ursula kept talking it came to me that maybe this was why Dora had acted a little strange when we were riding down Lester's road. She had braced against the dash and leaned away from that side of the road next the embankment.

"The truck rolled over several times," Ursula was saying, "before it finally came to rest. Dora had only cuts and bruises, but her son suffered head injuries and lay in a coma for five years before he died."

Ursula's voice was as flat as a stone.

"During those years her child was in a coma, Dora became increasingly dependent on alcohol, and to pay medical bills she grew marijuana and sold it."

Only a body who has never had any pain in their life could tell that story with no more feeling than Ursula had. Again she swiveled around in the chair, taking her nerves out on that paper clip. "An attorney took the accident case to court, and even though Dora had been driving under the influence when the accident occurred, he won an enormous settlement for her. The trouble is, Dora will not take a penny of that money. The attorney, with his entire family, is now on an extended cruise."

"You mean he took the money?"

"One would assume that he did. Dora foolishly refused the settlement and continued growing marijuana to pay the bills. As might be expected, she was apprehended, tried and convicted, but the judge knew her story and sent her to Priscilla Home rather than to prison. If she's not rehabilitated here, incarceration is inevitable."

I remembered Ursula had said Dora would be sent home if we didn't get a breakthrough soon, so I had to speak up. "It seems to me Dora has had a lot in her life to make her closed-mouthed. Even if she don't talk much, I for one think we should keep her here as long as it takes for the Lord to do his work in her life."

"*Doesn't* talk much," she said, correcting me. "Ethically, we have no choice. Dora needs to go through the grieving process, but since she won't talk to me, she has not taken the first step. It would be unconscionable to keep her here when we have a waiting list."

I determined right then and there that I would do everything in my power to see that Dora stayed at Priscilla Home until she found victory in Jesus. That meant I had some big-time praying to do!

Ursula rang the bell for Group. I followed her downstairs to the day room, where the girls were straggling in from the garden. We arranged ourselves in a circle with Ursula and her clipboard in the leader's chair.

"Where's Dora?" she asked.

"I'll fetch her," I said and got up to go look for her.

I found Dora in the garden, swinging a pick, digging out a huge rock. "Dora, Miss Ursula's beginning Group."

"Say she is?" And she went right on digging.

I just stood there, not knowing what to do or say.

When she finally got the rock loose, we picked it up and carried it to the pile beside the road. Dora leaned on the pick handle and pointed. "It's over there we'll plant taters . . . in that sheltered place." She pointed the other way. "The corn alongside the road. You don't plant corn till the oak leaf be the size of a squirrel's foot."

I nodded like I'd known that all my life and just waited, wondering how in the world I would persuade her to go inside.

Finally she shouldered the pick. "Say that self-rising Christian wants I should come to Group?"

I wanted to smile but didn't.

Dora led the way back to the house and set the pick down beside the door, and we walked inside.

Ursula waited until we sat down. "Dora, we were just getting in touch with our feelings. One way we do this is by bringing up memories from our childhood. Tell me, what memories would you like to share with us?"

I was surprised that Dora didn't hesitate to answer. "My memory is a muddy pond where fish can't live, only tadpoles and frogs that grunt in the night."

You might think the women would have laughed, but they didn't. They were probably as mystified by this strange girl as I was. I heard Linda muttering under her breath to Portia, "Is she off the wall or what?"

Ursula kept her cool. "Very well, Dora, don't think of memories; just tell us about an experience that made you happy."

Dora sat with both hands stuffed deep in the pockets of that old coat, and the words rolled out of her as easily as if she had practiced them. "Come a cold night, Papa and all the men from round about climb upland where there's a place above the holler with a stone-face shelter from the wind. They let loose their hounds, build a good fire, and uncork their jugs afore they set to lis'enin' to the chase. It's a man's pride to hear the sound of his own hound a-singin', for his hound's singin' is like nary another, and nothin'll pleasure him more than spendin' the whole night a-lis'enin' to that hound he's raised from a pup an' learned him good.

"Oncet the run is over and the bayin' begins, them men grab their guns and go after that coon or cat a-whoopin' an' a-hollerin' like a pack o' Injins on warpath. It pleasures me, too, a-hearin' them dogs and them men a hollering after them.

"Dogs is a wonderful thang to have. There's bird dogs that scares up a covey of quail an' the like; rabbit dogs, which ain't much; b'ar dogs, the bravest by far; deer hounds, the best of the lot for table meat—ever' one trained to foller just one scent an' no other. But mostly them hounds lie on the hearth an' dream dreams of goin' upland to yelp and yowl for them old coots—yelp and yowl to their heart's content."

We all just sat there, looking at Dora. You might think we should have clapped or said something, but if you'd been there, you would have known better. It felt like being in another time and place, or hearing sweet music for the first time. That was the spell she cast.

Ursula scribbled something on that clipboard and must have had enough of Dora because she turned to ask Angela, "Since your parents are missionaries and you've been brought up in a Christian home, tell us what led you to rebel against your parents and essentially against Christianity."

Angela was sitting with her hands cupped under her chin, framing her pretty face, saying nothing, keeping up her guard.

"Angela?"

"I'd rather not talk about that," she replied.

Ursula persisted. "Come now, you're among friends."

She didn't get anywhere. Angela sat looking back at her stony faced.

Ursula was the kind of person who didn't know when

to quit. "It's all right to have resentment against our parents," she was telling Angela, "but until we lay open our resentments, we can't resolve the problems."

That hit a nerve! Angela's eyes were full of fire. "It wasn't like that at all! My parents were wonderful, they still are—they were good to me. I'll not sit here—"

"Now, now. There's no need to be defensive. Of course, your parents were good to you, but what was there in your home environment that led you to abuse pharmaceuticals?"

"Miss Ursula, let's you get one thing straight. It wasn't my parents' fault. Do you understand that?"

"All right. Fine, so you don't think it was your parents' fault. We'll leave it at that, but what was it, then?"

"Well, if you must know, it was like this. When I was ten or eleven years old, my parents were bringing all kinds of people into our house to disciple them. You know—taught them the Bible. There were these two rough-looking characters who told wild tales about getting drunk and running from the law. It sounded exciting—their lifestyle fascinated me."

Ursula wasn't satisfied with that. "So they fascinated you. What else?"

Angela looked disgusted. "Nothing happened then, but I never forgot that man and woman."

Obviously, this was not the end of the story, but I for one thought Ursula should leave well enough alone. Instead, she was closing in for the kill. "But later, something did happen?"

"Well, yes, it did," Angela answered, her voice tight. "I need a cigarette. May I?"

"That can wait. Go on with your story."

Angela rubbed the palms of her hands on her thighs until she could begin again. "The mission board sent us overseas to Africa. We went to Kenya. I loved growing up there. When I was sixteen I was going to high school and had a lot of friends, but that's when we came back to the States.

"America was like a foreign country to me. Kids at school and in church all had their little cliques, and I didn't fit in. My parents were real busy with deputation and sometimes had to leave me at home by myself. That's when I started hanging out with street kids. They took me in without asking any questions or making any demands on me, gave me drinks, gave me drugs, and . . . I thought I had found what I was looking for. We hung out in the corner bar and, like it says in that song, everybody there knew my name."

That story made me feel real bad. Even at my home church, Apostolic Bible, we had our own little groups, and about the only people who reached out to newcomers were the Willing Workers. After anybody visited our church Clara would always take them a pie or a cake. But that homeless man Boris Krantz brought to church caused a big stink in our Willing Workers class. We didn't think it was a good idea to have such a man among our young people. *I wonder if he's still coming to church?*

I tell you the truth, I was learning a lot from these Priscilla women, things I wished the W.W.s could learn.

Ursula must have thought she had sorted out all the pieces because she was saying, "Angela, what you are saying tells me it will be harder to win you to Christ than it will be for someone who has not had your Christian experience."

"No, Miss Ursula," she said, her voice soft but steady, "I want my Christian life back."

My heart ached for that girl. And it ached for her parents. They were bound to be tore up over this.

Ursula was jotting down something on that clipboard and was ready to end the meeting. "Miss Esmeralda, do you have anything to add?" she asked.

"Nothing except to say we'll start right after breakfast to get the rocks out of that patch."

Linda stood up. "Miss Ursula, she's a slave driver!"

"Aren't I!" I said, pleased that my English was good.

Ursula corrected me. "Not *aren't I*, Esmeralda."

I laughed. "Ain't I, then."

"No, *ain't* is not a legitimate word. It is a contraction of 'am not.' What you should have said is, 'Am I not.'"

She was so serious as to be ridiculous, so I came right back at her. "The onliest contractions I know come with childbirth."

That broke up the meeting, and we all left laughing. All except Ursula, that is. I didn't think she knew how to laugh.

6

After breakfast the girls were ready to start work. There were a few snowflakes falling, but I thought maybe they wouldn't last long, not in April. Knowing Lenora and Evelyn were not physically able to work in the garden, I let them work in the house, polishing the furniture, dusting, doing some laundry, and so forth.

Since Ursula had already left to go to the bank, I had to stay in the office by the phone until she got back. As much as I liked to work in a garden, I needed some quiet time, so sitting in the office was good. I'd been praying on the run lately, and that didn't make for a good connection, if you know what I mean. I'd say, "Lord, make Ursula lighten up," or "Lord, send in the money," but that's not giving the Lord his due. It is not polite to keep making requests and only throw in a few thank-yous and praises here and there.

Ursula must have been in the office the night before worrying because there was a pile of ruined paper clips in the wastebasket. I tell you, when it comes to paper clips, that woman is a mass murderer.

Yes, I needed to be alone with the Lord, but in a way, I dreaded it because he would most likely rake me over the coals.

You've heard of the Ugly American? Well, this business of losing my temper and having bad feelings toward Ursula was turning me into the Ugly Christian. You see, I had sense enough to know the Lord was not going to change Ursula unless I got straightened out myself, and even then she may not change. In that case, I would need more grace than ever I'd had before, which was precious little.

Beatrice's letter was sticking out of my Bible, and I decided to read it again. I needn't have bothered. There was really nothing much in that letter. But the references at the bottom of the page made me curious, so I looked them up. They were from Matthew, and I knew the verses by heart: "Ye have heard that it hath been said, thou shalt love thy neighbor, and hate thine enemy; But I say unto you, love your enemies, bless them that curse you, do good to them that hate you, and pray for them who despitefully use you, and persecute you."

I tell you, memorizing those verses was one thing, but obeying them was where the rubber met the road. Ursula wasn't exactly persecuting me, but she was just so hard to take. It was her attitude that rubbed me the wrong way. All the same, she was a "neighbor" that I didn't love. To tell the truth, I would just as soon the Lord didn't get so personal with me. I knew he really and truly expected me to love her, and everybody who rubbed me the wrong way, but I was not one of those super spiritual saints who went around sweet and smiling with a halo on her head. God knew I couldn't fake it. If I'd had a halo, it would've turned green the first day.

And of course, Ursula was not the only one I'd get out of sorts with. When I thought about the way I'd get irritated with the W.W.s and make fun of some of them, I felt ashamed of myself.

I decided I'd rather not think about Ursula or those women. What I wanted to do was worship the Lord. Now, I don't have a solo voice, in fact, a bullfrog sounds better, but I don't sing for anybody else, just myself, so no harm's done.

I remembered Pastor Osborne saying the whole gospel is in that old hymn "Trust and Obey," and that you can't have the trust without the obey. Well, I guessed that was where I was wrong; I was stronger on the trusting than on the obeying, but I sang it anyway. I knew all the verses by heart as well as the chorus:

> Trust and obey,
> for there's no other way,
> to be happy in Jesus,
> but to trust and obey.

The phone rang. It was a woman answering the ad about the piano, and I got excited. She asked, "What kind is it?" I didn't remember, so I asked her to hold the line while I went to look. When I came back, I told her, "It's a Steinway, a baby grand."

"I'm looking for a Yamaha," she said. So that ended that. Needless to say, I was disappointed.

I went back to reading, thumbing through Matthew, reading more of the same—"turn the other cheek . . . go the second mile . . . blessed are the peacemakers."

Good heavens, there was so much in there that was hard to take. I had to get out of the Sermon on the Mount. Checking out the cross references, I turned to Ephesians. Well, lo and behold, the same kind of stuff was in Ephesians. At least the words weren't printed in red. I know it's all the word of God, but somehow, when it comes from the mouth of Jesus, it gets to me. Those Ephesian verses were on the right hand page, the bottom of the left column, and that's how I would remember where to find them the next time I wanted to hear about being meek and long-suffering, which anybody who knows me will tell you is not and never has been my long suit. "Forbearing one another in love . . . not letting the sun go down on your wrath lest you give place to the devil." *There's hardly a night lately when the sun don't go down on my wrath—with me mad as a wet hen.*

I'd had enough. I closed the Bible, leaned back in the chair, and started talking it out.

No doubt this is why you have not sent in the money, Lord. I for one have give place to the devil. You tell me here we're supposed to be kind, one to another, tender-hearted, forgiving one another. . . . No wonder we have not been getting along like Christians ought to. But Lord, don't she know these Scriptures, too?

To be honest with you, Lord, there's no way I can live up to what you're telling me to do here. In fact, I'm ashamed to say it, but I don't really want to give in to that woman.

If you think for one minute I felt good about this, I didn't. It's just that I knew myself. I'd tried before to love people that rubbed me the wrong way and it didn't work, so there was no use beating around the bush and making out like I could be the sweet, good Christian I ought to be. It just wasn't in me!

Someone knocked on the door. Evelyn said she and Lenora were having trouble with the washing machine, so I had to go down and straighten that out. Something was wrong with the timer, but I showed them how they could work it. Like a lot of things around there, that machine needed fixing.

When I came back upstairs, I was thinking about them—Lenora and Evelyn, so thin they both looked sickly, but so willing to help, so meek and mild. *I don't know if they're Christians or not, but they've got me beat a mile when it comes to acting like a Christian.*

I got to thinking about the things Clara and Mabel had said about the women I'd find up here, foul-mouthed and the like, and I looked forward to the day when I could set them straight. Priscilla Home residents, for the most part, were as polite as any one of the Willing Workers. I had not heard one four-letter word, not one swear word since I'd arrived. In fact, I was seeing most of these women as just souls the devil had led down that primrose path Papa used to talk about; caught them up and dragged them down step by step. The devil wouldn't be finished with them till he destroyed them one way or another.

You could look at the young girls and think, *That's some mother's daughter.* There was Angela all tangled up in sins of her own making, and her praying parents heartbroke. And then there were ones like Dora with that awful load of guilt sucking the life out of her. And Linda . . . Linda who thought she had the world by the tail. The Lord would sure have to help me love that one! Imagine her saying prison was wonderful . . . I guess it would seem wonderful if all those things happened to her that she said happened. But I was of the opinion she liked to hear herself talk, liked to top everybody else's story.

I got up and went in the parlor, where I could look down on the girls working. Getting out those rocks was not easy work, but they looked like they were getting along all right with it. I started to pray for each one, first Brenda, a fortyish woman who ran a beauty shop, if I remembered right. Although I called her by name and said the right words, I knew in my heart I was not on praying ground.

Going back in the office, I sat down again. *There's too much at stake here, Lord, too many souls hanging in the balance for me not to be on praying ground.*

I was so ashamed of myself. *What a judgmental, self-righteous hypocrite I am. Lord, you know I have got a short fuse; you know I'm proud and hard to get along with . . . Lord, whatever it takes to change me, do it. I'll do my part, but I can't stay here if—*

Right then it struck me. I didn't ever want to leave Priscilla Home!

I put my head down on the desk and prayed for the

Lord to help me. That's the best prayer a body can pray. I'd prayed it many a time, and he had never failed to come through with an answer.'

I must have used half a box of tissues before I got hold of myself. I sat back in the chair, still dabbing my eyes and blowing my nose when again somebody knocked on the door. It was Evelyn again. "Do you want us to fix lunch?"

"Well, I don't know what's in there to fix. I'll come look. I thought Miss Ursula would be back by now."

We had run out of meat the night before, and there wasn't much left of the vegetables. We still had some donuts. In the pantry I found some bread, and some cheese in the refrigerator. No mayonnaise or mustard. "Let's make grilled cheese sandwiches," I said.

I got to thinking about what we could have for supper. The girls would be hungry after working in the garden. I decided to put on a pot of dry beans to cook slow. "Do either of you know how to make cornbread?" I asked.

"I could try," Evelyn said.

Well, I couldn't risk not having cornbread to go with the beans, so I decided I'd make it. "Evelyn, you just keep an eye on the beans so they don't burn."

"Has the mail come?" she asked.

I had forgotten about the mail. The girls were always anxious to know if they had a letter, so I said I'd go see.

I walked out to the road past the pile of rocks the girls had heaped up from the garden. "Good job," I hollered, and seeing I was on the way to the mailbox, they all dropped what they were doing to follow me.

The mailbox was filled with circulars, two more applications from women wanting to come to Priscilla Home, and only one letter. It was for Portia.

As I handed it to her, Linda snatched it. "It's from her mother," she said. I reached for the letter and gave it back to Portia. She stuffed it in her shirt without reading it and went back to the garden. *That Linda! I could wring her neck!*

As I was coming back in the house, I heard the phone ringing and ran as fast as I could to answer it. I was surprised to hear Clara on the other end. "Esmeralda, we just wanted to hear from you. How're you doing?"

"Oh, just fine," I said. "Clara, I want you to thank the W.W.s for all those sheets and towels you sent up here. The girls were tickled pink with some curtains they found in one of the boxes."

"Well, the towels were old. I hope they're all right."

"Clara, those cotton towels are a whole lot better than the new ones made out of who knows what kind of material."

"I guess you have single beds up there, and we didn't have any sheets that weren't double."

"They work just fine. The girls just tuck them under. Now, listen, Clara, I want you to bring the W.W.s up here for a visit. We can make room for as many as can come. Once the W.W.s meet these girls and see the work that needs to be done in their hearts, they'll go home burdened to pray for them. It's real pretty up here, and you'll all enjoy the scenery. But now, Clara, Thelma will have to do the driving because these mountain roads are the mischief to drive."

"Oh, Esmeralda, we'd love to come!"

When we hung up, I leaned back in the chair, feeling good about Clara and the rest of them. They really were good women, and they did stuff nobody else would take the time to do. They may not have had all the smarts in the world, but maybe that was just as well.

In a minute the phone was ringing again. It was another caller about the piano. He asked the price, and when I said, "Five hundred," he hung up on me. That was discouraging. I went back in the kitchen and told the girls, "I guess we're asking too much for that piano."

Lenora shook her head. "No, you aren't asking too much."

I was surprised to hear her say that, mainly because she hardly says anything. She added, "Any Steinway is worth a lot more."

"But it's in such bad shape."

"I know," she said, her lifeless eyes the color of slate.

"You play, don't you?" I asked.

"I play," she answered.

Ursula had told me Lenora played in nightclubs until her drinking got the better of her, but I didn't think I should pry to find out anything more. "I wonder what's keeping Ursula?"

"Won't she be home for lunch?" Evelyn asked.

"I hope so."

But she wasn't. The girls came in from the garden,

and we sat down to the sandwiches and tea. Hearing the women talking with each other was encouraging, and I tried to keep a conversation going at our table with Dora, Linda, Portia, and the two from the kitchen. Linda did most of the talking. "When the cat's away, the mice will play," she was saying. "Miss E., when we finish in the garden, can we go down to the falls?"

"The falls?"

"Yeah. The falls are down in back of here, only there's not so much falls as rocks—big boulders the size of city buses. Musta been an earthquake or something that tore 'em loose and sent 'em down the mountain. Creek water runs in and around and under them. I climbed to the top one time. Climbing to the top takes some smarts because you have to pick your way up, but I got no problem with that. You can see way downriver from up there. Can we go?"

"We better wait for Miss Ursula and ask her."

"Oh, she won't let us go," Linda grumbled. "But maybe if you go with us she will."

"Well, I'll go with you, but she's the director; she's the one you'll have to ask for permission."

Linda groaned. "She'll say no."

❧

Ursula didn't come and didn't come. I was concerned that she might have run out of gas or something. But at about 3:00 she turned in the driveway, and I went down to meet her at the back door. "Did you get the loan?"

"Well, maybe. All their computers are down. I kept waiting, but they finally told me it was no use waiting any longer, to come back Monday." She sounded tired. "Anyway, the president of the board has to sign the forms, so they promised to mail them to Mr. Elmwood."

"Don't worry," I said, "the ten days are not up until Wednesday. This is only Friday."

"I know," she said. She looked beat.

"Have you had lunch?"

"No," she said, so I told her to go on over to her apartment and I'd bring her a sandwich.

While I was making the sandwich, Linda came in from the garden. "Did you ask her? Did you ask her if we can go to the falls?"

"Not yet," I said. "I will, I'll ask her. Better yet, you ask her. Here, take this tray over to her apartment."

"Her apartment is off-limits to us."

"I see. Then I'll take it." Linda walked with me to open the doors. "Good heavens, you girls have earned a treat. Look at all those rocks you've piled up there. We can use those rocks to build a wall or make a patio or something."

"You don't know when to quit, do you, Miss E.? You're a Type A if ever I saw one."

"What's a Type A?"

"It's a workaholic—somebody who don't never quit. You're a prime target for heart attack or stroke."

"Who told you that?"

"Miss E., if you had been in as many rehabs as I have, you could write the book on psychology."

I laughed and we parted at the door leading up to Ursula's apartment. Linda went back to the field.

The apartment was sparsely furnished, and the computer sat on the only table, with piles of papers and books. They were probably all necessary to writing proposals for grants, but they made for a big mess. Ursula thanked me, but I guess she was too worried to smile. Pale as a ghost with dark circles under her eyes. I wished she'd quit spending so much time on those appeals and get more rest.

She sighed. "Sit down, Esmeralda."

I took a pile of books off a chair and drew the chair up to the table.

Ursula was on the verge of tears. "Esmeralda," she began, "I must not fail in this job . . . I simply cannot fail." Handling that sandwich the way a sick person does who hasn't the strength or the will to eat, Ursula sighed and put it down. Her eyes were brimming; I handed her a tissue. "I've been here nearly two years and have nothing to show for it except a pile of bills. I want so much to serve the Lord . . ."

I did the best I could to comfort her—told her she *was* serving the Lord.

"Am I? Am I serving the Lord?" She lifted her eyes from the plate and looked at me. "I don't seem to be getting anywhere."

"Oh, come now—you're working so hard you're bound to succeed. You'll succeed, Ursula. I guarantee it!"

"I have to, Esmeralda . . ." She fingered the glass of milk.

I rattled on, hardly knowing what I was saying. "Well, now, Ursula, there's more than one kind of success . . ."

I don't think she heard me. "You see, my parents . . . well, my parents disapprove of what I'm doing. They want me to pursue an academic career such as they have. The only way I could persuade them to let me take this job was to present it as a practicum in my major, psychology."

Now, in my book, a woman her age should be able to make her own decisions. "Ursula, if I may ask, how old are you?"

"Twenty-nine next month. . . . You're thinking that I'm old enough to choose what I want to do without asking anybody's consent. Well, I am old enough to do that, but my parents aren't Christians, and I don't want to do anything that might keep them from coming to Christ."

"I see," I said, but I really didn't see that being tied to their apron strings would have anything to do with winning them to Christ.

"My parents are both scholars. Mother teaches humanities, and my father is a professor of antiquities."

"He teaches about antiques?" I couldn't believe it. "People go to college to learn about *antiques*?"

"No, not antiques. Father lectures in the university and all over the world about ancient civilizations."

"I see," I said. Ancient civilizations. That sounded as dry as moldy bread.

"Father wanted me to follow in his footsteps, and I would have, but I would've had to learn Semitic languages. I don't have his gift for languages. In fact, I failed Latin, French, and Spanish. I had to pursue graduate work in a field that had no language requirement. That's why I chose psychology."

I was seeing another side to Ursula and beginning to understand a little better why she was the way she was. Chances were, since she only knew English, she was determined to know every word of English in the dictionary.

"My parents are very disappointed in me. I have a brother who was a Rhodes Scholar. Now he's in the state department. When I accepted Christ and began to talk about Jesus, my parents were so alarmed they sent me to one of those places to be deprogrammed."

"Oh my!"

"I went through the program but came out still knowing that what I believe is true. My parents were devastated—*humiliated* would be a better word. They threatened to cut off my allowance, but education is such a priority with them, they permitted me to return to grad school and finish my last semester."

I really felt sorry for her. As for her parents, I could wring their necks! There was a photograph on the cabinet, and I picked it up. "Is this your daddy?"

"Yes, that's Father."

The picture showed him gray-headed with a dark beard, smoking a pipe and wearing a turtleneck. "He looks like a professor," I said and set the picture back on the cabinet.

"Now can you see why I cannot fail at Priscilla Home? They would never forgive me for wasting two years here when I could be well on my way in a doctoral program."

"Is that what you want to do—study for a doctor's degree?"

She hesitated. "No, Esmeralda. No, it isn't. I just want to make a go of it here at Priscilla Home."

I could've told her a lot of stuff that would help her succeed, but I figured this wasn't the time. Ever since I came to Priscilla Home it looked like everything except the counseling sessions were just thrown together. When the women were not having a one-on-one with Ursula, for the most part they wasted time—stayed outside smoking. "Ursula," I ventured to say, "what would you think about writing us a schedule so that every day is planned and duties are assigned?"

"I do have a schedule for counseling sessions. The last resident manager took care of scheduling other activities. She was incompetent, and I suggested that she make a career change, which she did."

"You mean scheduling is my job?"

"I thought you knew that."

"No."

"I should write job descriptions," she said wearily.

"Well, then, I'll try, but I'll need your help. What would you think of having the first hour of the morning set aside for prayer and praise?"

"Prayer and praise? Do you think they're ready for that?"

"I do."

"Very well." She was too worn out to give it much thought.

"After prayer and praise, then there's work in the house and yard—I could sign them up for that. After lunch we could have a Bible study."

"Will you teach it?"

"Me? I'm not a Bible teacher."

"Well, you're the only one available. I'm tied up all day long counseling."

"Ursula, I've never taught anything!"

"Well, think about it."

Think about it? There is no way under the sun I could set myself up as the Priscilla Home Bible teacher!

Suddenly I remembered the falls. "The girls—I mean, the *ladies*—want to go to the falls. I'll take them if it's okay with you."

"All right, you can take them. Tell them to be careful."

"Good. I'll tell them. Now, Ursula, eat your sandwich and drink your milk—and why don't you take a rest while we're gone?"

"I might as well."

I picked up the tray to take it back to the kitchen, but when I looked back at that poor, sad girl, my heart went out to her. I put down the tray, went around the table, and gave her a hug.

❦

7

The trail to the falls led us through rhododendron thickets with trees towering overhead. Shaded as we were and with a stiff breeze whipping about, I was chilly, but the girls led at such a pace I figured we'd warm up. I was bringing up the rear with that girl Brenda from Alabama. She's a hairdresser and offered to do my hair any time I liked.

Brenda told me her *real* husband, as she called him, had been a nice man until some bimbo at work wooed him away from her. "Tommy and I were getting along good, went to church, had a nice house almost paid for. The kids were grown. Then he met that bimbo at work, and she wouldn't leave him alone. Miss E., young girls go after older men because they have got more money than the lowlifes their own age."

Here was this middle-aged woman telling me that after that man left her, she'd fallen apart and started drinking. If they had went to church all their married life like she said, how come they let this happen? Well, I can tell you.

Going to church can be an end in itself—just a habit—a place to see friends. And if it's not, it's like I've always said—going to church is not enough when it comes down to the nitty-gritty of facing the things life throws at you. A body needs to be close to the Lord—needs to be one-on-one with Jesus every day to be up to meeting whatever comes down the pike. Reading some little devotional and letting that pass for a quiet time just won't hack it. I tell you, I have learned the hard way. I slack up on studying my Bible and cut short my prayer time, and things go to pot. It happened right there at Priscilla Home.

Brenda smoked a lot, so she got out of breath. We stopped to rest, only she lit another cigarette. From what she told me, since her husband had left her, she'd gone from one man to another. "Miss E., I guess I keep thinking I'll find another Tommy, but I've given up. There are just not any more Tommys out there." She sucked on that coffin nail and blew the smoke away from me. "I see Tommy every once in a while in the mall or some place with that woman's children. She had three and now they have one together."

Seeing she still loved that man, I could tell she was sliding into a big-time pity party if I didn't put on the brakes.

Brenda ground out the cigarette. "My mother says I've disgraced the family and I'm not welcome in her house." Her chin was trembling. "She never even invites me for holidays or anything. The children won't have anything to do with me. I don't ever hear from them, not even on my birthday or Mother's Day."

I started applying the brakes by saying we'd better

catch up with the others. We got up and hit the trail again.

It was not an easy walk but the kind you would expect on a mountain footpath, rocks and fallen logs, marshy places. When we reached the stream, the footpath turned into a very rugged trail following alongside the stream up to the falls. I did pretty well climbing over rocks and roots until it came to a nearly impassable place. Instead of climbing farther, I decided to stay right there on a flat rock that jutted out into the water. "Brenda, you go on ahead with the girls."

Holding on to a branch, I stepped out on that slab of a rock and was welcomed by sunshine again. I got settled with my back to the sun warming my bones and thought I would pray for Brenda and the other women if I could. So far as I could tell, Priscilla Home wasn't helping her or any of the others very much. There were still a few girls I didn't know well—a stout woman named Wilma, a truck driver from eastern North Carolina, tough as nails. Emily, who came from Missouri and claimed to be a professional ice skater. Well, I didn't know about her. There was another girl from Virginia, Nancy. She was a nurse.

It was hard to find the time to really get to know these women, but Portia was the only one I found too weird for words. Ursula told me she'd hitchhiked all the way from Florida—walked the last miles on the Old Turnpike with a foot of snow on the ground and a gale blowing hard. Landed at the door at 3:00 in the morning with only the clothes on her back and cigarettes. Ursula couldn't turn her away, and after Portia's application was filled out and her mother sent her medical deposit, Ursula had no excuse not to let her stay on.

From where I was sitting, I could see the avalanche of boulders above and wondered what catastrophe had caused all those rocks to tumble down the mountain like that. *Lester might know,* I thought, and remembering him, I wished I could get away to check on him.

High up on the boulders I could see one wide waterfall, and on the creek's way down there were smaller ones. A few yards above where I sat, there was one with that clear, cold water spilling over rocks, swirling and splashing white all around the slab I was sitting on.

God's glory was everywhere—the sun and the breeze playing on the trees and the stream, birds flitting here and there chirping. I felt like singing praises to the Lord, so I turned to see how far away the girls were; it wouldn't do for them to hear my foghorn of a voice. I could hardly hear them shouting to each other, so I figured they were far enough away that my singing wouldn't cause permanent damage to their eardrums. With all that beauty around me, I sang "How Great Thou Art" like I was on stage with only God listening.

Below my rock, there was a wide pool with the trees reflecting in the water, shimmering nervous-like. The water was so clear I could see trout facing upstream, waiting for an unsuspecting bug to come their way. It was the kind of pool children skip rocks on. Beatrice and I used to do that when we were little kids. *Poor Ursula,* I thought, *as a kid she probably never skipped rocks or did anything much except keep her nose in a book—probably read the dictionary all the way through.*

I sat there thinking about the things Ursula had told me; I was beginning to understand why Dr. Elsie had said I could help her. I didn't have book learning, but I did have experience.

Undoubtedly, Ursula had never in her life had to trust the Lord for money. When a body goes through life living on the allowance their daddy gives them, they don't have to depend on the Lord to provide. They miss a lot. In my book, they miss one of the best ways of getting to know God. *Wouldn't it be something if I could help her get her daddy off her back.*

I looked at the avalanche and could see Dora in the lead almost at the top. Wilma wasn't far behind. The rest of them were here and there, holding on to each other, scrambling to find a foothold or trying to decide if they could jump from one rock to the next. Evelyn looked like she was holding her own with the rest. I didn't see Lenora.

I turned to look back at the pool below. There was a fisherman down there making his way upstream, casting for trout. He was decked out in waders and all the paraphernalia city men buy to go fishing. There's no telling how much money they spend just to catch one or two fish that they could buy in the fish market for two or three dollars. Wading in that cold water over slippery rocks is not my idea of a good time.

I kept watching him casting, hoping he'd make a strike, and he did. Reeling in the fish, he seemed to be an expert at netting it. I watched him take out the hook, and as he dropped the fish in that wicker box strapped on his side, he looked up and saw me. He tipped his hat in a friendly kind of way, and in a not-too-friendly way I acknowledged him with a nod. After all, you can't be too careful with people you don't know.

As he was making his way upstream toward me, he cast a couple times more and came close enough that I could see he was an older fellow, probably retired. For sure, old enough for Social Security. That hat was decorated with all kinds of hooks and flies, probably a fortune in lures. He wore glasses and had a neat, trimmed mustache. You don't see men smile the way that man was smiling. I guess it was catching the fish made him smile.

The boulders up behind me would make it impossible for him to fish any farther than my rock, and I wanted to see him catch at least one more before he had to stop. He handled that rod with a wrist motion that cast the line out over the pond, which was not an easy thing to do. I had to laugh; I caught myself praying he'd catch one! Well, sure enough, he angled that line just right for a trout swimming along looking for a bite. Once it took the bait and darted this way and that, the fellow started reeling him in. To see that rainbow trout splashing out of the water, flashing in the sun, fighting against the hook, was something right out of a wildlife magazine. Even after the man scooped it up in the net, that little bugger still fought, flipping and flopping.

The fisherman took his time removing the hook and getting the catch in his box. Then he set out again. The water was getting deeper, nearly up to his waist. Casting one more time, he didn't get a taker, so he reeled in his line and made his way toward the bank. I thought he would take the footpath back the way we came, but instead he was making his way along the trail beside the creek, coming my way. Ducking under limbs and climbing over rocks, he finally came out at the place where I had come onto the rock.

"Good afternoon," he said in a gentlemanly kind of way. "It's a fine day for fishing."

"So I see," I said without sounding too interested.

"May I join you?" he asked.

"Well, I guess you can. This rock don't belong to me."

He smiled and, holding on to a limb, swung down from the bank to my rock.

Now, I wasn't in the habit of striking up conversations with strange men, but there was just something about this man that would tell anybody he was a gentleman. Of course, Jack the Ripper was probably a gentleman when he wasn't killing women.

The fisherman told me his name, Albert Ringstaff, which sounded German to me, and I have not got much use for Germans.

Once on the rock, he stood there with water from his waders trickling down in little rivulets. Gazing out over the pond, we saw a fish plop up. "Hmm, I should've waited for that one," he remarked. "May I sit down?"

"Like I said, this rock don't belong to me."

He smiled, laid his rod on the rock, and settled himself down a few feet from me. Then, out of the blue, he said, "I heard you singing."

I thought I would die on the spot!

He turned around to look up the mountain. "Do you know those ladies climbing the rocks?"

I told him I did and that we were from Priscilla Home. But I could hardly look his way I was so mortified he had heard me singing. He told me he lived up on the mountain and knew Dr. Elsie. Said he knew about Priscilla Home, although he had never been there. The way he talked, he had a slight accent, and that made me pretty sure he was German.

"Can you use some fish?" he asked.

"Well, maybe." I didn't want to appear too anxious.

When he asked me how many ladies were in residence, I told him that with the director and me there were fourteen.

He lifted the lid of his fish box and looked inside. "I was very fortunate today. The wildlife service has just stocked the stream—put tons of fish in the water—so I caught a number of speckled and rainbow trout. If you can use them there might be enough to make you a meal."

"Oh, you keep them for yourself."

"No, I'm not much of a cook. I usually catch and release, but if I see I'm going to catch enough, I save them and give them to the neighbors."

I wanted those fish in the worst way. "Well, if you insist," I said. "Thank you. We'll clean them and have a fish fry tomorrow night."

Seeing I didn't have a bucket or anything to put the fish in, he said, "I'll take them up to the house for you."

We could hear someone thrashing through the bushes coming back down the trail. It was Lenora. She was muddy from slipping and sliding on the trail, and her face was scratched. Stopping to catch her breath, she held on to the limb above my rock and steadied herself. "I couldn't make it up those rocks," she explained.

I didn't know whether or not to introduce her to Mr. Ringstaff, but since he was giving us the fish, I decided I should. "This is Miss Lenora Barrineau, one of our residents," I told him.

The man's mouth fell open. He was so shocked he repeated her name. "Lenora Barrineau? Do you mean *the* Lenora Barrineau?" He stood up, holding out his hand to her.

What's this? Lenora looked like a scared rabbit!

"Miss Barrineau, do you remember me?"

Embarrassed, Lenora turned her face the other way, and for a minute I thought she was going to break and run.

Mr. Ringstaff grabbed her hand. "You *are* Lenora Barrineau, aren't you?"

"Yes."

"Then you remember me?"

"Of course, I do, Mr. Ringstaff," she said, still hanging on to that limb, trapped with no way to escape.

Thunderstruck as he was, Ringstaff didn't let go of her and was so excited I was afraid he was going to fall off that rock and take her with him. "Miss Barrineau—I can't believe it's really you!"

A nervous little smile showed on her face and then vanished.

I knew she was embarrassed looking the way she did, muddy from head to foot. With neither hand free, she brushed her head against her shoulder trying to wipe her face. "Please pardon my appearance," she stammered.

"The trail proved to be too much for me. If you will excuse me, I need to get back to the house and clean up."

"Oh, please," he begged. "Please, come sit with us a few minutes."

As much as she didn't want to let go that branch, the way he begged left her little choice. He carefully helped her onto the rock, and I moved over to make room for her to sit down between us.

Ringstaff couldn't take his eyes off her. "How long has it been?" he asked. "When was the last time I saw you—Moscow? Milan?"

"I don't remember," she said softly and drew her knees up under her chin.

"Oh, I think it was Milan—must have been fifteen years, well, almost fifteen years ago."

Lenora smiled slightly and laced her fingers together, holding on to her knees.

I felt like a fifth wheel. This gentleman was someone from her past, and maybe what they had to say to each other was none of my business. To tell the truth, curiosity was about to kill this cat, but I made an excuse and started to get up. "I need to see about the ladies," I told them. The man jumped up and helped me get off the rock onto the bank. Like I said, he had been brought up right.

All I did was climb far enough to be out of sight and earshot. As I sat waiting for the girls to come down, I couldn't get over the way Mr. Ringstaff seemed to spark something in Lenora. *It might be good for her if I asked him to stay for supper,* I thought. All we had were beans, but we had plenty, and I was going to make the cornbread. *Well, we'll see.*

8

Mr. Ringstaff couldn't come for supper because that evening he was driving to Greensboro, where he would spend the night and take an early flight to New York the next day. After Lenora had gone upstairs, he stayed a few minutes on the porch, and I gave him a rain check for the supper he was missing. "I'll be back next week," he told me, "and I'll be in touch."

Of course, I was dying to know who this man was and what business he had in New York. There was no doubt Lenora knew all about him, so the temptation to ask her was strong, but I didn't. As frail as she was, asking her anything personal might send her further back into her shell and spoil what chances we might have to help her. When I'd set my mind to find out a mystery such as this one, I was pretty good at it. I thought, *The next time I talk to Dr. Elsie, I'll ask her about Ringstaff. He's her neighbor; she'll know.*

Ursula looked better after resting a while, and she seemed encouraged that someone else had called about the piano. "I told him it's in poor condition," she said, "but he didn't seem to be put off by the price. He's coming tomorrow to look at it."

I had made rice pudding to go with our meal and planned to take some to Lester the next day when we returned the horse and plow. The garden needed a lot more grubbing before we could plant, and we were already past planting time. Of course, we had no seed or anything else. *Maybe there is not to be a garden, after all,* I worried. *If the Lord don't send in the money to pay these bills, we'll have no need for a garden. We'll be closed down.*

I couldn't bear to think about that happening, but I had to admit, we weren't offering much in the way of spiritual help for these women. On that account the Lord might be finished with Priscilla Home. I felt guilty that I hadn't done my part. I'd been so busy about the garden and everything I hadn't put first things first. There was one thing I knew I could do, and I promised myself I'd get cracking on that the next day.

❧

Saturday morning we had our first Praise and Prayer session. Each of the women had been issued a new translation of the Bible, one easier for them to understand than the King James, and we were sitting around in the day room ready to get started.

I hardly knew how to begin. "Well," I said, "what do we have to be thankful for?"

There was dead silence.

I was about to say something myself when Dora volunteered. Can you imagine—Dora!

"He has give me ever'thang a body ever needed," she was saying. "The sun to warm my back, the moon and stars spread over me of a night, good water to drink, good air to breathe, a mill on the branch to grind my corn, a cookstove and bed pots. I got no quarrel with God. He's been good to me."

She didn't mean to be funny and, to my surprise, nobody thought it was. Nobody laughed or even smiled. I guess we were all kind of taken back by what she said and the way she said it.

The effect had not worn off when I cleared my throat and suggested we open our Bibles to the Psalms. There's real soul food in the Psalms. "Let's pick verses to praise the Lord with," I told them. "Mr. Splurgeon says, 'We ought not to leap in prayer and limp in praise.'"

That pearl of wisdom went right over their heads. They were too busy turning back and forth trying to find the Psalms. "The Psalms is smack dab in the middle of your Bible," I told them.

"I found it—the Palms!" Wilma exclaimed.

I hesitated but decided it wouldn't do not to correct her. "It's Psalms, Wilma, not Palms, okay?"

"Sure looks like Palms," she said and laughed.

To get the thing going, I picked the first verse of Psalm 103: "Bless the LORD, O my soul: and all that is within me, bless his holy name."

Angela, curled up in the corner of the sofa, added, "And forget not all his benefits."

Good, I thought. *At least somebody understands*

what we're trying to do here. But then there was a long silence. I didn't know what to do. They were turning pages, looking for something to read, so I waited and prayed somebody would come up with a verse.

Wilma, the truck driver, started reading a long psalm with every verse ending in "his mercy endureth forever." By the time she had read half a page, she stopped. "That ain't what you want, is it?"

"It's all good, Wilma. Go right ahead."

And she did.

Melba, one of the best cooks in the house and a hairdresser like Brenda, found the psalm she was looking for and waited for Wilma to finish before telling us, "I can say this one by heart. I learned it in Vacation Bible School when I was eight years old." She recited the Twenty-third Psalm without a hitch.

"That's the one they used at my daddy's funeral," Nancy said. "He died the day I graduated from nursing school." She read a praise verse, then explained, "Emily left her glasses so I'll read another one for her." Emily, the slender redhead sitting beside her, was Nancy's roommate. They all said she was a professional ice skater, so I reckoned that was true.

I felt really good that the women seemed to be liking what we were doing. They kept pawing the pages until I reckoned maybe half of them had read a verse or two.

"Miss E.," Angela asked, "could we sing a chorus or something?"

"Sure," I said. She and Nancy put their heads together and came up with a chorus about being a sanctuary for the Lord. Angela led off with a voice like an angel's. I tell you, she sang as good as any of those big-time singers traveling all over the country making big bucks. Why, it wasn't no time till she and Nancy had us all singing that chorus, only you can bet your bottom dollar I didn't let loose full force; I just hummed along. The words were so pretty and the girls sang so sweet it would have made the angels clap their hands, except as how probably none of the women could honestly claim to be a sanctuary for the Lord. It's like Splurgeon says, "Fools can sing, but only those who are taught of God can be holy."

During the singing, Portia left the room to go to the bathroom, and her roommate, Linda, jumped at the chance to tell us about her. "Portia calls herself Satan's child, so don't look for her to sing Christian songs."

No one laughed, and I for one had to bite my tongue not to jerk a knot in that blabbermouth.

Portia didn't come back until we were giving our requests for prayer. We prayed for the women's children, their husbands, ex-husbands, boyfriends, and their parents, but oddly enough, no one asked for victory over their own addiction.

As Dora and I left the house to get the plow and horse ready to make the trip back to Lester's, Linda followed me. "Miss E., can I go with you?"

"No, you need to stay here and work in the garden."

"I've got something to tell you."

"Can't you tell me right now?" I motioned to her to lift the other end of the plow to help me put it in the trunk.

"No, I can't tell you right now. It's a long story, something important you should know. I can tell you in the car."

She just wants to fill me in on more gossip, I figured. "Well, if it's something about another resident here, we'll go to that person and you can tell it to them as well as to me."

Linda laughed. "That would take all the fun out of it." Then she blurted out, "That tattoo Portia has covers the entire front of her body—you oughta' see it! It's a rose bush with buds where you might expect—"

"Linda, I don't want to hear this!"

"You don't want to hear that she left home when she was fourteen because of her stepfather—how he messed with her?"

"No! I do not want to hear another word of this!" I was getting madder by the minute and walked fast toward the garage, trying to shake her. She kept right on my heels. "Linda, we're not here to dwell on the past. We're here to think about the future we can have if we let the Lord into our lives."

That garage was full of junk. I was looking to see if there was a gasoline can in there. We needed gas for the van.

Linda would not shut up. "Portia's mother is a Christian, and every time Portia calls her, her mother sends her a bus ticket or a plane ticket to come home. Of course, Portia never goes home; she just cashes the ticket and spends the money. She could go home now if she wanted to. Her stepfather left her mother some time ago, so she's got no excuse not to go home."

"Linda, that is none of your business nor mine!" I found the gas can, but it was empty.

She laughed and followed me back to the car. I tell you, there was evil in that girl! I knew I shouldn't let her bug me; after all, she wouldn't be at Priscilla Home if she was a saint. Like Splurgeon says, "It takes holy hearts to make holy tongues" and Linda was a long way from having a holy heart.

But I couldn't shut her up!

"One reason Portia got that tattoo is to keep Christians away from her. No self-respecting Christian will have anything to do with somebody has got tattoos like that."

"Then why did she come here to this Christian place?" I asked and opened the car door.

"The only reason she came here was to have a warm place to spend the winter." Linda was holding on to the door to keep me from closing it.

"Linda, that's not true. Portia came from Florida, where it's much warmer than it is here. She wouldn't leave Florida and come to the mountains for a warm place to stay."

"Oh, yes, she would. Priscilla Home is free room and board."

"How did she find out about this place?"

"The trucker who let her off in Rockville, he told her about it."

Any way you looked at it, Linda's story didn't ring true. "Linda, the Bible says, 'The tongue is a fire, a world of iniquity. It is set on fire of hell.'"

She laughed. "Then you better watch out, Miss E., you might set the woods on fire."

"I wasn't thinking of me," I spluttered.

She knew she was getting under my skin, and that tickled her to death. "Oh no?" she said. "You don't strike me as one of those goody-goody, mealy-mouthed women who can't dish out a tongue-lashing now and then."

I couldn't deny that. Right that minute it was all I could do not to light into her and give her a dressing down she'd never forget. Instead, I pointed to a hoe leaning against the dumpster. "There's a hoe, Linda. Now get cracking in the garden."

"Wait, there's one more thing." She wouldn't let go of the door. "Miss Ursula caught Portia smoking in our room, and you know the rule, three strikes you're outta here. Portia's one down, two to go."

I was so provoked with that girl it was a good thing I was leaving. "Let go the door," I said and yanked it shut.

With the door shut, the windows rolled up, and the motor running, I waited for Dora. Seeing she couldn't bend my ear any longer, Linda lit a cigarette and moseyed out to the garden without the hoe.

Sitting there, stewing, I told myself I shouldn't let this be another one of those days when the sun went down on my wrath, but to tell the truth, I knew it would take more hours than a day had got to cool me down!

❧

It was another one of them foggy mornings, so Dora and I decided it would be better if she rode ahead of me.

That way it would be easier to keep her in view, and she could set the pace.

Driving slowly down the Old Turnpike, I had plenty of time to think about Linda. It didn't take a rocket scientist to know the Lord had allowed her to get in my face for some reason. I figured he was dealing with me about this getting mad business. Well, we'd just have to see.

We made pretty good time, considering that horse's gait, and arrived at Lester's by late morning. He was sitting on the porch and looked pretty good. When I asked him how he was, he said he was tolerable, so I took him at his word. Dora led the horse beyond the house where he could graze, and I took the rice pudding into the kitchen and put it in his refrigerator. Everything was neat as a pin in there. The woodstove had the room warm, and on the stove was a pot of pintos with a hunk of fatback.

A man like Lester you don't lecture about eating healthy.

I came back on the porch, and he asked me if I could use some seeds. I coulda dropped my teeth! On the bench beside him were some paper bags and a few small jars. "I saved these seeds from last year's crop," he told me and opened one of the sacks to show me squash seeds. "I only save seeds from the tomaters an' such as I like best. Once they git dry, I put 'em away till it's time to plant the next year. I got aplenty."

There were onion sets, beans, peas, cucumbers, and a bunch more all neatly packaged and labeled. "Lester," I protested, "we can't take your seeds."

"I got plenty more, and tomater plants a-comin' on. Come May 20, that's the time to set 'em out."

"May 20? I plant my garden on Good Friday."

"Up here you best wait till there's no more chance of frost. May 20 is soon enough to plant."

"Well, that's a relief to hear. We've got a lot of work to do to get the ground in shape, and I thought we were way past planting time. I don't know how to thank you, Lester. Do you like fish?" He said he did, so I told him, "We're having a fish fry tonight, and if there's any left I'll bring you some in the morning on our way to church."

"Church? They always take them Priscilla folks into town for church."

"Not tomorrow. We're going to that little Valley Church down by the river." I didn't tell him, but we didn't have gas enough to take the van into town for church.

"Well, you'll hit it just right. Valley Church has preachin' ever' second Sunday, and tomorrow's second Sunday."

Dora was ready to go, so I thanked Lester again and said I'd see to it he got some fish if any was left after supper. He thanked me, and I got back in the car. We turned around, and I waved to him as we headed out to the Old Turnpike.

Well, it looked like the Lord meant for us to have a garden. Who'd of ever thought all the seeds and stuff we needed to plant would be dropped in our lap free and postpaid!

9

When we got back to the house, there were visitors. Turned out it was the man who had called about the piano, and he brought his wife. As I came into the parlor the woman was running her fingers over the keyboard, saying, "It's not fit to play."

He said, "I know a feller in town can fix it."

"Maybe he can, maybe he can't. Either way it'll cost us an arm and a leg."

"Lookee here at this wood, Isabel. It looks like mahogany. And lookit this here plaque." He was rubbing his thumb over it. "Bronze—solid bronze." He squinted to read the writing. "It says this here piano was give by a woman in Charlotte."

"Like as not she give it away because nobody would buy it."

"She was probably rich, Isabel, and had no need of it. Buy it and you'll be the only woman in Rockville with a baby grand."

"We don't have room for it."

"We'll make room," he said. "We'll take out that old couch—"

"We'll do no such a thing. That was my granny's couch."

"It was wore out afore she died."

"It's a priceless antique," she told him, and turning to me, "Men don't know value when they see it, do they?"

I didn't have to comment, because she kept running her fingers over the keyboard and shaking her head.

Making the sale seemed out of the question, but I thought it might help if we lowered the price. At least it was worth a try.

Ursula must have been thinking the same thing because she said, "If the price is—"

"I wouldn't have it if you give it to me," the woman snapped.

The man threw up his hands. "Well, there you have it. Come on, Isabel."

After they left, I followed Ursula into the office. We sat down, but she was too discouraged to talk. And I couldn't think of one thing that would cheer her up. Getting seeds to plant wouldn't mean anything to her. Finally, I said, "We have the trout for supper," as if that would do the trick.

"What about tomorrow?" she asked. "Do we have anything for Sunday dinner?"

"Oh, I can scrape something together," I said, knowing full well the cupboard was bare.

"On top of everything else," she said glumly, "we have a new resident coming today. One more mouth to feed."

Ursula was feeling so low, she'd have to stand on a soapbox to reach bottom. "Well, Ursula, we won't go hungry," I said as cheerfully as I could.

She put her head in her hands and grumbled, "Still presuming on the veracity of God—"

"Run that by me one more time."

"Never mind," she said. "Shouldn't you go check on the ladies?"

Before going to the garden, I went in the kitchen to see if I could find anything there to make a meal for the next day. There were a few donuts, some of the staples, and oatmeal, but little else. I ate a stale donut and went on out to the garden.

The girls were chopping and hoeing, shaking clumps of grass and tossing them onto a pile. Only Linda was goofing off, sitting under a tree, filling her lungs with death-dealing nicotine. Tobacco companies will never go out of business so long as there's the likes of Linda still living. Seeing I was coming her way, she hollered, "I got no tool, Miss E.!"

At the garden I reached down and took a handful of dirt. It had the smell of good soil, and the feel of it, soft and crumbly in my hand. It had the makings of a good crop if the Lord sent enough rain and sunshine. "Come on, Linda, we need to make a scarecrow."

She sucked in a long draw on the cigarette and let it out slow. "A scarecrow? What for?"

"To scare crows, what else?"

The girls heard that and laughed.

"Oh yeah? Then Portia's gotta help me."

"No, I'm going to help you. See if you can find an

outfit for him in the clothing room. We'll need a hat and coat and pants."

She ground out the stub of cigarette and moseyed back toward the house, muttering who knows what under her breath. I had had about as much as I could take from that girl. Splurgeon said, "Idle people are dead people that you can't bury," and Linda fit that bill to a tee.

"Company's a-comin'," Wilma hollered, and the girls looked up from their work. I could hear a car or truck coming up the road. The way it was backfiring and kicking up dust, I figured it was a pickup.

It was a pickup, and it turned in at our drive. *Must be the new girl,* I thought.

It was. I beckoned to the girls to come welcome her, and we met the truck at the back door. An old man got out, worry written all over his face; he went around to the other side and opened the door for the girl. She was biting her nails; looked like she might not get out the truck. *Like as not she didn't want to come here in the first place,* I thought. Well, that was nothing new. When a girl's family or the court sent her here against her will, there was no reason she'd want to be here.

Her granddaddy, or whoever the old man was, went to the back of the truck, threw back a tarpaulin, and lifted out her one and only suitcase. Ursula came out the door and introduced herself and me. The man said, "I'm Martha's husband."

I coulda dropped my teeth! That girl was not thirty years old, and he was in his seventies if he was a day!

"We're from Williamsbu'g County, South Ca'olina," he told us in that slow drawl people have got in the Low

Country. "Cha'leston's 'bout fo'ty miles from where we stay."

I doubted Ursula could understand him. She told him to bring in the girl's bag, and the three of them went upstairs to check Martha in.

The rest of us sat on the stoop or stood around taking a break. Linda came bouncing out the back door with clothes for the scarecrow. "Will these do?" she asked, holding up a nice tweed jacket and corduroy pants.

I took a good look at them and told her, "No, somebody can wear these things. Go put 'em back."

She flopped down on the step and told Portia to give her a cigarette. Portia handed her a pack. Without so much as a thank you, Linda pulled out one, lit it, and put the rest of the pack in her shirt pocket. "I'll take that stuff back after they're done with the new girl. Where's she from?"

"Near Charleston," I said.

"Where's that?"

"South Carolina."

"Never heard of it."

Dora was looking off beyond the trees and started talking as much to herself as to us. "She comes from flat land . . . flat land where alongside sandy roads, red oaks blaze in winter sun . . . where moonlight shadows make marble of that white sand . . . and pine trees moan in the wind. . . . It's one place still left with trees. There's giant live oaks a-growin' there since after the flood, an' there's mysteries in them shaggy moss beards a-trailin' down from their limbs. . . . There's mysteries, too, in that still black water a-floatin' them big-bottomed trees—the air so heavy a blue heron can't hardly lift off an' fly. There's woods spirits in them places with stories that have not yet been told nor ever will be."

Linda laughed and flipped the ash from her cigarette. "Dora, you're weird. You never been outside of Tennessee before now; how do you know all about where that girl comes from?"

Dora kept looking off beyond the trees, and in her dreamy way of talking, told us, "You might say I been there. Papa . . . he papered the sidewalls of our cabin with ever' purty picture he could find in magazines and calendars people give him. . . . He papered them walls to keep out the cold. Mighta kept out some cold, but mostly them pictures brought outside places inside . . . San Francisco, Paris, Rome, New York City . . . Charleston, too.

"I loved them pictures; they give me something to study on. But mostly I hated them. They showed me why they done what they done to the trees an' all the wild thangs a-livin' in the woods. They done away with trees an' livin' creatures to make room for their big houses and paved-over parking lots.

"There's big houses ever'where, with steep roofs and wide green yards. You ought to know they build them big houses to hold their tables—white willer ones on the porch and inside the front room, small dark tables aside every soft chair. A low, flat, four-legged one stays put before them settees people sit upon.

"Room after room there's tables—long ones polished and set with candles; round ones with marble tops a-holdin' silver pots an' the like. The eatin' table has got chairs all around with candles that's never lit and false flowers, just for show. Another eatin' table is in the cook room with colored mats an' doodads set in the middle.

"Go along upstairs and in the hallway there's a drop leaf made of curly maple all covered over with lace an' a-holdin' a lamp. Up an' down the hallway there's bedrooms, an' ever' bed has got tables either side. It's a sin and a shame what they have done to give shelter to more an' more tables.

"Two hunnert years ago, the first McCutchen to come to the holler cut down a walnut tree, sawed the lumber, seasoned it, and planed a board to make the table my papa left to me. A body needs only one table. A good stout table for eatin' is one and the same for butcherin' a deer or making bread dough, canning beans, or writin' a letter to the court. I got me such a table so I don't need no big house.

"Home is in my mountain holler with trees an' wild thangs all aroun' and nary a road paved. Ever' place else is for tables an' cars an' the like."

Well, I tell you the truth, I think we all felt pretty foolish. Who in the world but Dora would think of tables being the reason for big houses, yet when you come to think of it, we have got the idea that we need a lot more tables than we ever use. And it's also true that big healthy trees get cut down to make room for houses and such. Developers gobble up woods and farmland where critters have lived for generations and chase them out to live or die the best way they can. There oughta be a law against such as that.

We could hear the girl's husband coming down the

stairs, so we made room on the stoop for him to pass. He was taking that worried look with him. He said to me, "I will be much obliged if you can find your way cl'ar to take ca'e of my Martha." His eyes were misty. "She's all I got, and all our girl-child has got."

I promised him I would take real good care of her.

We all stood in the driveway watching that sad old man as he drove up to the road and turned on to the Old Turnpike. We watched until he was out of sight and then I said, "Let's call it a day, girls."

I went inside and saw that Lenora and Evelyn had cleaned all those fish and was ready to start frying them. I showed them how to salt and meal them and how to get the grease hot before they put the fish in the deep fryer. Evelyn asked if she could make the cornbread, and I allowed she could since I had showed her how.

Then I went to my room, took a long, hot bath, put on clean clothes, and worked on my hair a little. In that climate a bad hair day was the rule, not the exception. I lay back in the chair hoping to doze off, but before I fell asleep the supper bell rang.

That supper was out of this world! There's nothing like fresh trout cooked right. Evelyn was so proud of the way the cornbread turned out, she ate more than she usually did. Ordinarily, she would just play with her food, pushing it around on her plate. We had plenty of fish, but to make sure we had some to take to Lester, I set aside my second helping.

Ursula had the new girl, Martha, sit at her table, and I heard Ursula promise her that she'd have a roommate the next time another resident enrolled. The girl wasn't saying nothing and just picked at her food.

After supper, I washed my hair and rolled it up, then pressed my skirt to wear to church the next morning. With that done, I was free to relax. In my robe I sat in the chair and started reading my Sunday school lesson. That made me think about the Willing Workers back in Live Oaks—most of them would be doing the same thing. We were all brought up—well, maybe Thelma wasn't brought up like the rest of us since she came from Chicago—to know Sunday begins Saturday night. After getting all cleaned up and our shoes polished, we'd read the lesson. And here I was reading the quarterly, even though the same Sunday school lesson was not likely to be taught in the Valley Church where we were going. In fact, it was such a small church they might not even have Sunday school.

There wasn't much to be said for that lesson, so I read my Bible and prayed awhile. I must have fell asleep because about 11:00 I woke up. As often happens when I doze off like that, I became wide awake and couldn't go back to sleep.

Finally, I decided I might as well make myself a cup of tea and go downstairs and read a magazine. When I got down there, the new girl, Martha, was sitting in the day room all by herself in the dark. I turned on a lamp and asked her if she'd like to have a cup of tea.

She shook her head.

I sat down and set the cup on the end table. That made me think of Dora. I picked up a magazine, one of them with home-decorating pictures. I had never before noticed how many tables are in houses. Dora was right. They're full of tables.

I thought I better tell the new girl that lights were out on the third floor at 11:00. I did, but still she sat. In a few minutes, she lit a cigarette, and I had to tell her she couldn't smoke inside. As she reached for the ashtray to put out the cigarette, I told her, "You can smoke outside."

She ground out the cigarette and kept sitting there. I figured the first night at Priscilla Home must be hard for a newcomer, so I decided I'd sit up with her until she felt like going to bed. According to the admissions rule, she had been detoxed and sober for seventy-two hours, but she was still real nervous. I offered again to make her a cup of tea, but she didn't want any.

I put the magazine down. "Do you have children?" I asked.

"One," she said.

"Boy or girl?"

"Girl."

"How old is she?"

"Five."

"Your husband, does he farm?"

"He's seventy-five years old," she answered bitterly; she picked up her cigarettes and went outside.

I'd hit a nerve. Well, I wouldn't ask her any more questions, just stay with her until her nerves settled down. Of course, if I had known we'd be sitting up until the wee hours of the morning, I might have thought twice about that. Finally, about 3:00, Martha got up to go upstairs. I thought it best not to follow right on her heels. I heard her take the first two or three steps, and then she stopped.

Uh-oh, I thought. *Has she changed her mind? Is she coming back in here?* I kept listening for her to come back or go on upstairs, but she didn't move. I wondered if I should go see what the holdup was. In a few minutes, I heard her take to the stairs again. I listened to make sure she made it up the second flight to the third floor, and then I got up and went upstairs to my room.

There wasn't much use in going to bed, but I laid back the covers and crawled in. I had hardly got settled when I heard a big racket right over my head on the third floor—sounded like the place was coming apart! I threw on my robe and went running up there. The racket was coming from Martha's room. I dashed in and flipped on the light switch. The bed was shaking like crazy, and Martha was thrashing about like some rag doll.

"Martha! Martha! What's the matter?"

She grabbed my arm, her eyes wide open and wild. I couldn't do a thing to stop what was going on!

Suddenly, Nancy was by my side and trying to help me. Together we struggled to hold on to Martha so she wouldn't hurt herself, but we couldn't stop the fit she was having.

"Nancy, what's wrong with her?"

Nancy shook her head. "I don't know."

"A seizure?" We couldn't hold her down. The whole bed was bouncing about.

"It's not a seizure—she's wide awake."

What we were seeing was like one of them horror movies, only there was no blood-curdling screams. The whole room seemed charged with some kind of evil power, and that poor girl—never in my life have I seen a body so terrified! I just lit into praying as hard as I could. "Lord, help us. Lord, in the name of Jesus, help! Lord, help us! Help us, Lord! In the precious name of Jesus, help! Help!"

How long that went on, I can't tell you. It seemed like forever before that power, or whatever it was, let go of Martha. Before that bed stopped shaking, it had rocked clean across the room and was up against the bed on the other side.

As things calmed down, that poor girl just lay there staring at us and whimpering. I kept telling her, "It's all right, Martha, it's all right."

Nancy took hold of my hand. "Miss E., let me look at your arm." Martha's nails had broke the skin on my wrist, and it was bleeding a little bit. "I'll get a Band-Aid," she said and left for her room. I picked Martha's blanket up off the floor, straightened it out, and spread it over her.

When Nancy came back with the Band-Aid, we pushed the bed back where it was supposed to be. She offered to stay in the room with Martha for the rest of the night, but I told her I'd stay and call if we needed her. Nancy didn't want to leave me, but I insisted. She went back to her room, and I lay down on the other bed in Martha's room.

I felt zapped but knew I wouldn't sleep. Who could sleep after a thing like that? I did thank the Lord that whatever it was, it was over, and I prayed it wouldn't happen again. I was also very thankful that the other girls had not woke up. Excitement like that would put the house in an uproar. And I thanked the Lord for Nancy. Having a nurse in the house was a life saver.

Martha's breathing worried me; it was heavy and unnatural. Poor thing. I hoped she was going to be all right after this.

As the early morning hours wore on, I lay there trying to understand what we had been through. I didn't want to put a name to it, but if I was to guess, I'd have to say the devil was in back of it. But why?

I was thinking I would have to tell Ursula, but before the sun came up, I had decided not to tell her and let the chips fall where they may. For starters, Ursula had enough to worry about without this. In the second place, I couldn't explain what had happened. And in the third place, Ursula would probably send Martha home. I, for one, didn't want that to happen. I had promised Martha's husband I'd take care of her, and the Lord helping me, I intended to keep my word to that old man.

Of course, if it happened again, I'd be in Dutch for not telling Ursula.

10

Sunday morning dawned bright and clear. Decked out in our Sunday best we didn't look like the same crew who had been working in the garden. I'm sure I had bags under my eyes from not sleeping a wink the night before, but Martha looked okay. After all, she did get some sleep, such as it was.

The girls piled onto the van with me behind the wheel and Ursula in the jump seat. On the way down the mountain I tried to prepare them for what kind of service this church might have. "I don't know what we'll find here," I told them. "This church may not be like any you have ever went to."

"Gone to," Ursula said.

"Not 'went to'?"

She shuddered. "No, Esmeralda, not 'went to.'"

I could hear reactions in back of me. It wouldn't take much for some of the women to tell Ursula off about correcting me, but I was determined to keep cool and ward off anything like that. I thanked Ursula like it didn't bother me, and went on explaining what we might find in the Valley Church. "Like I was saying, this church might be a lot different from what you're use to. If there's shouting, anything like that, it's nothing to laugh at. We don't make fun of nobody's religion."

Ursula repeated what I had just said. "We don't make fun of *anybody's* religion," she said.

"That's what I said."

"No, you said, 'We don't make fun of *nobody's* religion.' That's a double negative."

"Well, whatever," I said and shut up. Making light of it did not come easy. I could hear Linda having a good time with this, and the women yelling at her.

I didn't say another word until we got to the turnoff to Lester's place. "Where are we going?" Ursula asked, and I told her we were taking Lester some fish.

When we got to Lester's, I let Dora off. While she took him the fish I drove down past the apple tree and managed to turn the van around okay.

"You mean somebody lives in that shack?" Ursula asked.

"Sure. It's small, but Lester has a nice little place there—told us we can pick blueberries and grapes when they come in." Even as I said that, I thought to myself, *That is, if we're still in business come July or September.* I didn't even know where Sunday dinner was coming from. There was nothing in the kitchen to make even a halfway decent meal.

From Lester's place it wasn't far to the Valley Church. As we were pulling into the lane, the church bell was ringing, and we could see this little white church with its steeple and bell tower. It put me in mind of that old song about the church in the wildwood. Picnic tables were about the yard, and I spotted two out houses, one on either side of the church and half hidden in the willows. We rolled up in an area near the stream, and I parked the van where a couple of pickups and a car were parked.

Opening the van door, Ursula got off first. As the girls were piling off, I stopped Nancy and asked her to wait a minute. After everybody was off the van, I told her it would be best if we kept to ourselves what had happened the night before. I also asked her if, when we went inside, it might not be a good idea for us to sit on either side of Martha in case something else happened. She agreed.

The shallow river running in back of the church and the morning mist floating above it made me shiver in my sweater. A breeze rustling the willows had a chill in it, but despite the cool weather, wildflowers were blooming blue all over the meadow.

Our group stood around together while a few people were making their way inside. Linda pulled out her cigarettes and lighter, but I shook my head. She scowled and put them away.

I was pretty sure we wouldn't hear a sermon such as Pastor Osborne would be bringing at Apostolic Bible but, like Splurgeon said, "Carry an appetite to God's house, and you will be fed."

After it looked like everybody was inside the church who was going inside, we trooped in. Our group swelled attendance to twice the number sitting there—men on one side, women on the other. Most of the men wore white shirts buttoned to the neck, and there wasn't a necktie among them. A couple of them wore overalls. Two young boys sat with the men and turned around to gawk at us coming in. None of the grown-ups turned around to look.

I managed to steer Martha in between Nancy and me with Ursula on my left. The rest of our group ranged over several pews on the women's side. Once we got settled, I enjoyed sitting there, waiting for the service to begin. Although there was a musty smell from the church being closed up all week, the walls and rafters were of pine; if they would open the windows, we'd get a strong, clean smell. The old benches were made of long-gone chestnut, and with the sun streaming in, they had a soft, warm look about them. Square in the middle of the aisle was a pot-bellied stove smelling of the ashes left over from winter use.

I could hear the stream flowing over the rocky river-bed; as I listened, I heard one rock thumping, thumping, thumping as the water poured over and around it. I wondered how many years that thumping had been drumming a rhythm, keeping time with the flow of the river.

There was no sign of a preacher anywhere. The only creature on the platform was a wasp buzzing about the window. I picked up a fan that had fell on the floor. The fan had a picture of the Good Shepherd holding a lamb in one arm and a shepherd's crook in the other. It was exactly like the ones we used to have in our Apostolic Bible Church before it was air-conditioned. I wished Beatrice could see it—it would give her a trip down memory lane. Next time she called I was going to ask her to give me the name of a town where I could write to her in care of general delivery. Then I could write little things like that and not waste our telephone time.

Looking at my watch, I figured it would be two or three hours before Beatrice and Carl would stop for church out there in Arizona or wherever they were. And it was past time for the W.W.s to be starting class. Poor Clara would be up front trying to make the announcements, and the rest of them women would not shut up and listen until they got finished telling all the news in town. Then Clara would have to repeat what she had already said. She'd give all the lowdown on who was sick and what was wrong with them. There'd be a lot of talk about every case while Thelma counted the collection. Somebody would pray, and then they'd get down to the Bible study. By then half the time would be spent.

I had to hand it to Clara, she had patience. Of course, she grew up with most of those W.W.s. They may not have had all the smarts in the world, but they did have a heart for the Lord. No matter how much they squabbled over something, when the chips were down, they came together and did what had to be done. In my book, hearts meant more than smarts, but for the most part the W.W.s were took for granted. I knew it would mean a lot to them to get to come up here—they didn't get to go many places. And I hoped Priscilla Home got straightened out before they came. It would be so good to see them. But, I tell you, as much as I missed the W.W.s' fellowship, I would not have changed places with a one of them. Never in my life had I felt more needed than I did right then.

Still waiting for something to get started, I thumbed through the hymnbook. It was one of those that has shaped notes. I had never seen that kind, and it made me curious to know the why and wherefore for shaped notes.

Finally, three women on the front pew stood up and turned around to face the congregation; nice-looking women in house dresses and wearing cardigans. One of them had a pitch pipe, and she blew on it to find the note for each of the singers. They all hummed their note, then began singing. "Some glad morning, when this life is over, I'll fly away . . ."

It was country singing at its best—"I'll Fly Away" in three-part harmony. It's hard to hear music like that and not pat your foot, but nobody did that I could see. The ladies sang all the verses, and when they ended, I could have clapped. I tell you, that trio was not half bad.

But they weren't done. Going through the same tuning business, they sang out on "Unclouded Day." The gospel singers I'd see on TV slapped their thighs, snapped their fingers, and wiggled, keeping time with the music, but not this trio. Neither did the congregation show any enthusiasm; they just sat there being respectful, or bored, one.

I wondered how Ursula was taking this music. I knew the girls liked it. Even after all Martha had been through, she would glance at me, smiling, showing she was enjoying every minute.

Nobody seemed concerned that the preacher had not showed up. No doubt the regulars were used to him being slow in coming. If he was a circuit preacher, there was no telling how far he was traveling to get there. For me, I was enjoying the singing and didn't much care that he hadn't showed up.

When "Unclouded Day" ended, the pitch pipe came out again, and in a few minutes we were hearing, "We'll Understand It Better By and By." That one I took to heart. With little or nothing to cook for dinner, no money coming in, our not selling that old piano, it was something in the way of comfort to know that some day we would understand why.

There seemed to be no end to the songs those ladies knew by heart. By the time they had sung several verses of "I'm Bound for the Promised Land," we could hear a pickup rattling down the lane. The trio took their seats, and an old man in overalls stood up, raised his face toward the rafters, and commenced singing in a throaty voice:

I'll meet you in the morning, by the bright riverside;
When all sorrow has drifted away;
I'll be standing at the portals when the gates open
   wide,
At the close of life's long, dreary day.

On the chorus, men chimed in doing the bass parts. It looked to me like having that old man sing that song was a regular custom in the church, something he did at every service, probably at the sound of the preacher arriving.

The truck came to a screeching stop by the creek, and in a few minutes somebody was coming onto the porch, scraping his shoes on the steps before coming inside. I had a hard time resisting the urge to look around. In a minute, he strode down the aisle, tall as a Georgia pine, with a shock of gray hair and a flowing beard. Hugging a black Bible the size of a wallpaper catalog and holding a bundle of clothes in the other arm, he could have passed for any one of them Old Testament prophets. *He's eighty-five if he's a day,* I thought. Dressed in a white shirt that could've used a little bleach, a suit coat, work pants and brogans, he mounted the platform and stashed the bundle behind the pulpit. Without apologizing or saying anything, he lit into praying. It was a long, loud prayer mostly thanking God for letting him live to see another day. Then he commenced his sermon.

"God has give me a word," he announced. "Hit's about the Pharisee and the Republican. Now you know me to be a all-out Republican, but all politicians be sinners a-plenty, and I don't put one mustard seed of my faith in them. Ever' bit o' my faith is in the Lord God Aw'mighty, maker of heaven an' airth."

An amen came from the men's side of the room, then all the men amened him.

"My papa told me we was once Democrats; always had been, even when Democrats lost ever' election. But when a Democrat made it to the White House, he bein' president, promised not to send our boys into war and then he done it. Next day, my papa marched over to the county courthouse and signed up Republican, and we Baileys 'ave been Republicans to this day. You'll not never find no Bailey man a-votin' any ways but Republican.

"Now, brethren, you all know Rockville's newspaper

is Democrat on ever' page, up one side and down t'other. Papa would not have that paper in his house. He sent away for the *Union Republican,* an' ever' week that paper come to our mailbox aside the road. I took hit myself as long as it was wrote.

"One day Papa was a-fightin' the mud on the Old Turnpike. You know when the road's knee-deep in mud it can be the mischief of a way to get to market with a load o' corn. Old man Rivers told him, 'Bill, if you was to vote the Democrat ticket, they'd pave this hyar road for you.' Well, sir, my papa told Rivers in words I dare not use from behind this sacred desk, 'Rivers, I have waded this mud all my life, and I'll wade it up to my armpits afore I'll vote the Democrat ticket!'

"Enough o' that," the preacher said and thumped his Bible, rolled it open on his forearm. "Now this hyar story about the Pharisee and the Republican has got to be a true story, no question ast. I take hit that Pharisee must 'ave been a Democrat; he put on a good show, took ever' opportunity to let folks know how good a man he was. Prob'ly sat on the front row in the biggest church in town, a deacon or elder, one—paid his tithes, wrote big checks, and waved 'em about so ever'body could see. Prayed a good deal—out loud an' long prayers, the kind you fall asleep on. That's the kind o' feller he was. But human nature bein' what it be, most folks would vote for him over that God-fearin' Republican.

"Well, I tell you right now, as for me an' my house, we vote fer the Republican. He know'd he was a sinner, an' he done the only decent thang a sinner can do—he felt so bad about it, he beat his bosom an' ast the Lord to be merciful to him fer he was a sinner.

"Now, that's the man to vote fer. For shore he's the man Jesus voted fer. Jesus said that Republican went home saved.

"Now I'd like to go on a spell 'bout this, but we 'ave got more of the Lord's business to tend to today. We have got dinner on the grounds and a baptizin' to boot." Raising both his long arms and with a twang in his voice, he laid out the blessing: "The Lord bless thee and keep thee. The Lord make his face to shine upon thee, and be gracious unto thee. The Lord lift up . . . lift up . . ."

Some man in the congregation prompted him, "'His countenance,' preacher."

"Ah, yes, his countenance . . . " But the poor preacher couldn't remember the rest. "Amen!" he hollered, and the men answered back, "Amen."

The preacher came off the pulpit and was down the aisle and out the door in less time than it takes to tell it.

As we stood up, the ladies in the trio came over to me and Ursula. I introduced the two of us as well as Martha and Nancy and told them we were from Priscilla Home. They invited us to stay for dinner, but Ursula politely declined. They insisted. Nettie, the alto, said, "We have got more food than we'll ever eat."

I can tell you right now, we were in no position to turn down a free meal, and when the women repeated their invitation, Ursula gave in and said we'd stay for dinner.

Since church let out, the men's outhouse was doing a steady business, but before any of the ladies used theirs, they asked us if we'd like to go. I needed to go bad so I went first.

The women's outhouse was a two-holer, but I didn't expect to have company in there. There were lids for the holes; at least no snake or varmint could crawl in thataway. There were spiderwebs in there that I had to knock down before I could sit. From what you've probably heard about outhouses you might expect a Sears catalog to be in there, but this one had three rolls of toilet paper wrapped in plastic. I laughed to myself. *I bet Ursula would have a accident before she'd use a outhouse.*

When I came out, Nancy manned the pitcher pump for me to wash my hands, and I told her to pass the word that the outhouse was a two-holer. That would speed up the process of getting everybody comfortable before we ate. Ursula looked nervous about the girls waiting in line, taking turns, but they were all giggling, having the time of their lives going in and out the outhouse.

The men stood around talking to each other while the women brought out platters of fried chicken, potato salad, green beans, corn pudding, pickled peaches—you name it, they had it—piles of food. When the girls saw Ursula and me helping with setting out the dishes, they joined in, carrying cakes and pies to one picnic table and cold drinks to another. Portia was unwrapping paper plates and cups. Her tattoo was pretty well hidden by her coat, but when it peeked out, Nettie caught a glimpse of it and I saw the shock on her face. To her credit, Nettie got over the shock right away and started talking to Portia about how glad they were to have visitors.

Once everything was ready, Preacher Bailey made quick work of blessing the food and dived right in to help his plate. Looked like he was starved. The ladies ushered those of us from Priscilla Home in line behind him.

Ursula and I served our plates, and Nettie asked us to sit at her table with the other ladies. As our girls came from the line they found tables in the sun. All the men and boys were going over to tables on the other side of the church. That was good. Drugs make some women man-crazy, and it would've been bad if they took to flirting with those mountain men.

As we were eating, one of the women in the trio brought up the subject of the preacher, sort of apologizing. "Preacher Bailey has been preaching since he was a young boy," she said. "It used to be there was not a preacher around could hold a candle to him when it came to preaching and living a God-fearing life."

Heads nodded in agreement.

"But as you can probably see, he's failin'. Gets a little mixed up. But we all love Preacher Bailey. He baptized all my people back to my granddaddy. Funeralized them, too. Baptized me when I was ten years old, right here in the river. Remember that, Nettie?"

The lady across the table chimed in, "Me, too."

Nettie wiped her fingers on the napkin and reached for another piece of fried chicken. "Most churches in this district have let him go for one reason or another—age maybe, or maybe because they've taken on town ways. We keep him because we love him." Heads nodded again. "Being as how so many of our members have moved to town," she continued, "it doesn't really pay Preacher Bailey to come so far for the little bit we can give him."

At that point I put my foot in my mouth, saying, "I noticed that you didn't take up an offering in the service."

"Never have, never will," Nettie replied, stiff as a poker. "We go by the Bible: 'Don't let your left hand know what your right hand is doin'.'"

"I see," I said, and shut up and ate.

Food never tasted so good. When our plates were nearly empty, one of the ladies went to the dessert table and brought Ursula and me each a slice of caramel cake and blackberry pie. Now as far as sweets go, I might as well rub them on my hips because that's where they're going, but I ate every crumb.

When Ursula and I were taking our plates to the trash can, she said we should remember this kindness—if we got the money from the bank, we should invite the Valley Church people to dinner at Priscilla Home. I thought she might be whistling Dixie, but I went along with her, saying that was a good idea.

Everybody pitched in to clean up after the dinner. There was chicken and potato salad left over as well as two cakes half eaten. The church ladies went into a huddle and when they came out, one of them told Ursula they wanted us to take the leftover food to Priscilla Home if we could use it.

Ursula protested. "Oh no. Surely you can share this good food among yourselves." But the women insisted and, under the circumstances, Ursula had the good sense not to refuse again.

While things were winding up there, Martha came over to me and whispered, "Miss E., I need to talk to you."

"All right."

"Could we sit in the van? This is not for anybody else's ears."

"Okay," I said, and we went back to the van and climbed in.

"It's about last night," she began and then hesitated. "This is hard for me to talk about, Miss E. You'll just have to bear with me. . . . I'm ashamed to tell you this, but I didn't come to Priscilla Home for the right reasons." She took a deep breath, her voice not quite steady. "Miss E., when I came to Priscilla Home it was not to get help for my drinking problem; I came here to kill myself."

"Kill yourself!"

"Yes, to kill myself. I'd been thinking about it for a long time. For months, in fact. But I didn't want to do it at home where my little five-year-old daughter would prob'ly find my body. Even if she didn't find me dead, I didn't want her to ever find out that I had killed myself.

"For a long time my husband had been after me to come to Priscilla Home where I could get help for my drinking problem, and I finally decided this would be a safe place to do it. Nobody up here would know me, and if I did it right nothing could stop me. I didn't want to botch it, you know. Doing it up here away from home would help my husband keep the truth from Samantha.

He'd just tell her I got sick and died, something like that.

"That's why I was sitting up last night. I was waiting for everybody to get to sleep, then I was going upstairs to the bathroom, lock the door, and cut my wrists. But then you came downstairs and kept sitting there. I waited and waited until finally I decided you weren't going to leave; I'd have to go on upstairs and do what I had to do."

Locking her fingers together, her knuckles white, she whispered, "Miss E., as I was about to go up the steps, I saw Jesus."

Jesus? Good heavens, was this girl having the D.T.s?

With her eyes looking desperate, Martha searched my face. "Maybe you don't believe me, Miss E., but I saw him, plain as day." Her chin was quivering. "I saw Jesus. He was standing in the door of the laundry room."

I tried to get the picture, but for the life of me, this was beyond anything I could imagine! Whatever it was, it was real to her, and I would've liked to believe her, but it was a bit much. I was about to ask her what he said, when she told me, "Seeing Jesus, I knew I was not going to kill myself. I can't tell you how I knew that or anything else about it, but I know I saw him—it wasn't a dream. I saw Jesus just like I'm seeing you right now. It wasn't a dream, Miss E., it was Jesus himself."

Never before in my whole life had I heard anything like this, except maybe on those televangelist TV shows, so I had my doubts. But I wasn't ready to put the kibosh on what she was telling me, not just yet. I needed to hear her explain what all that hullabaloo was that went on in her room. "What about that racket in your room?"

"Miss E., that was the devil! I was never so scared in my life! If you had not come in there when you did, I don't know what would've happened to me." That girl was trembling all over; even her voice shook. "Did you hear the voices?" she asked me.

I shook my head.

"The voices were telling me, 'Kill yourself! Go ahead, do it! Do it!' All the time they were attacking me, throwing me around, they were screaming. You mean you didn't hear them?"

"No," I said.

"I thought they were going to kill me!"

Ursula was coming toward the van with the leftover food; we would have to stop talking. "Martha, I think it would be wise for us to keep this business to ourselves, don't you?"

"Oh yes, Miss E., this was something just between the Lord and me. The only reason I'm telling you is because you were there. And believe me, Miss E., I'll never drink another drop so long as I live!"

I opened the door for Ursula. "Esmeralda, these people have been so nice to us I think we should stay for the baptism, don't you?"

I agreed and we stashed the food in the van. "Looks like they're ready to begin."

We walked down to where the people were gathered at the water's edge. Preacher Bailey had taken off his coat and was standing barefooted with one of those young boys half naked and shivering in the cold. The old man who had sung the solo in church heisted the tune, "Shall

We Gather at the River" and sang so loud he drowned out the rest of us.

I couldn't get my mind off what Martha had told me. I didn't know what to think, and it's hard for me to put stock in things I don't understand. Of course, it's like Pastor Osborne says, when we measure what we do know against what we don't know, we find we're much more ignorant than smart. I think that's especially true when it comes to spiritual things. Sometimes I watch them TV preachers and see all the things they claim as gifts of the Spirit, miracles and so forth, but I don't see none of that going on in Apostolic Bible Church. I'm satisfied with what we have got at Apostolic, but who am I to say that the Lord is not working in different ways with other people. As for Martha's experience, I would have to let it rest. It was beyond my understanding.

When the man was done singing, Preacher Bailey, with his thumbs in his suspenders, had words to say before he went on with the baptizing. Placing one hand on the head of the shivering boy, he started in talking, his voice as solemn-sounding as a judge giving out a death sentence. "Charles Allen Hughes, have you come to the light? Do you know you are a borned sinner?"

With his arms wrapped around his naked chest and shaking all over, the boy nodded his head.

As well as freezing, he's probably scared out of his wits, I thought.

"Say it, boy!" the preacher shouted. For an old man he had a booming voice.

"I am a sinner borned," I heard the boy say.

"Charles Allen Hughes," Preacher Bailey shouted again,

"holler it out loud an' clear fer all these hyar witnesses to hear an' believe ye to be honest in yer callin'!"

I felt sorry for that young'un. Looked like he might pass out. With teeth chattering, he hollered, "I am a borned sinner, Preacher Bailey!"

"A sinner needs a Savior. Have you got one, boy?"

"I have, sir," he screeched.

"And who mought that be?"

"Jesus Christ the righteous."

"How did Jesus save you, son?"

"By dyin' on the cross an' a-sheddin' his precious blood."

"Did you lay all yer sins an' miseries on him?"

"I did, sir."

"Was yer heart in it?"

"It was, Preacher."

"Before all these witnesses a-gathered here this day, I declare you borned again," the Reverend boomed. "Charles Allen Hughes, you have been borned into the family of God. Walk in the light, keep your eyes fixed on Jesus, hold fast to the cross, and serve the Lord with gladness."

With all of that said, the two of them waded into that icy water, all the way to the middle where the stream was deepest and the current swiftest. Holding Charles Allen Hughes with one arm under him, the preacher clasped his hand over the boy's face and shouted, "I baptize thee in the name of the Father . . ." Then he ducked him under the water and up again. Spluttering and strangling, the boy did not have time to recover before Preacher Bailey was shouting, "And in the name of the Son," dipping him yet again. The boy floundered in the stiff current but surfaced, blue-lipped and snatching at Bailey's suspender. The third shout went forth, "And in the name of the Holy Ghost!" Sousing him good, the preacher brought Charles Allen Hughes up again, held onto him until he was upright, then let go.

The boy looked dazed; he slipped and floundered but found his footing before the current got hold of him. White-faced and blue-lipped, he stumbled ashore where his mother stood holding a towel. Giving a quick wipe of his face and hair, she wrapped the towel around him, handed him his shoes and clothes, and told him to hurry and get dressed. He struck out running for the church.

The preacher was not far behind him with his wet clothes clinging to his sparse frame and a towel around his shoulders. In back of him must have been a deacon, carrying his shoes.

The baptism over, I was ready to leave, but the girls were wandering down along the river where it curved to go around a big rock. The stream was wider there, making a pool, and the flat rocks that had been washed ashore formed a little beach. The girls were moseying around, curious about the stones, picking them up and examining them. I was surprised to see Ursula join Lenora exploring the beach. I guessed we wouldn't be leaving right away. Watching the two of them, I thought about Lenora's mystery man. I wished I knew when Albert Ringstaff would come back, and I hoped I could make good on the rain check for dinner I had given him.

Dora commenced skipping small rocks, sending them over the flat surface to the other side. Emily tried her hand at that; then Wilma and Melba took turns. Emily got the knack of it quicker than the others. There was a gracefulness about that girl. Maybe she was, after all, an ice skater.

Seeing them all enjoying themselves in God's creation made me feel good. I bet most of those girls had never seen a place like this—never known the first thing about enjoying something that don't come from a bottle, a needle, or a pill.

Thank you, Jesus, I prayed. *Thank you for giving us Sunday dinner and supper, too. Thank you, Jesus.*

For the moment, my cup was full and running over.

11

The visit to the Valley Church set the house buzzing about all that went on there. They all wanted to know if we could go there the next Sunday. "Maybe," I said and let it go at that. Unless we got money for the gas before the weekend, we would be going to the Valley Church. Even though the preacher wouldn't be there, that trio would sing and maybe there would be praying.

All afternoon the girls sat on the porch talking about it—the trio's singing, the preaching, and the baptizing in the river. Most of them had never used an outhouse before, so Wilma kept us in stitches about learning the art of "out-housing" as she called it. Melba asked me if we couldn't invite the trio to come for a singing at Priscilla Home, and I said Ursula and I had already talked about having them come for a meal so maybe that would work out.

Monday morning we used the last of the dry milk for breakfast and had just about finished up everything there was to eat. Ursula called the bank, and they told her the computers were still down but to come in anyway and wait in case they got them up and running again. Even if they got things fixed, there was only a very slim chance that the loan would come through and the money be deposited in time to buy groceries for dinner. I was wracking my brain trying to think of something we could have for lunch. We could make pancakes if I could scrounge up enough syrup.

Ursula was over in her apartment getting ready to go to the bank and I was on my way to the day room for a Praise and Prayer session when the phone rang. I answered, and it was an attorney whose name I didn't catch. He wanted to speak to the director, so I asked him to hold while I went over to the apartment to tell Ursula to pick up her phone.

On the way I figured some creditor had set a lawyer on us to collect a bill or file a judgment against us. Well, Ursula couldn't blame me if that was a creditor whose name she had not given me when I went asking for extensions.

Ursula let me in. She was dressed and pulling on her jacket. When I told her a lawyer was on the phone, her face fell and I could see she dreaded picking up that receiver. I started to leave but she motioned for me to stay.

After identifying herself to the caller as the director, all she did was listen, so I didn't have a clue as to what this call was about. In a minute or two Ursula began scrambling through papers on her table to find information he must have asked for—numbers, things like that—and she was nervous or excited, one.

I hardly dared hope it was a foundation calling.

She asked one question: "Is it safe to write a check on our account today?" That got me excited, because it sounded like money in the bank!

Ursula was on the phone about ten minutes, saying four or five thank-yous before she put down the receiver. She kept holding on to the phone, looking across the table at me, and her chin was trembling, her eyes brimming.

"What is it? Ursula, what's the matter?"

She took off her glasses and wiped her eyes.

"Esmeralda, that was Attorney Phillip McIntosh." She was so emotional she could hardly talk. "He was calling to tell us . . . to tell us we've been left a legacy. A legacy of forty thousand dollars! *Forty thousand dollars!*"

"What!" I couldn't have heard that right.

Now she was really historical, crying and laughing at the same time.

"Forty thousand dollars? Are you sure? Who? What?" I was on pins and needles, but Ursula was too historical to talk. I grabbed some tissues and handed them to her.

"You remember a Mrs. Hirsch . . ." she blubbered and blew her nose. "She . . . Mrs. Hirsch . . ."

"I remember her," I said. "You told me her daughter came through the program here and was saved."

"That's the one," she sobbed.

"That daughter was killed, wasn't she? Killed in an automobile wreck."

"Correct."

"And her mother has been sending us checks . . ."

"Until months ago." She was wiping her glasses and sniffling; I handed her more tissues. She put the glasses back on, adjusted them, and blew her nose again. "Mrs. Hirsch has died, and in her will she left her entire estate to Priscilla Home—forty thousand dollars!"

I honestly couldn't believe my ears!

"It's true, Esmeralda. It's true! The attorney said as soon as he got off the phone with me he would deposit the money electronically to our account. He said we can write checks on it today."

"He did? Oh, praise the Lord! Praise the Lord!"

"There's just one thing—if the bank's computers are still down . . ."

"Ursula, I think we can trust the Lord to make those computers get cranked up, don't you?"

We both laughed. Ursula sniffled. "I'll call the bank right now to see if that electronic transfer will go through." She put the phone to her ear and frowned. "There's no dial tone."

"I left the phone off the hook. I'll run over there and put it back on."

I was so happy I could have flown across the yard. *Thank you, Lord, thank you! Thank you, Jesus!*

As I hurried through the day room, all the girls were waiting for me to start Praise and Prayer. Linda yelled after me, "You're late, Miss E. What happened to you?"

"Just wait," I said, hurrying up the stairs.

When I got in the office, I put the phone back on the hook and practically fell down in the chair. I was actually weak in the knees. *Forty thousand dollars!* Never in my entire life had I felt so absolutely flabbergasted!

To think the Lord would do this for us when my faith had been on such a roller coaster going up and down, getting nowhere. In spite of that, here the Lord gave us all this money. I just started bawling!

It was the money, all right, but it wasn't just the money. It was the Lord's way of telling us he wasn't through with Priscilla Home. That was the icing on the cake.

I had to get back downstairs, so I tried to pull myself together. I went in my bathroom to wash my face. I didn't know how much I should tell the girls because I didn't know how Ursula felt about including them in this.

Drying my face I could see that my eyes were awful red.

I would have to tell them something.

I went back downstairs and was surprised to see Ursula sitting there with the girls. Her eyes were red, too. "I want to tell the ladies," she told me, and I was glad to hear that because it relieved me of maybe saying something I shouldn't. "I called the bank," she told me, "and the computers are up and running. The transfer will go through."

Well, Ursula didn't spare them any of the details. It was a kind of confession about her not trusting the Lord to provide. The girls were dumbfounded, as much by seeing Ursula emotional as by hearing the good news of the forty thousand dollars.

Linda broke the spell. "Does this mean we get a town visit this week?"

Ursula wiped her eyes, put her glasses back on, and answered, "Yes, we'll see that you get to town sometime this week." Then she excused herself and went up to the office.

A murmur was going around the room, the women discussing what they had just heard. To get Praise and Prayer underway, I asked them if they remembered anything from our last session. Instantly, two roommates, Nancy and Emily, answered at the same time, "His mercy endures forever."

Talk about surprise—I was bamboozled! That came from the long psalm Wilma had read—every stanza ended with "His mercy endureth forever." And I had thought her reading that was a big mistake. Just goes to show you how the Lord works. It was easy to understand why God's mercy would mean a lot to these women. "Well, we have certainly experienced his mercy today, haven't we, girls? I gotta tell you, I had just about give up on the Lord sending us enough money to pay our bills. Here he's given us more than enough."

Of course, the devil wasn't going to let that pass. Linda piped up with, "Oh, you're saying Jesus will give you anything you want, just so long as you're a Christian?"

Wilma took her on. "No, Linda, it don't mean that and you know it don't mean that."

This could lead to a war of words if not fists; I had to head it off if I could. "Girls, all I'm saying is, you can stand on God's promises with both feet." And I added what Splurgeon said about that: "The Lord has never forgot a single promise to a single believer."

Portia was looking at me with eyes that held more pain and misery than ever I'd seen in one so young. She whispered something to Linda, and Linda with a grin on her face asked me, "Portia wants to know, what if you don't believe—is there a promise in the book for a sinner?"

It bothered me that Portia couldn't ask her own question.

Linda egged me on. "What about that, Miss E.? I say the only promise God has got for sinners like us is hell-fire and brimstone."

Words seemed to pop right in my head. "Portia, the Lord sends rain on the just and the unjust, those who believe in him and those who don't. That shows you he loves everybody, even people who don't believe in him."

I couldn't tell if that meant anything to her or not. Linda wasn't satisfied. "She wants to know if there's any *promises* for her." And poking Portia in the ribs, she laughed. "Portia, you're stupid. I told you the only promise God has got for you is hellfire."

"No, Linda, you're wrong," I said, trying to keep my voice down. "Jesus made a promise especially for unbelievers as well as believers. Let me find it here," I said and started looking for the verses. They were in Matthew on the left-hand page, in the right column, at the end of a chapter, so I found them pretty quick and gave out the reference.

Waiting until they all found the place, without think-ing, I asked Portia to read the verses. I should have thought twice before asking her. Linda answered for her. "Miss E., you know better'n to ask Satan's child to read the Bible!"

I felt like telling Linda off, but she would love that

and use it to make matters worse. "Emily, will you read them?"

"I don't have my glasses."

Well, it looked like I was striking out, so I read them. "'Come unto me, all ye that labor and are heavy laden, and I will give you rest. Take my yoke upon you, and learn of me, for I am meek and lowly in heart, and ye shall find rest unto your souls. For my yoke is easy, and my burden is light.'"

Linda didn't give the words time to soak in. She blurted out, "It don't read like that in this Bible."

"Well, that's because you have a newer translation than mine. Miss Ursula gives you Bibles in modern English because that's easier to understand."

Linda hooted, "Portia, you listen to me. This Bible we got is full of mistakes—"

"Now, Linda, that's not true."

She wasn't listening. "Oh, by the way," she said, "yesterday that preacher ducked that boy three times, right?"

"Right. He was baptizing him in the name of the Father, Son, and Holy Ghost."

"That means you Christians believe in three gods, right?"

"No," I said. Remembering how it was taught to me, I told her, "There is only one God but there are three persons in the Godhead."

"Explain that."

"Well, I can't rightly explain it, but that's what the Bible teaches."

Linda was really getting a kick out of this. "So you believe everything in the Bible is true?"

"I do. The Bible is the Word of God."

"Ha! It's been translated so many times it's as full of mistakes as Swiss cheese has got holes. And you still think it's the Word of God? How do you know that?"

My neck was getting warm. "Well, Linda, I can't give you all the reasons why we know it's the Word of God, but it works for me."

She looked around the room grinning. "Well, it sure don't work for me!"

"Have you give it a try?"

"Sure. Lots of times. I been saved four times."

"Well, I think it'll help if you'll just read the Bible for yourself. What say you all read the Gospel of John—maybe a chapter or two a day—and underline the word *believe* every time you come across it. Okay?"

I didn't know how the girls reacted to that because the bell rang and they all dashed outside to smoke.

I can't tell you how upset I was at not being able to answer Linda any better than I did. As I gathered up keepsakes that had fell out of my Bible and put them back in there, I fretted, *What we need is a preacher, somebody who can teach the Bible and give these women answers to their questions.*

I left my Bible on the couch and went up to the office. Ursula was writing checks to our creditors. "I called the bank again, and the forty thousand came through a few minutes ago. Would you like to take these checks into town?"

"Yes, but first we need to buy some groceries. There's nothing here for lunch."

"Well, I'll give you a check for the groceries. You can run into town this morning and buy them, and this afternoon one of us can go in and pay the bills."

"Okay. I'll give the girls, uh, the *ladies,* their work assignments, then I'll make a grocery list."

When I came through the day room, Portia was curled up in a corner of the couch looking through my Bible. The other women were waiting for me outside and polluting that good mountain air with tobacco smoke. That is one nasty habit. Why any woman would want to go around smelling like the American Tobacco Company is beyond me. But I wasn't going to let a thing like that spoil my day—not this day—not with forty thousand dollars in our bank account.

I was in the middle of making work assignments when I glimpsed Evelyn ducking behind the dumpster, and I was curious to know why. "She's throwing up," Linda told me.

"Is she sick?"

"No, Miss E., she's not sick," Nancy said.

"She throws up all the time," big-mouth Linda informed us.

That puzzled me, but I didn't want to follow up on it in front of all the girls. Nancy, being a nurse, didn't think Evelyn was sick, so I would leave it at that.

"Now, Lenora," I said, "Miss Ursula will be busy in the office this morning and I have to go into town. I'm leaving you in charge of checking the rooms upstairs to see that everybody has made their bed and hung up their clothes. After you're done with that, see if you and Evelyn can straighten up the craft room. It's a big mess."

The rest of them knew what was to be done in the garden; if I was to get back from town in time to fix lunch, I didn't have a minute to spare. I made a quick list, got the check, and hit the road.

To tell the truth, it was a relief to get away for a little while. It gave me enough peace and quiet to get my head and my heart to agree again. That's a big problem with me. My heart wants to go one way and my head another. Beatrice always told me I had more heart than head, but I took that with a grain of salt because most of the time Beatrice put me up on a pedestal right up there with the pope. If she had been in Praise and Prayer and heard all them questions Linda asked that I couldn't answer, she'd know she was right; that my heart was okay but it was my head that was out of line.

It's surprising what forty thousand dollars in the bank will do for your faith. *Nothing doubting,* I told the Lord, *what we need is a preacher—somebody who can answer questions about the Trinity and all the like of that.* Good heavens, if the Lord would send us forty thousand dollars, surely he would not mind giving us somebody who could teach the Bible.

I wished Beatrice would call so I could tell her about the legacy. That thing of her depending on public phones to call me was a nuisance. *Don't Carl know it is un-American not to be holding a cell phone to your ear in all public places?*

I laughed and barreled down the Old Turnpike, belting out "Standing on the Promises." Coming around a curve, I slammed on brakes to keep from running over a partridge and her brood. That mama didn't mind the brakes squealing—just moseyed across the road like always, her chicks following along behind, but when I commenced singing again, that scared the daylights out of her and she shot through the woods like a rocket! I had to laugh.

In the store I hurried as fast as I could with the shopping. At best, we would have a late lunch. Naturally, when you're in a hurry, they have only one cashier working and there's a line a mile long. I can't stand to wait any time, much less when I'm running late. Ordinarily I'd tell the manager he needed to get another girl on checkout, but I guess I was too happy to make a fuss. While I was standing in that line, I ran through my list to make sure I had bought everything. We would have hot dogs for lunch since that was something we could fix quick. For supper we'd bake the ham and have cabbage and potatoes. We might even stir up a couple of the cake mixes.

When I finally got through the checkout, I went to get the car. All that working in the garden had my bones in an uproar, so, with forty thousand dollars in the bank, I gave myself a treat by driving up and having the bag boy load the groceries. It was worth the fifty-cent tip.

Driving home I was still excited, but being alone in the car was a good time to be praying. I thought about

Angela, Brenda, Melba, Portia, Evelyn—there were so many needs. But I couldn't keep my mind on praying. A body needs to wind down to pray right. *I have got to find the time to pray more, Lord.* There was so much going on at Priscilla Home, I couldn't keep up with it. My mind was racing from one thing to another.

Albert Ringstaff—now that was something I wanted to get to the bottom of. Him turning out to be someone who knew Lenora was a big surprise. Him asking "Was it Milan or Moscow?" where he last saw her was a big mystery. *Good heavens, there's no telling what we have got here.*

The Chevy had made it up the Old Turnpike, and I tooted the horn as I was turning in the driveway. The girls dropped their tools and flocked toward the back door to meet me.

12

By the end of the week we had accomplished a lot—Dora had borrowed the plow again and laid off the rows getting the garden ready to plant. You should've seen the scarecrow those girls made! It wasn't a "he" it was a "she" with a burlap body and lots of stuffing in all the right places and dressed in the tackiest evening gown and shawl I ever saw. They named her "Goldilocks" because Brenda and Melba, our two hairdressers, had dyed a mop head yellow and made it into stovepipe curls for Goldilocks's hair. Earrings Emily had made from jar rings dangled from both sides of the head, and somebody had found throwed-away pie pans to hang on her to scare the birds away.

Friday I drove the van into Rockville and let the girls off at a strip mall. Dora didn't want to go to town, so Ursula scheduled a counseling session with her. Lenora went with us, but it was beginning to rain and she didn't get out of the van. The only thing I needed was mouthwash, and I bought a large economy size. After my trip to the drugstore, I sat in the van with her, waiting for the others to finish shopping.

I talked but Lenora didn't. Finally, I got the courage to ask her in a roundabout way about Ringstaff. "I guess Mr. Ringstaff had business in New York."

She nodded her head.

"I thought he was retired."

"He is," she said, but that was all. Her pale skin and that lank-looking hair made her look older than her fifty-odd years. Fingering a button at her throat, she seemed lost in her own little world.

I didn't know where to go from there, so we just sat, not talking. The rain was coming down pretty hard. I kept an eye out for the girls as they went from one store to another. I hated spying on them, but they weren't allowed to go in a drugstore where they could get over-the-counter dope. Of course, they could get some of that stuff in the grocery store as well as beer and wine, but we couldn't deny them the right to a grocery store. Once we got back home Ursula would check their purchases to make sure nothing outlawed at Priscilla Home was brought in the house.

Even though it was raining, I asked, "Lenora, would you like an ice cream? There's a store on the corner."

She shook her head.

"Wasn't it nice of Mr. Ringstaff to give us those fish? He's quite a fisherman. I wonder what kind of work he was in."

"He worked for a piano company in New York."

I had it on the tip of my tongue to say, "So that's where

you met him, New York?" but I didn't. Instead, I said, "I guess his company called him back to New York."

"From time to time, they do."

I figured Ringstaff was a piano salesman. "Maybe he can help us sell our piano."

"Oh no," she said, and a spark of life showed in those dull eyes.

"Mind you, we wouldn't expect him to do that for nothing; we would pay him for selling it."

"No, don't do that," she said rather forcefully for a woman who never had anything to say.

"Well, I won't burden him with it, but it's a shame to let it keep on taking up room in the parlor."

"Before you do anything, let Al—Mr. Ringstaff look at it."

"Okay," I said.

On the way home, everybody was happily showing their purchases to each other and talking up a storm. Angela sounded off on "Old Time Religion," and they all joined in. Then it was "Sanctuary" and half a dozen more choruses.

Raining like it was, I took it slow and easy on the Old Turnpike and kept thinking about Ringstaff. The only thing I got out of that conversation with Lenora was the fact that he worked for a piano company, but I was more curious about the connection between him and her. Did he meet her in a nightclub where she worked? He didn't look like a man who hung around nightclubs—he had more class, but you never could tell. . . . He didn't strike me as a married man. *Probably divorced or a widower*, I thought. I did wonder if those two could be more than friends. Before she caught herself, Lenora had almost called him Albert. No, I decided, he was older than her, and she was an alcoholic who popped pills. A man like him wouldn't be interested in a woman like Lenora. . . . Even so, I remembered how excited he got that day on the rock when he first saw her.

Solving this mystery was not going to be easy.

Back at the house we ran around closing the windows to keep out the rain. That done, I helped Ursula go through the packages of stuff the girls bought in town. Linda was bragging about shoplifting. "In high school my friends would tell me what they wanted from such and such a store and I'd go get it for them. I was good at it, I tell you—so good I was banned from the mall. After that I just went to the next town to do my shopping. Before you know it, there wasn't a town within twenty miles that didn't ban me from their stores."

Wilma picked up on that. "If you were so good at shoplifting, how come you got run outta all those stores? You musta got caught lots of times."

"Linda, did you steal this bra?" I asked as I poked it back in the bag.

"I'll never tell," she said and laughed.

Portia turned her back to Linda and whispered in my ear, "It's paid for, Miss E. I paid for it." Of course I knew it was paid for because the sales slip was in the bag. I didn't let on that Portia had said anything to me because I knew Linda would get even with her one way or another.

It bothered me no end the way Linda bullied that girl. Sooner or later I'd have to do something about that.

Ursula took a small package from Evelyn's bag and put it in her desk drawer. Evelyn was a sweet girl, and I was surprised that she would bring in outlawed stuff. Ursula didn't say anything to her and allowed her to go on upstairs with the rest of the girls.

When they were gone, she showed me what Evelyn had brought in—a package of laxatives. "Evelyn suffers from anorexia nervosa, an eating disorder," Ursula told me. "She is starving herself by consuming little or no food. If she eats anything she purges with laxatives or uses self-induced vomiting."

I had read about that in one of them supermarket scandal sheets. Pictures of those skinny women was something awful. They looked like warmed-over death.

"I've evaluated her case," Ursula was saying, "and there's very little we can do for her. She probably needs psychotropic medications."

"Has she been to the doctor?"

"She's been to a number of doctors—been hospitalized several times critically ill. And she's been in and out of mental health programs."

"She's such a sweet girl."

"*Lady*, Esmeralda, *lady*, not girl." She leaned back in her chair and started talking like a textbook. "Perfectionism is a part of the problem. Failing to be perfect is unbearable to an anorexic patient. In counseling her I have reinforced Evelyn's positive qualities to reduce her fear of failure and to build a positive sense of self. I've also given her an assignment to keep a journal of her food intake, her thoughts, and feelings associated with her eating behavior."

"What causes her to be like this?"

"Our society. Society values thin bodies for females, and some young women become obsessed with having a thin body. Evelyn wants to become an actress, so she emulates fashion models. No matter how thin she becomes, she perceives herself to be fat."

"That's hard to believe," I said. "Mirrors don't lie."

"Another factor in this equation is a history of being controlled by an authority figure. Evelyn was brought up by foster parents who never let her out of their sight. The one thing she could control was her intake of food, and it has become her obsession."

I was amazed at how much Ursula knew. She was really smart, and I tried to understand everything she was telling me.

Ursula put the laxatives in the medicine cabinet and locked it. "At Evelyn's age, there is very little we can do for her. If we could have reached her when she was in her early teens, we could have helped her. Probably now all her organs are affected by the lack of nutrition. The prognosis is not good. Patients eventually die."

"Oh, Ursula, there must be something we can do."

"About all you can do, Esmeralda, is use Evelyn's spiritual belief system to reinforce the concepts I have endeavored to convey. We will pray for her and give her the plan of salvation, but apart from that, Evelyn is a hopeless case."

"Ursula, nobody is hopeless!"

I left the office about as disturbed as a body can get.

Boy, I was going to pray for that girl! I might not have understood all that gobbledygook Ursula gave me, but I was sure of one thing—Evelyn was not a helpless victim. It all boiled down to her choosing to do what she was doing. *Once the Holy Spirit starts dealing with her, maybe she'll take the responsibility for what she's doing to herself.*

I was looking for Dora, and when I couldn't find her I poked my head in the office and asked Ursula if she knew where she was.

"Oh yes," she said. "Dora got upset during the counseling session and ran out of the house about an hour ago. I don't know where she is."

"What upset her?"

"It was nothing. I asked her to write a letter to her son who died to tell him she was sorry and ask his forgiveness."

"Oh," I said. *She thinks that's nothing? That's enough to push Dora over the edge!* I hurried upstairs, hoping I'd find her on the third floor.

The rain sounded thunderous on the roof and battered against the sides of the house. I called, "Dora!" but got no answer. She was not in her room, not in the bathroom—nobody had seen her on the third floor. I ran downstairs and looked for her in the kitchen, on the porch, in the parlor. Then I hurried down to the first floor, checked the laundry room, the crafts room, even the guest bedroom, but she wasn't anywhere down there.

I threw on a jacket, pulled the hood over my head, and

raced outside. Leaning into the strong wind, I crossed the parking lot to the garage.

Dora was not in the garage nor in back of it. I looked up the driveway. With the stormy winds blowing and the thunder crashing, there was no use yelling out her name. I was getting drenched. I looked over toward the garden up to the road but didn't see her anywhere.

Where in the world is she? Maybe she's on her way back to Tennessee. But no, we would have met her on the Turnpike when we were driving home.

The falls! It hit me like a ton of bricks. *That's where she is! She's gone up there to kill herself!* I could just see her throwing herself down those boulders!

13

There was nothing I could do but go after Dora and pray I found her before it was too late. I headed straight for the footpath. By the time I reached it, I was wet to the skin, and the footpath had become a gully gushing torrents. I splashed along in it and alongside it, crawling over fallen limbs and logs, slipping on the rocks, stumbling in the mud. I lost my shoe to the mud, retrieved it, washed it off as best I could, and hurried on.

With so much noise from the driving rain, it was some time before I could hear the roaring of the river. When I reached it, the river was swollen out of its banks and plunging downstream, forcing its way over everything in its path. With water streaming down my face, I tried to scan the rocks for a glimpse of Dora, but trees blocked the view. Despite the roar of the wind and water, I cupped my hands and screamed "Dora!" but was drowned out.

Maybe I can see better from that rock that juts out in the stream—the one I sat on.

I scrambled to find the trail that led to the rock. No

such luck; the river was overflowing the trail. I quickly studied the situation and saw how I could wade to the rock by holding on to branches and limbs. I sloshed through mud and water up to my knees, but I made it. I made it, yes, but that slab of rock was under water so swift it would be suicide to venture onto it. *Lord, help me!* I prayed.

I was getting very scared thinking Dora might have already reached the top and flung herself down. *Lord, don't tell me she has—don't tell me she's dashed to death on those boulders!* Frantically I searched the river below to see if her body was being carried downstream. She could be lodged somewhere out of sight. I searched that wide place in the stream, my heart in my mouth for fear I'd see her body bobbing around in the swirling water.

I tried to tell myself I was overreacting, but I knew I wasn't. Dora was so chock full of guilt and pain it was a miracle she hadn't killed herself before now.

Scared as I was, I had to find her. That's all there was to it—I *had* to find her! There was only one thing to do—climb up to the falls. Since the trail alongside the river was flooded, I would have to find a way up to higher ground. Not far beyond where I was standing, there was a ledge that would take me to the high ground if I could make it. It was slippery as all get out, and with my shoes full of water—well, anyway, I had to try. Hikers had gone up that way, so there were footholds as well as brambles to hold on to. *Lord, you know I got to do this . . . help me now,* I prayed.

I slipped and slid climbing up that ledge, but I did make it to the top. Everything up there was soaking wet, but I was out of the reach of the river. I probably had scrapes and bruises that would show up later, but I was just thankful I had made it this far without killing myself.

Rhododendron was all over, but with the rain filtering down through the trees, the way was easier to handle than when it was pelting down full force. I tackled the first of them thickets head on. There was some kind of animal track tunneled through the laurel or rhododendron, whatever it was, and I got down on my hands and knees to crawl through to the other side. There was hardly enough room for me with all my weight problem, and the ground was marshy, all muck and mire. It made me nervous crawling through what might be home to all kinds of creepy things. I came out on the other side muddy from head to foot, but I felt pretty proud of myself. *That wasn't too bad.*

After that, the going was straight uphill with me thrashing through underbrush, old jack vines, and briars, fighting my way toward the top. When my heart started pounding and my head buzzing, I just kept on climbing, slipping and sliding but getting higher and higher. Even though I was panting like a bloodhound on a hot day, I was beginning to think coming this way was easier than going by the riverside trail where there were all kinds of obstacles I could never climb over or go around.

Then, lo and behold, I come smack dab up against a roadblock as bad as the worst of them—boulders, one after another piled high with no way to get past them. One was split in half, but the crack was too narrow to crawl through. Grappling to find a way, I groaned, *Oh, Lord, this can't be!*

All of a sudden, I was flat on my face! I guess my feet got tangled up in all those ferns and stuff. That fall just about knocked the breath out of me. And the mud! I just rolled over in it, sat up with my back against the rock, and was about to bust out bawling. *Stop it!* I told myself. *This ain't no time to get historical!*

But I come pretty close to it, I tell you. Somewhere I had lost my hood, I was soaked to the skin, and water was pouring down my neck like it could add something more to my misery. Smarting from it all, I had to jerk a knot in myself. *You can't just sit here, Esmeralda. You got to find a way.*

It sounded like the rain was slackening. At least the thunder was just rumbling overhead, not crashing down like before. I was dragging myself to my feet when I thought I heard something. I listened hard, hoping to hear it again. Sounded like some animal caught in a trap. I pulled myself up, made sure of my footing, and commenced to go around that boulder one more time.

Feeling my way, I came to that crack that halved one of those boulders. That's when I heard the cry again. It had a peculiar sound—not so much like a trapped critter. *Can that be Dora?* I wasn't sure, but I cupped my hands and hollered as loud as I could. "Dora!"

The only answer I got was the wind and rain thrashing through the trees.

Well, I didn't waste a minute. I was going to make it through that crack if it was the last thing I ever did! With all that lard I'd put on, it would be hard, but I had come too far not to try. I squeezed in between the two halves of that rock and pushed myself sideways a foot or two. The crack got narrower. I panicked. *What if I get stuck in here!*

About that time I heard that cry again. Really, not a cry, not a scream—it was more like a wailing. Like nothing I ever heard before. But it had to be a human—it had to be Dora! I sucked in my breath and forced myself through that crack another foot, then another. My heart racing, I kept hearing her—the wailing coming from high up on the falls.

It was dark in there between the rocks and, feeling my way, my hands felt nothing that wasn't slimy. That did not help my nerves one bit. Inching along, I wasn't hearing Dora anymore. The longer that went on, the more I wondered, *Maybe it ain't Dora, after all.*

It seemed like forever before I glimpsed light at the end of the crack. Pushing and pushing, I kept squeezing myself through until I fairly popped out on the other side.

Trembling all over, I rubbed my bruised elbow and looked around. Up ahead I saw a break in the trees, which meant I was almost at the top. If I could make it up there, I could break out of the woods and be at the falls. If Dora was up there, I would find her. *It would help if only I could hear her wailing some more.*

It didn't take me long to cover that last lap. I stumbled out of the woods out of breath and shaking like a leaf. Looking all around to find her among the boulders, I didn't see a thing. I listened, but all I could hear was the roaring falls. As I kept looking, I had the color of that old hunting coat in my mind's eye. *Lord, please gimme a glimpse of that old coat!*

Then I heard something. Not the wailing but shrieking. Downright shrieking! Even above the roar of the falls, that shrieking was loud and clear. It came from *somebody,* and it came from the other side of the river. I cupped my hands and screamed, "Dora! Dora! Where are you, Dora?" The shrieking kept up, uninterrupted.

I didn't spot the coat, but I did see a ledge overhanging the bank on the other side; something just told me she was under that ledge. I would have to get over there to make sure, and getting over there would be dangerous. Even more dangerous than the slippery rocks were the wide channels worn down in the stone where floodwater rushed swift and deep. Yes, it was dangerous. And yes, I was scared, but I had to believe the Lord would not have brought me that far if he hadn't intended for me to go all the way.

The shrieking had stopped. I yelled one more time and listened, but all I could hear was the deafening roar. I knew she was there, and I was determined to get to her, so I decided the safest way to get over there was to sit down and slide across the rocks on my bottom. No, I was in no shape to take such risks. If I slipped I would go bouncing down the falls to my death, or at best wind up with broken bones or a busted head.

I eased out onto the nearest rock.

Even with the rain peppering down, sliding over one rock after another was not as hard as I imagined it would be. The hard part was when I came to a channel too wide for me to step over and no way around it. The only thing to do was stand up, take a deep breath, and jump. I stood up, prayed, prayed again, then jumped! Landing on the other side, I fell to my knees, which shook me up pretty bad. I didn't try to get up right away. In a few minutes, I looked up, and there! I saw Dora huddled under that shelf. With her arms wrapped around her knees, she was rocking back and forth. I scrambled to get closer, and when I was close enough, I heard her moaning.

As I made my way down to the shelf, Dora seemed unmindful of me and everything else outside herself. I could have used a hand getting down to where she was, but without any help, I managed to crawl part way, then roll under there alongside of her. Breathing hard, my nose running, and me still shaking, I couldn't talk.

If Dora noticed me, she didn't show it. She looked terrible—downright wild—and sounded worse. That moaning was coming from somewhere deep, deep inside her, from someplace nobody could reach. I had seen plenty of people get historical, even go berserk, but I had never seen a mortal soul in the state she was in. Who could understand the hell that must have been going on inside her.

I didn't know what to do. To tell the truth, I was in no shape to do anything but lay there trying to get hold of myself. Water was dripping down on us from the shelf overhead, and that old wet hunting coat gave off the smell of a long-haired dog, but after all I had went through, the space under that rock felt like my own personal "Rock of Ages, cleft for me." I was safe and I wouldn't worry about getting back across those rocks and making it home.

The thunder was rumbling off in the distance, rolling

away across the hills. Maybe the rain had spent itself or was moving on, too.

After a while I was breathing more easy; I could live with the buzzing in my head. Looking up through the opening I had climbed in at, I saw that the rain was letting up. Dora was no longer moaning—with her head buried in the crook of her arm, she was whimpering like a whipped puppy.

In a little while her rocking slowed. I waited and waited. Finally, it came to a standstill. There was no way of knowing how this would turn out, but as far as I was concerned, it was all in the Lord's hands. Feeling cramped in that narrow space, I shifted onto my side to better see outside. Mists were rising from the rocks. *The sun must be coming out.* If it was, it wouldn't have long to go before it set. *If we're going home, we shouldn't wait too long.*

After a while, Dora unlocked her arms from around her knees and rolled out from under the shelf. *Is she going to leave me under here?* I wondered. I pulled myself closer to the edge and was ready to try to get out by myself, but Dora reached down, took hold of both of my hands, and pulled me to safety. She saw me settled on the rock before she sat down herself.

You would think I would feel awkward, us sitting there not saying a word, but I was so relieved that Dora was alive and that I had not killed myself, no matter what might happen later it would have to be a piece of cake.

I could tell by her eyes that Dora's grief was not yet spent, but maybe the worst of it was behind her. She seemed content just sitting there, watching the clouds breaking up and scattering, the pale sun showing its face.

The longer we sat there not saying a word, you'd think I would get nervous again, but I didn't. Maybe I was too wore out to get nervous, or maybe it was because Dora was a strong woman and I knew she'd take care of me. But the truth is, I was feeling that warm peace that comes over me sometimes for no reason at all. I did wonder what Dora had in mind. Was she going back to Priscilla Home, or would she just see me there safely then go on her way hitchhiking back to Tennessee?

The sun would soon go in back of the trees; if we wanted to get out of the woods before dark, we didn't have much time. Still I didn't say anything. Dora probably knew it was getting late; she had to be the one to make the move.

In a little while, I don't know why, I just started in singing. I didn't care that my voice box was all out of whack—I just sang from my heart those precious words:

> No one understands like Jesus,
> Every woe He sees and feels;
> Tenderly He whispers comfort,
> And the broken heart He heals.

I felt so helpless. *If only I could take that poor girl's hand and put it in the hand of Jesus.* I felt downright weepy, singing,

> No one understands like Jesus,
> When the days are dark and grim;

No one is so near, so dear as Jesus,
Cast your every care on Him.

I did a pretty good job of not showing my feelings, but I tell you, my heart was so full I just ached. I wanted to put my arms around her and hold her, but you don't mother Dora, not a strong woman like her.

The wind was picking up, and I shivered in those wet clothes. Leaning back on the rock, propped up on her elbows, Dora lifted her face toward the sky and said, "Sing it again, Miss E."

And I did.

After I finished, Dora stood up, took my hand, and pulled me to my feet. We started back across the rocks.

14

I was so beat, I doubt that I could have made it back to the house without Dora's help. She held on to me going across the falls over those slick rocks and didn't let go until we were on safe ground. Safe ground? Well, you might call it that, but she had to blaze the way ahead of me going down through the woods. I was amazed at the way she zigzagged through the brush, making a path out of no path. When we came to that roadblock, she had me hold on to her waist as she climbed around one boulder and scaled down the steep side of another. Then she guided me around rhododendron thickets, and in half the time it had taken me to climb up there, she had us back on the trail that led up to the house.

As we were coming up to the back door, I was relieved to see the light on in Ursula's apartment. That meant she was up there doing her paperwork and we could slip in the house without her catching us. We could hear the girls talking and laughing on the front porch, so Dora and I slipped inside unnoticed.

When we reached the second floor, Dora said to me, "Once the moon is right, we'll plant the garden."

That was her way of telling me she was staying on. "Good, Dora," I said, and she went up the stairs to the third floor.

I went in my room, anxious to get out of those wet clothes and into a tub of hot water. My bones were telling me my age and letting me have it for what I had put them through. Hungry as I was, food could wait. I turned on the water in the tub and started taking off my clothes. There's nothing like a hot bath to take care of body aches and pains. As I soaped myself I discovered more scratches, scrapes, and bruises than Brer Rabbit got in the briar patch. One knee was scraped pretty bad. I gave my hair a good scrubbing and rinsed it under the shower. Then I turned on more hot water in the tub and lay back in water up to my neck. Oooh, that felt good!

As I lay soaking, I thought about the ordeal I had been through. I guessed no woman my age should attempt such a thing, but I'd always had good legs and, well, all I knew was I *had* to go up there. It was the Lord sent me, otherwise I would not have made it.

I heard the screen door bang a couple of times. *The women must be coming back inside.* I sure hoped Ursula was staying in her apartment so I wouldn't have to explain anything to her. I kept listening to hear if she came into the office. She didn't. That was a relief—I could soak as long as I wanted to.

Fifteen minutes later, I was still in the tub when somebody knocked on my door. *Uh-oh,* I thought, and yelled, "I'm in the tub."

"It's just us," one of the girls answered.

"Okay, just a minute." I got out, dried myself, and put on my robe. Opening the door, there stood Brenda with a supper tray and half a dozen of the women crowding around. "Oh my, what's this?"

"It's supper. Can we come in?"

"Sure." I opened the door wider to let them in. "I can go to the table—"

Brenda laughed. "No way, Jose, this is room service!"

"Room service? How come?"

"Dora said you got caught in the rain," Linda said. "Now tell us the truth. Where've you been?"

I let that question hang. "Well, if you insist on serving me in here, I'll take the chair and you all sit anywhere you can find a place." They piled onto the bed or sat cross-legged on the floor, and with the tray on my lap I lit right into those chicken and dumplings.

Martha picked up Bud's picture from off the TV. "This your husband?"

"Yes, that's Bud." I knew they were curious to know if we were divorced or what, so I told them Bud had passed away, that he had been wounded in Vietnam and was sick a long time before he died.

"How long has he been dead?" she asked.

"Seventeen years this fall."

Martha handed Bud's picture to Melba to be passed around and asked, "Did you ever think about getting married again?"

"Yes, I've thought about that," I said.

Linda piped up, "Why didn't you?"

"Why *didn't* I get married? Don't you mean why *don't* I get married?"

"That's the spirit!" somebody cheered, and Linda growled, "Whatever."

"Why don't I get married?" I repeated. "Good reason." I held off on saying what that reason was, taking a sip of coffee and then taking my time buttering a biscuit.

"What's the reason?" Linda demanded. "Why didn't you get married again?"

"Nobody asked me."

That cracked them up! Once we got over laughing, I told them, "Well, to tell the truth, Bud was the best, and once a body has had the best they can't be satisfied with anything less."

"Cut the crap!" Linda said. "We want to know where you've been, Miss E. Miss Ursula had us out looking for you. She's probably up in her apartment right now talking to the police."

Wilma hooted at that. "Linda, that's a lie! This storm kept Miss Ursula in her apartment all afternoon. She didn't even miss Miss E. until supper."

Angela giggled. "Miss E., I told her you were in your room fasting."

"Now why would you say a thing like that?"

"First thing I could think of."

"Now, Angela, you know better than that. You should have told the truth."

"Didn't know the truth. I asked Miss Ursula where was Dora and she cut me short—said Dora would be back. I put two and two together, and if I was right about where you were, I sure as shootin' wasn't going to tell her!"

"Now, Angela . . ."

Linda wouldn't let up. "Miss E., you went after Dora, didn't you?"

Wilma came to my rescue. "Linda, that's for her to know! It's none of our business."

"Says you!" Linda snapped, and got up. "I gotta take a leak."

"You can use my bathroom," I told her.

Brenda handed my empty cup to Portia for a refill, and as she got up to go to the kitchen, I told her I took it black. Brenda went on to say, "Miss Ursula said Mr. Ringstaff called and she's invited him for Sunday dinner. Since Melba and I are doing the cooking, we'd like to come up with something special—you know, a company meal."

"I know he would like knackwurst," Lenora said.

"Whatever is that?" Melba asked.

Emily was sitting on the floor next my bedside table, so I motioned to her. "There's a dictionary right next to you, Emily. How about looking that up for us?"

"I don't have my glasses," she said and handed the dictionary to Nancy. Emily never seemed to have her glasses, especially during Praise and Prayer. I figured that was an excuse to get out of being involved. "Emily, did you read the Gospel of John and underline *believe* as I asked you to?"

"I couldn't; my glasses are broken."

This was getting to be a habit. Now she was telling me they were broken, and she hadn't even started to read John. I would have to do something about this.

Nancy was having trouble finding the word. "Does that start with a k?"

Well, I thought, *maybe Emily don't have the money to get them fixed.* Until I knew better, I would give her the benefit of the doubt. Of course, most of those women never seemed to lack money for cigarettes. At the price they had to pay for them, they could max out a credit card real quick.

Be that as it may, if Emily was going to get the help she needed, she would have to get those glasses fixed and read the Bible. Emily's roommate, Nancy, would know if money was the problem. If it was, I would take care of that. I'd give money to Nancy. I could trust her not to let Emily know where it came from, and in that way Emily wouldn't be embarrassed. Besides, I didn't want word to get around that I was a soft touch. A con like Linda would sure take advantage of that.

Nancy finally found *knackwurst* in the dictionary and read the definition aloud: "Knackwurst: a short, thick, highly seasoned sausage."

"Scratch that," Brenda said. "The only sausage we've got is Vienna. We'll make ham or something. I wish we had some green tomatoes. Fried green tomatoes is my Alabama specialty. What's your specialty, Miss E.?"

"Well, people seem to like my fried apple pies. That's what I always take to church suppers."

Portia came back with the coffee. My bottomless pit was right beside my chair so I fished around for my wallet and as a joke came up with a nickel tip for Portia. I kidded her, "Don't spend it all in one place." That poor girl didn't know what to make of it. She just thanked me and held that nickel in her palm like a little child.

I blew on the hot coffee. "Girls, as soon as I finish this second cup, I'm going to hit the hay."

"That's a hint," Angela said, and they all started getting up to leave. "By the way, are we going to the Valley Church Sunday?"

"No, we'll be going into town." That brought on a big groan. I laughed. "Well, who knows, in town I might find myself another husband."

"But you've had the best—what more do you want?" somebody said, and they all laughed.

As they were leaving, I asked Nancy to wait a minute. After the others were all gone, I closed the door. "Nancy, can you tell me, is Emily short of money?"

"Well, yes, Miss E., she is short. In fact, she doesn't have a dime."

I reached for my wallet again. "Can you keep a secret?" I asked as I counted out a few bills. "Here, I want you to see that she gets her glasses fixed, only promise me you won't let her know where this comes from."

Nancy didn't take the money, just quietly shook her head.

"Oh, come on now. I can well afford this."

Nancy shook her head again.

Poking the bills at her, I asked, "You mean this isn't enough to cover it?"

"Miss E., her glasses aren't broken."

"No? Then what—"

I was about to spout off about Emily's excuses when Nancy told me, "Emily can't read."

"What? You mean . . . ?"

"Yes, it's true. Emily can't read."

194

"Oh . . . oh, I see. Well, didn't she go to school?"

"She went to school all right, but she never learned to read. They kept her back a couple of grades, then just passed her on."

"How did you find out?"

"One night I heard Emily crying in her pillow, and I wouldn't give up until she told me the whole story. It's her vision. Emily was in high school before they finally sent her to a specialist to have her eyes tested. The doctor discovered that she sees only the top half of letters. I guess it was too late to do anything about it, or maybe it can't be corrected. Anyway, that's when she dropped out of school."

"Oh my."

"It's been hard for her here since the program involves reading. And she's so afraid somebody will find out about it she's been thinking about leaving."

"We don't want that."

"Miss E., she seems better now that you're here. You've made this a happier place."

I never could handle compliments, so I changed the subject. "Nancy, tell me, is Emily really a professional ice skater?"

"Yes, she is, Miss E., and a good one. She showed me her scrapbook where she's won a lot of competitions. She spent two years with an ice show that traveled the country. They had to let her go. She's a heroin addict. She's tried to get off it—been in treatment three times before—but nothing has had any lasting effects. Her insurance only paid for thirty days of treatment a year, and the policy had a three-year limit. After three years, her drug treatment option was canceled. She was lucky to find Priscilla Home, because it's about the only place for women that doesn't charge."

"Do you think she's being helped here?"

"It's hard to tell. There isn't much Miss Ursula tells her that she hasn't heard before. Emily's so nervous in Praise and Prayer I don't think she gets much out of it."

I thanked Nancy for telling me and followed her to the door. "I'll keep this to myself, Nancy, and if you can think of any way we can help this girl, please let me know." I pressed a five-dollar bill in her hand. "I'm sure Emily can use this."

❧

I went into the bathroom to doctor my scratches, feeling sad about Emily. *How hard, how embarrassing it must be not to be able to read.* I doctored several places and applied a few band plasters. Brushing my teeth, I prayed I would find some way of helping that poor girl. After gargling the last of the mouthwash and tossing the bottle in the wastebasket, I rubbed on some liniment, slipped my gown over my head, and went back in my room.

Still thinking about Emily, I ran the brush through my hair, set the alarm, and decided I'd have to sleep on it.

By the time my head hit the pillow, I was asleep.

❧

Saturday morning, I was so wore out, I didn't hear the alarm and slept through breakfast. When I realized what time it was, I threw on my clothes, grabbed my Bible, and dashed downstairs for Praise and Prayer. The girls were all in the day room waiting for me. Emily and Nancy were sitting beside each other on the couch, sharing a Bible. I wished I had not told the girls they were to study the Gospel of John independently, because now, if Nancy could study with Emily, it would solve the problem.

Then I got a bright idea: Why not have all of them pair off and allow two women to study John together? Nancy and Emily would be partners then, and it wouldn't matter how the others paired off.

Well, it didn't work out quite like I hoped. "Girls," I said, "what would you think of choosing partners and studying the Gospel of John together?" They liked the idea, but before I could pair them off, Martha said, "Just count off by twos and let one side choose a partner from the other side."

So we did it that way, only Nancy and Emily were both "twos." Nancy chose Lenora and Emily chose Portia. At first I wondered why Emily chose Portia, but the more I thought about it, the more I realized why. If Portia found out Emily's secret, she was one person who would never let on she knew, not even to Emily if she could help it.

After Praise and Prayer, I left my Bible on the couch and went upstairs to the kitchen to help Brenda and Melba plan the menu for Sunday. Once we got that settled, they told me they had a surprise for us—they were going to set us all up to a shampoo and set that afternoon. I was tickled pink to hear that and went back down to the day room to pass the word.

Most of the girls had scattered, but Portia was still sitting on the couch and had my Bible on her lap, paging through it. I figured she had taken a fancy to all those little mementos tucked inside. Well, I didn't mind if she read them. There was some good stuff in there.

❧

That afternoon, Lenora let Melba cut and style her hair, which made her look 100 percent better. Maybe with a new hairdo she would take more interest in her appearance. With a little effort and a few more pounds, Lenora could be a nice-looking woman.

❧

The service in town was good. The people were friendly, and the girls seemed to enjoy it, so we were in a good mood coming home. Brenda and Melba had got up at the crack of dawn to get the dinner ready, so all we had to do was put the meal on the table as soon as Mr. Ringstaff arrived.

When we pulled in at Priscilla Home, his car was already there.

15

Mr. Ringstaff stood talking with Ursula while the van was unloading. With him not all decked out in five-hundred-dollars' worth of fishing gear, he looked a lot different. Wearing a dark suit, a sensible tie, polished shoes, and a carnation in his lapel, he looked more like a salesman.

I don't care much for salesmen. They come on strong with a big smile pasted on their face and start the shakedown with jokes. In my case, they size me up as a little old lady who has not got bitty brains, and if flattery don't work with me, they sober up and get religious. All they're thinking about is the commission they'll make. You can see dollar marks every time they blink their eyes.

On the other hand, Ringstaff didn't seem to fit that bill. For one thing, he was too laid back to be a four-flusher. Ursula was doing all the talking, and he was doing all the listening. His looks were a cut above average. Don't get me wrong, he was not handsome like the pictures you see in magazines of men advertising whiskey, but he was an all right looking man. On a scale of one to ten I'd put him somewhere above the middle. He was losing his hair, which gave him a forehead that wouldn't be satisfied until it reached the crown of his head, but what hair he had was more pepper than salt. And his mustache was full-grown and clipped right. He was not very tall, but in my book that was not a strike against him. I hand it to any man his age who has kept himself trim and don't carry around a potbelly. Ringstaff was definitely not one of those gluttons whose mouth pops open every time his elbow bends.

Lenora was the last one getting out the van, and he reached his hand up to help her. "Oh, Miss Barrineau, how good it is to see you again."

She thanked him and quickly followed the other women going toward the back door, but Ursula called her back over.

After I had took inventory of Ringstaff's features, it came to me that whatever appeal he had was not so much in his looks as in his manner. Without being a dandy, he had a lot of polish, if you know what I mean. Just the way he stood listening to Ursula told me he was a quiet, gentle-natured man who "knew the propers," as Mama would say. Of course, I didn't so much like that he was wearing a carnation in his lapel. But just as I thought that, I heard him say, "Oh, I forgot," and he removed it, explaining, "I'm an usher in church."

Ursula didn't sound like her usual self; she was putting on the dog and asking Lenora very politely to take Mr. Ringstaff to the parlor.

Why don't she ask me to do that? I'm the resident

manager. That woman treats me like I fell off a turnip truck.

"I have to run up to my apartment for a few minutes," Ursula was saying, "then I'll join you."

I led the way inside with the two of them right behind me. At the top of the stairs I excused myself and went into the kitchen to help the girls, and Lenora took him into the parlor.

I put the biscuits in the oven, turned up the gas under the pots to warm the food, and prayed nothing would burn, boil over, get scorched, or turn out uneatable. The tea and coffee were ready, and Brenda and Melba were setting out the plates and glasses on the serving counter, so I left them in charge while I ducked in my room for a pit stop. I wasn't going to take off my girdle or change shoes as I usually did. I dabbed some powder on my nose and gave my hairdo a lift here and there.

I wondered if Ursula had come inside yet. No doubt she was still up in her apartment trying to fix her face to impress Mr. Ringstaff.

Once the biscuits were done, we put the dinner on the serving counter and rang the bell. All the girls filed in and took their places at the tables, but Ursula and Lenora were still in the parlor with Ringstaff. *What's keeping them?* I wondered. "Ring it again, Melba."

She did, and the three of them moseyed into the dining room, taking their own cotton-picking time, their minds on whatever they were talking about. Hearing that little German accent Ringstaff had made me think, *Nazi.* I seated the three of them at my table.

Since Ringstaff was a man who went to church, I didn't think he would mind if I asked him to say the blessing. He obliged, and I tell you right now, Nazi went right out of my mind. Nobody could pray like that man and not know the Lord! He didn't rattle off one of those "Let's get it over with" blessings we say from memory—the words were all his own, short but heartfelt. Like Splurgeon said, "Prayer requires more of the heart than the tongue."

Ursula led the way through the serving line; you could smell that girl's perfume a mile away. I followed behind Ringstaff, and Brenda and Melba served him a generous helping of baked ham, sweet potato soufflé, green beans, applesauce, and biscuits. It didn't look like anything had burned, boiled over, or turned out uneatable, but you never know until you taste it, and the man was smiling as if he liked what we were serving him, so that was a relief. You can never tell about foreigners; they eat stuff we've never heard of.

Once we were all seated, Ringstaff unfolded his napkin, laid it in his lap, and looked across the table at me. "Miss Esmeralda, we were just looking at the piano. That is a very fine instrument you have there."

"Oh?" I said, surprised.

"Yes. It's a Steinway, and in my opinion a Steinway is the best piano money can buy. Your baby grand is exceptionally fine. It was made in Hamburg, Germany, in 1930."

I laughed. "No wonder it's falling apart."

He smiled and there was a twinkle in his eye. "Not this

one. It hasn't been used in a long time and needs repairing, but our pianos rarely fall apart." His hands came into play, those long fingers motioning as he spoke. "A Steinway is built with an iron plate, over strung strings, with a thin, sensitive soundboard all handcrafted. At Steinway, four hundred men work nine months to produce one concert grand." His eyes fairly sparkled as he talked about it.

"Mr. Ringstaff is a piano tuner for Steinway," Ursula informed me in that smug way she has got.

So he's not a piano salesman, I thought, *just a tuner.* But I was in for a surprise. Lenora came out of her shell and corrected Ursula. "Mr. Ringstaff is Head Concert Technician."

"What does that mean?" I asked.

"It means he travels all over the world with famous concert pianists to care for and tune their pianos."

"Oh," I said. That's the most Lenora had ever said at one time in my presence, so I was glad to hear her open up and say something.

Then, before she retreated back into her shell, she added, "Mr. Ringstaff is not only the best piano technician in the world, he is a genius." Her voice was soft but confident. "He works sheer magic for artists who are too temperamental for anything less than the best."

He was quick to dismiss the compliment by saying, "Miss Barrineau, you were never temperamental."

Slightly frowning, she touched her finger to her lips, and he got the message. By way of changing the subject, he said, "Most maestros are temperamental, but I enjoyed working with them. I could tell you lots of stories."

"Please, Mr. Ringstaff, tell us one," Ursula purred.

Ringstaff dabbed his mustache with the napkin before he spoke. "You would recognize this artist if I told you his name," he began. "He is world famous, but I will just call him 'Maestro.' It happened in Berlin . . ."

As he told the story of a piano string that broke just minutes before this Maestro, as he called him, was to begin a concert, I was thinking, *What a wonderful story-teller he is.* His facial expressions and the way he used his hands beat all I ever saw. I could have listened to him all night.

"In a crisis like that, I always tell myself to stay calm, and I always pray, 'Lord, help me in this situation.'"

There! I glanced at Lenora and, upon my word, those slate gray eyes seemed to be coming alive.

Once he finished the story and went back to enjoying his meal, Ursula announced, "Mr. Ringstaff has offered to bring his tools and work on our piano."

Well, I didn't have much hope for that piece of junk, but for whatever reason, I figured it would be good to have a Christian man visiting Priscilla Home.

❧

After dinner, Ursula told Lenora to come out on the porch with her to visit with our guest while the girls cleared the tables and cleaned up in the kitchen. I got up to go in the kitchen, but Mr. Ringstaff took my arm and steered me out onto the porch. He was smiling and telling me, "Miss Esmeralda, you must have had some interesting experiences to share with us." He made me feel like I was somebody, and that told me more about him than anything else he might say or do.

I tell you, we had a wonderful afternoon visiting on the porch. He wanted to know what it was like being brought up in Live Oaks, so I told him about Beatrice and me, how we had to quit school and go to work. I told him about marrying Bud and him dying the way he did. Finally, I said, "That's enough about me," but he wanted to know about Apostolic Bible Church, so I told him about Pastor Osborne and the Willing Workers—about the Lord bringing Maria to us. I was set to tell him that whole story when I cast an eye at Ursula. My talking so much was making her fidgety, and I smiled to myself. *Too bad she don't have a handful of paper clips to do in.*

But it was time for me to get out of the limelight. "Mr. Ringstaff," I said, "what kind of wood goes into making one of them grand pianos?"

I don't know if he caught on why I put the ball in his court, but I knew he loved talking about pianos. He commenced right away. "Miss Esmeralda, pianos have what is called a soundboard. That is the soul of any piano. The Steinway soundboard is either a close-grained Alaskan sitka or an Eastern Seaboard or European spruce."

I turned in my chair and pointed to the tree on the corner of the lawn. "There's a blue spruce."

"So I see," he said and admired it a minute. "Wood from a spruce like that has unusual stability and vibrancy under stress. It will give a free and even response throughout the entire scale."

I felt good about knowing the tree was a spruce. *I doubt Ursula knows a spruce from a hemlock.*

Ursula, desperate to get in the conversation, asked, "What holds a piano together?"

"The ribs. They're made of sugar pine to give strong support to the bridges and soundboard. Now, the bridges are made of hard rock maple and notched for each string."

"Hard rock maple can't hardly be split," I said.

"True. The action parts are also fitted with a hard maple interior dowel. We force-fit the dowel so that there is a minimum of moisture content. That makes for stability in every climate."

"A man was in here the other day, and he thought our piano was made of mahogany," I said. "To me, it don't look too much like mahogany."

"You are quite right, Miss Esmeralda. It isn't mahogany, it's rosewood. That is a very fine and beautiful case."

Good heavens, was I ever feeling my oats!

"The rim and case of every Steinway are double bent," he was saying. "That is, both the inner rim and the outer rim are bent and pressed together."

"You don't use machines," I commented matter-of-factly.

"No. All the components are fitted by hand, glued and maple-doweled before the installation of the sound-board."

I was really enjoying myself; Lenora was hanging on to every word, but Ursula looked like she could bite a ten-penny nail in two. Ringstaff must have seen the situation because he got off the subject of pianos to talk about something Ursula knew. "So, Miss Ursula, you are a psychology major?" The rest of the conversation was textbook gobbledygook, but I didn't mind. I'd had a very good time.

It was almost suppertime when Ringstaff said he must go, but he looked reluctant to leave. I think he had enjoyed the afternoon as much as I had. When he went around the back to get his car, the three of us remained on the porch, not saying a word. As he came around the house and up the driveway, he tooted the horn, and we waved back.

❧

Of course, my joy was not to last. Monday morning after Praise and Prayer, Ursula called me into her office. "Esmeralda, something distressing has come to my attention."

"Oh?"

"Linda tells me that when Dora stormed out of the house the other day, you went after her. Is that correct?"

I tried to hedge. "Oh, come, Ursula, you know Linda lies."

"If this is not true, tell me. Did you or did you not go after Dora?"

"Well, yes, I did. I felt I had—"

"And where did you go?" Looking over the top of her glasses, her eyes were so fixed on me I guess I was supposed to squirm.

With no way around her, I confessed. "Dora was up at the falls."

"And you followed her up there?"

"I did."

"In the rain?"

"Yes, in the rain."

Ursula fished out a paper clip from a tray and, twisting it all out of shape, leaned back in her chair. "Did it ever cross your mind that a woman your age is in no condition to attempt such an operose venture?"

"No. I can't say as it did."

She popped forward in the chair. "Fatuous, absolutely fatuous! A reckless, egregious disregard for cautionary procedure!"

For all I knew she could have been cussing me, but the Walking Dictionary was not finished. "Did it not occur to you that should you fall and break a limb, it would tax all the emergency service resources we might engage to bring you out?"

Anything I would have said would only add fuel to the fire, so I didn't answer. As Splurgeon says, "If a donkey brays at you, don't bray back at him."

Leaning herself back in her oversized chair, she succeeded in straightening that paper clip into a straight piece of wire, then toying with it, asked me, "What exactly did you accomplish by such intrepid heroics?"

"Exactly? . . . I don't know, Ursula. I do believe it was the Lord's will for me to do what I did, but we don't always know the reasons why, do we?"

"No, I guess we don't." I thought she was softening, but then she threw me a curve. "The Priscilla Home Board would not see it your way." If she was threatening me, she was wasting her breath. When I didn't say anything, she tossed the paper clip in the wastebasket and wheeled around. "I have decided to dismiss Dora."

"Dismiss Dora!" I nearly came out of my chair!

"Precisely. She has been most uncooperative, and now this tantrum that has endangered not only her life but also yours is unconscionable. You can tell her to pack her things."

"Ursula, you can't mean that. Maybe this tantrum, as you call it, is the breakthrough you've been waiting for. Think about it!"

She reached for another paper clip.

"Besides," I told her, "we need Dora in the garden. The rain has just about ruint the rows she's laid out—"

"Not ruint!" she said in that cold, unfeeling voice she had got. "Ruined."

"Okay, ruined," I said as calmly as I could. "Ursula, Dora's the only one can handle the plow and get the garden back in shape."

"Esmeralda, I never approved of your bringing that animal on this property and having our residents digging in the dirt. We are not a farm colony."

"Think of it as therapy, Ursula. Outdoor work gives us a good appetite and we sleep better."

"There is more to this program than eating and sleeping." She was bending that paper clip this way and that but looking out the door as if she was thinking. I sensed she might be reconsidering about Dora.

"Don't we give the residents three strikes?" I asked.

She didn't answer me. "Now that you mention it, there is another matter that has been brought to my attention."

Oh no, I thought. *What else?*

"I want you to go in your bathroom and see if you can find your mouthwash."

"Mouthwash?" I was puzzled, but I got up and went in there to check it out. I did remember that I couldn't find the new bottle I had bought, but I thought I must have left it in the van when we came home from town. I had forgot to look there.

Well, it wasn't in the bathroom, so I went back in the office. "I must have left it in the van."

"Your mouthwash has been consumed," she told me.

"Consumed?"

"Yes, consumed. Portia stole it out of your bathroom and drank all of it."

"Stole it out of my bathroom? When?"

"The night you came from the falls. Linda tells me several of the residents descended on your room, and you allowed them to visit with you."

"Well, yes, I did but—"

"That was most unprofessional. Linda tells me that when Portia went to the kitchen to bring you another cup of coffee, she slipped into your bathroom and took your mouthwash."

"Now, see here, Ursula—it was Linda who went in my bathroom—Linda, not Portia."

"We found the bottle in Portia's backpack."

"Then Linda put it there!"

"No. Portia did not deny the charge."

"Ursula, you don't understand—"

"Esmeralda, I understand perfectly. If you had read

my guidelines, you would be aware that an alcoholic will drink anything that has an alcohol content—cough medicines, mouthwash—anything containing alcohol. This offense is strike two for Portia. One more and I will have no choice but to dismiss her."

"Oh, Ursula, you're making a big mistake!"

She ignored me. "By this experience I hope you have learned the wisdom of making our personal living quarters off-limits to the residents. Do you understand?"

"Ursula—"

"It was most unprofessional for you to allow them to congregate in your room." She stood up, dismissing me.

❧

I tell you, I went to bed that night all shook up. *Portia didn't drink my mouthwash—but that poor girl is so bullied, so afraid of Linda, she'll take the blame. . . . Whatever made Portia the coward she is must have been terrible. That poor child is soul tired—sunk so deep she can sink no more. Oh God, do something—give her a glimmer of hope peeking through that fog she's in. Help me, Lord. Help me help that girl!*

16

That night after Ursula said Dora must leave and also gave Portia another strike, I couldn't sleep. It was all so unfair. Didn't Ursula have sense enough to know that it was her who caused Dora all that torment? That business of having her write a letter to her dead child was the worst thing anybody could have done. It wrung the heart out of Dora; she could have killed herself. *A temper tantrum, my eye! Ursula knows I'll not tell Dora to pack her bags. Before I'd do such a thing I'd pack my own bags. Besides, this is Dora's first strike, and she gets three.*

As for Portia, I knew good and well that Linda had stolen the mouthwash, drank it, put the bottle in Portia's backpack, then tattled to Ursula. I knew that, but I could not prove it. I figured Portia took the blame because Linda kept her so browbeat she would be afraid not to. *I can't figure out how Linda has such control over that poor girl.*

I wrestled on the bed as long as I could, then I got up and was in the kitchen making myself a cup of tea when

Angela came in. She was breaking a rule being up at that hour of the night, but I was sick and tired of Ursula's rules. "Can't sleep?" I asked.

"No." She was making a cup of coffee in the microwave.

In a few minutes it was ready, and she stirred in some sugar. "I need somebody to talk to."

"Will I do?"

"Who else can you talk to around here?"

We went down to the day room. I sipped my tea and waited for her to say something. Leaning back in the chair and closing her eyes, she nursed the coffee mug in both hands and said nothing.

After a while, I said, "I guess you heard what's happened to Portia."

"Linda told us. Miss E., Portia didn't take your mouthwash."

"I know."

"Everybody knows it was Linda. I really yelled at her, but it didn't do any good. She has Miss Ursula conned; she believes anything Linda says."

"Can we prove Linda did it?"

Angela sighed. "No, I guess not."

"Portia didn't deny she did it."

"She was scared, Miss E." Angela toyed with the cup, took a sip, and looked like she was tickled about something. "Dora says Portia has worms."

"Dora says Portia has got worms?"

Angela smiled. "That's what she calls it. Dora says they're 'fear worms.'"

"Fear worms? I never heard of such a thing."

"Well, you know Dora—that's just the way she talks. Portia's full of fears, and they're eating away at her. Dora says fear worms will kill you."

"Well, why—why is Portia so afraid?"

"Linda says her stepfather did a number on her when she was little. I don't believe much Linda says, but that may be true. Portia was afraid to stay at home and afraid to leave. Once she left, she was afraid of everything and everybody. She lets anybody do anything they want to do to her. That's the only way she can survive on the streets."

Hearing that made me sick. "Why doesn't she go home? Linda said that stepfather has left her mother."

"I guess she's afraid he'll come back. She's afraid of everything."

What was left of my tea was cold, so I set it on the table and stretched out on the couch. I couldn't make sense of all this. It upset me so, I couldn't even pray. I just lay there dreading another day like this one.

Angela started in again. "Miss E., I've crossed the line."

"What do you mean?"

"Just that. I've gone too far for the Lord ever to take me back. Remember that place where it says 'he gave them up'? Well, he's given up on me."

"No, I don't think that's true."

"Miss E., I've done everything in the book."

"So?"

"There's another place that says when a person knows what being a Christian is and then turns their back on the Lord, that person can't ever repent and be saved."

"Where does it say that?"

"I don't know, but it's in there."

Vaguely I did remember something like that in the Bible, but for the life of me, I couldn't remember where it was. *Hebrews, I think.* But I didn't have my Bible, and the one on the table was a new version. I knew I'd never be able to find it in there. Anyway, I did not want to believe it was true of Angela, but what could I say?

That young girl with her hair rolled up in curlers, no makeup, and wearing a nightshirt with the picture of some rock group on the front, was yet probably the prettiest girl in the house. And to think that somewhere her parents were trying to carry on Christian work while she was living all-out for Satan. I hoped that here in the middle of the night they were asleep, but chances were they were tumbling and tossing, worried to death and crying out to the Lord about her. I've been told the prayers and tears of godly parents make it impossible for their child to perish. Maybe that's true and maybe it ain't, but I wanted to believe it was true. I didn't want to believe the Lord had give up on Angela. I asked her if she had ever been clean before.

"Miss E., in five years I've been clean three times. Being clean never lasted more than the week or two I spent in jail. Never lasted any longer than it took me to hit the streets again. For five years I was either stoned, getting stoned, or getting over being stoned . . ."

"Well, you're clean now. How long have you been at Priscilla Home?"

"Six weeks."

"So you've been clean six weeks?"

"Well, yes, I have. But it hasn't been easy. When I first came, it was awful hard—you can't understand what that craving is like unless you've been there. The worst is behind me, but once I leave here. . . . This is the longest I've ever been clean."

"How do you account for that?"

"Well, I guess it's being in this Christian environment. Besides, I know I'd get kicked out if I relapsed."

"Has the fear of being kicked out ever stopped you before?"

She laughed. "No. I've been kicked out of a couple of rehabs."

"You don't think the Lord has something to do with you staying straight for six weeks?"

"Oh, I know my parents have been praying for me."

"Well, Angela, if you have crossed the line like you think, why are you bothered about it?"

"Why? Miss E., anybody who thinks they have gone too far would be upset same as me."

"Maybe, but chances are they wouldn't be."

"What do you mean? Why wouldn't they be upset?"

"Well, in my opinion, the reason you're upset is because the Holy Spirit is working on you."

"You think so?"

I didn't have to answer that, but I was pretty sure.

"Well, you might be right," she admitted. "I feel real bad about the way I've been living. I know I hurt my mom and dad, but like I say, unless you've been there you can't know what it's like. Everybody who works in a place like this ought to have been strung out on drugs for a few years so they'd know what it's like."

"You think so? In other words, say you want to work with prostitutes; does that mean you have to *be* a prostitute before you can help them?"

"Well, no, I guess not."

"Oh, Angela, I believe drugs is more than anybody can handle by their self, but Jesus can give you the victory."

"I wish he would just take away this craving."

"It don't always work out that way, Angela. But if he don't take away the craving, he'll give you the grace to overcome it."

"Miss E., I wish I could believe that."

"Well, I don't know what more to tell you, except it ain't enough just being sorry for your sins, you have got to repent. Instead of turning your back on the Lord like you been doing, you have got to turn your back on the devil."

"I've heard all this before, Miss E."

"I reckon you have, but right now you are making a choice. Either you're going to trust Jesus—believe that what he did on the cross will save you from your sins—or you can be stubborn as a mule and keep right on going the way you been going."

She didn't say anything, so I quoted some Splurgeon to her: "Choose your love, Angela, then love your choice."

In a little while, she got up and said she was going to bed.

"Well, good night, Angela."

She came over to the couch, gave me a peck on the cheek, and said, "Thanks."

Disappointed that there was nothing more accomplished, I sat there wondering if I should have asked her to pray with me or something. I remembered the night Maria died and Dr. Elsie asking Lucy, "Did you draw in the net?" Lucy had drawn in the net. Maria had received Christ. But Angela?

My heart was as heavy as lead. *Lord, please, please, I've done all I know to do. Help Angela . . . help Portia. Set them free, Lord.*

I felt like my prayers were bouncing off the ceiling. Maybe it wasn't right to be lying on the couch praying, so I put a cushion on the floor and got down on my knees.

But I couldn't pray; I was so choked up all I could do was groan. Crowding in on me was Dora, Portia, Angela, Evelyn starving herself; Lenora living in a shell, Emily who couldn't read; they were all too much for me. Martha might have the victory, but only time would tell. And what about Linda? *Linda. Lord, I don't know if you sent her here or if the devil sent her. What do you expect me to do? No, I can't say that I love her. I know I ought to, but Lord . . . ?*

Like I said, all this was too much for me, and I wasn't getting anywhere praying. Kneeling like that, my legs were falling asleep, so I got up and lay back on the couch.

❧

Daylight was coming on before I faced up to what was wrong. A body can't pray when there's something between the soul and the Savior. It wasn't just Linda. *It's Ursula, ain't it, Lord? I have got to do better by*

Ursula, don't I? Lord, it's so hard . . . so hard to take that woman.

Dr. Elsie had said I could help Ursula. How could I help her when I not only didn't like her, I had such bad feelings toward her I could spit in her eye!

A long time ago, Pastor Osborne had told me the best way to handle burdens is to focus on Jesus. I had tried that before and it worked, so that's what I did. I called to mind many of the things that Jesus said, like, "Come unto me all ye that labor and are heavy laden." One thing right after the other came to mind. "My sheep hear my voice and I know them," "I will never leave you nor forsake you," "My peace I leave with you," "Ask . . . that your joy may be full," "I will come again and receive you unto myself."

I don't really know how long those bits and pieces kept coming to mind, but although they made me love Jesus, they didn't change the way I was feeling about Ursula and Linda. I tell you, I was ready to throw in the towel!

And then, believe it or not, a tidbit came out of the blue and slipped in my mind clean as a whistle. "My grace is sufficient for thee."

I don't mind telling you, I busted out crying! I just let them tears roll. Even after the wake-up bell rang I didn't stop. Grace, grace, marvelous grace. That's what I needed—grace. I didn't get up from that couch until I heard the toilets flushing up on the third floor. I blew my nose, dried my eyes, and went on up to my room.

I made up my bed and then took care of things in the

bathroom. I was dog tired but felt at peace. Since Mr. Ringstaff was coming to work on the piano, I put on my prettiest top with my best slacks. I was thinking about Ursula and Linda, trying to figure out some way to make the most of the situation. They both liked my fried apple pies. I decided I had time to make some, so I tied on an apron and went in the kitchen.

While I was rolling out the dough, I was humming that old hymn, "Nothing between My Soul and the Savior." I didn't have much confidence that fried apple pies would do much to improve the situation, but at least I was making a step in the right direction.

17

After breakfast Ursula said to me, "Are you going to tell Dora to pack her bags?"

That surprised me. I thought Ursula had given up on sending Dora home.

"Ursula, what Dora did is not like stealing or drinking. It's not a federal offence. In my book going off to be by herself don't even deserve a strike."

"Obstinacy does not become you, Esmeralda."

I followed her into the office. She was looking for her keys.

One thing I knew for sure, Ursula didn't want the job of telling Dora to pack her bags. Dora has a way of making the high and mighty feel low and foolish.

The only way you can win with a person like Ursula is to finagle. She was the kind who can't lose face, so I gave her a way out. "Ursula, don't you see there's been a breakthrough with Dora like you were hoping for? You uncovered a deep and festering wound buried inside of her. Don't you think she needs to stay on here to give us the time we need to show her how Jesus can heal that wound?"

I honestly thought she was struck by what I said, so I added, "Splurgeon said, 'Uncover your wounds to him, who so tenderly binds them up.'"

"Oh. So it's your *Splurgeon* again." She went back to searching for the keys. "I'm in a hurry—can't you see I'm in a hurry? I've got to get to the bank."

I followed her running down the steps. The girls sitting on the stoop getting their nicotine fix parted for us to pass. In the garage I opened the car door for her. "Ursula, about Dora—if we're going to have a garden, I need her help."

She turned the key in the ignition. "Oh, all right, Esmeralda. But I warn you, if anything like this happens again, Dora will be dismissed!"

As if she needed my two cents' worth, I told her she was doing the right thing. "And Ursula, about Portia—"

"I don't want to hear another word about that. Portia is cognizant of the fact that she now has two strikes against her and that's that!" She backed the car out, turned it around, and gunned it toward the road.

Ursula had hardly driven out the driveway when Ringstaff arrived. He pulled in behind the van, and I didn't want to look anxious so I went and studied the garden for a few minutes, then took my time moseying down where he was at. He had got out the car and was putting on a gray lab coat over his clothes. When he saw me coming he smiled. "Good morning, Esmeralda. What a beautiful morning!"

"It is, isn't it," I said. "You fixing to work on our piano, Mr. Ringstaff?"

"My name is Albert," he said with that twinkle in his eye, and lifted the hatchback of the station wagon. "I brought my tools."

I saw he could use some help getting that six-foot-long toolbox into the house and upstairs to the parlor, so I beckoned to the girls, and several of them snuffed out their cigarettes and came over to help.

We saw Ringstaff settled in the parlor before we went downstairs for Prayer and Praise. There was a full day ahead of us planting the garden, and I didn't want our session to run overtime. We wasted no time getting underway, and things were going well. Angela led us in a few choruses, and everybody seemed to be taking part. Even Emily quoted us a verse from memory. No doubt Portia had helped her memorize it, and I was pleased that their partnership was already working out so good.

Then Linda, yes, Linda, that fly in the ointment, came up with another big question. Twisting that disgusting baseball cap around on her head, she said to me, "Miss E., you Christians say that Jesus had to die for our sins. Why? If God is so good and loving like you say he is, why can't he just forgive sins? Besides, how come a good God let his so-called Son be crucified?"

At first I felt like I could answer that. After all, the Bible says, "Without the shedding of blood there is no remission of sins."

But that didn't satisfy Linda. "Well, why? What has blood got to do with it?"

That unnerved me, because it wasn't easy explaining about all the animal sacrifices in the Old Testament and how they figured in this thing. I tried, but when I was finished, she said, "I don't get it."

Well, I stumbled around trying to convince her, but I didn't get anywhere. What troubled me was that all the other girls were listening, real interested in the give-and-take of this thing. They deserved better answers than I could give. I felt bad about it, but I had to drop the subject and just go on leading Praise and Prayer.

Out of the corner of my eye I could see Linda tormenting Portia by holding two fingers before her face and mouthing, "Two strikes." More and more I did believe that girl was the devil's secret agent in Priscilla Home. One thing was sure, the devil was the father of all her lies.

When Praise and Prayer was over, Portia asked if she could look at my Bible, so I handed it to her. I figured she had run out of cigarettes because she didn't go outside with the others to grab a smoke before work duty. But it wasn't the first time she had borrowed my Bible and curled up in the corner of the couch to thumb through it and read all the keepsakes I had got between the pages. A slip of paper fell out, and I picked it up and glanced at it. "I always meant to frame this," I said and handed it to her. It was the poem about us having only one life.

I left Portia and went to find Dora. Already she was gathering up tools from the garage. I asked her if she would take care of supervising the planting while I checked to see if I could do anything to help Mr. Ring-staff. She said she would.

Lenora had followed me out to the garage to find out what her work assignment was, and I told her she could clean the parlor. "We won't run the vacuum right away, not while Mr. Ringstaff is working on the piano," I told her as we were coming back to the house. "Maybe you could straighten out those bookshelves and water the plants."

I looked around trying to find Evelyn but didn't see her. "Lenora, do you know where Evelyn is?"

"She was in the bathroom."

"Throwing up?"

"I think so."

Well, I didn't have time to deal with that. "When you see her, ask her to start folding the laundry, if she feels up to it." I was thinking I could slip in there and have a good talk with Evelyn in the laundry room.

In the parlor, Ringstaff had his head inside the open piano, examining the works.

"How you coming?" I asked.

He raised his head and smiled. "As I expected, we need to replace strings, and it looks like we may have some trouble with the hammer shanks." He sat on the piano bench and touched one of the keys. "Strings vibrate with measurable cycles," he explained. "The pitch of a concert grand is usually such that the middle A string vibrates at 440 cycles per second."

I didn't understand anything he was saying, but it's a good sign a man is an expert when he enjoys talking about his work.

"Mr. Ringstaff, would you like some coffee?"

He smiled. "Only if you call me by my name."

It was hard for me to do that, even though he insisted, so I laughed and asked Lenora, "Do you call this man by his first name?"

Rearranging the books, she did not so much as turn away from the shelves. "That all depends," she said.

I laughed. "That goes for me, too," I said and went to fix the coffee.

In the dining room there was a cabinet with china in it that was used only for company. Surely, serving this gentleman who knew maestros and such called for putting on the ritz. As well as taking out cups and saucers, I got plates for serving my fried apple pies. There was a silver tray in there that someone must have donated, and in a drawer were linen napkins. I warmed the pie, filled a cream pitcher with milk, and found a matching sugar bowl to serve the sugar in. I tell you, after I got that tray fixed, room service at the Waldorf couldn't look any swankier.

When I brought in the tray, Mr. Ringstaff was bent over the piano works, his long, slim fingers poking around in there. "Ah!" he said and straightened up.

I made sure he was comfortable on the couch before I went back to the kitchen to get coffee for Lenora and me. There were a couple more pies left over from breakfast. I figured it would help Lenora's figure to eat another one and that I might as well keep her company. After all, a body that carries as much lard as mine can easy handle another pound.

It was a wonderful morning. Mr. Ringstaff couldn't

get over raving about my fried apple pie. He even asked me to let him know the next time I made them. He was such a good talker. I was enjoying his stories about big shots with foreign names who play the piano, and was really sorry when he turned the conversation to Priscilla Home. He wanted to hear all about its history, and when I was done telling him that, he asked about our program, our schedule, and our plans for the garden.

After I was talked out, to my surprise, he was able to draw Lenora into the conversation. "Lenora, when last I heard, you were becoming quite a recording artist."

"Oh, Al—Mr. Ringstaff, that was a long time ago."

"Albert. My name is Albert, remember? We miss you on the concert stage."

"I guess you heard?"

He nodded. "Yours is a common experience among artists. Hours of rehearsal, the pressure of performing, the endless traveling. And, I suppose worst of all, after the applause one goes back to an empty hotel room."

"Yes," she said, her voice so low, so full of misery I could hardly hear her. "That was the worst of it. After a concert, after the aficionados, the parties . . . all the falderal, one goes back to a hotel room in a foreign city alone." She put the cup back on the tray and got up to go back to the shelves.

"Please, don't go," he begged.

"Lenora, those books can wait!" I added.

Reluctantly, she sat down again, and Ringstaff spoke to her very softly. "I know of no career as demanding as that of a concert pianist, but Lenora, you have given the world great pleasure—lasting pleasure. You communicate music in a marvelous way. I shall never forget your triumph at the Mozart Festival in Vienna. That was a joyous occasion. Do you remember how many encores?"

"The audience was very kind," she said, "but that's all behind me now." She sighed. "Right now, Albert," she said, her voice shaking, "all I want is a drink."

He didn't say anything.

"Let's have some more coffee," I said and picked up the tray.

Back in the kitchen, I had to heat the coffee, and while I waited, I was replaying all that conversation. I told myself I should have guessed that Lenora was more than some honky-tonk piano player. *I wonder if Ursula knows she was a concert pianist?* I didn't believe she did because she usually told me things like that.

When I came back in the parlor, Ringstaff was asking Lenora, "They tell me you've been playing in New York supper clubs. Is that right?"

"Yes, supper clubs," she said, as if she despised it. "When I could no longer be counted on to show up for concert engagements, my agent quit. Nobody else would represent me. I came back to New York, and the only work I could find was in supper clubs."

"I'm sorry," he said softly.

"They put up with drunks in places like that . . . but they do have their requirements. They would have me play nothing but the old standards . . . I had none of them in my repertoire."

"Could you not play adaptations of the classics by moderns? Rachmaninoff?"

She shook her head. "They would have nothing but

the standards. I now have a repertoire of two thousand or more. Oh, Albert, it was wretched. That music does nothing but entertain."

"True, it entertains, but it doesn't satisfy, does it? . . . Yet, Lenora, as you said before, even classical music that does satisfy doesn't give one a life. It's life you want, isn't it, Lenora?"

"It's too late for me now."

"It's never too late to have life—a complete life."

"Please, Albert, I know what you mean. You're a spiritual man. I envy you for that. I haven't forgotten that you were intrigued with the Bible and spoke in churches, all of that. I tried to find spirituality. I tried Eastern mystics, other religions, but they did nothing for me . . ."

I knew I should excuse myself and give them privacy, but I couldn't very well do that without being rude.

"May I tell you something?" she was saying. "When I failed at taking my own life, I remembered you and I decided to try one more religion. I looked for a Christian place, hoping I would find here at Priscilla Home the kind of life you have."

That stabbed a knife in my heart because I didn't much think she had found what she was looking for at Priscilla Home. Lenora probably sensed my embarrassment because she added, "We enjoy our Praise and Prayer sessions. There is one young lady here who asks provocative questions."

"You mean Linda?" I asked.

"Yes, Linda."

"Oh, she does. She has stumped me with questions about the Trinity, the Bible, you know—why it's the

Word of God. And who knows what she'll come up with next."

"Miss E., that was an interesting question she asked this morning. Tell Albert."

I put down my cup and tried to repeat the question as best I could. "Linda asked me why couldn't God forgive us without Jesus having to die on the cross. Wasn't that what she meant, Lenora? Why couldn't God just forgive us when we ask him to? Well, Mr. Ringstaff, I mean, Albert, I done my best to answer, telling her about the sacrifices and everything, but that didn't satisfy her."

"I see. Well, the answer isn't as complicated as it may seem. Let's see if this will help. What if you were murdered, and the murderer was convicted for killing you. Would a judge be just if he acquitted that criminal? Could he take the liberty of saying to the murderer, 'I forgive you; you may go free'?"

"No. Of course, not," Lenora said.

"Neither can God arbitrarily forgive us our wrong-doing. If he did, he would not be the just God we know him to be."

"But Albert, God is a God of love, or so they say. If Jesus was his Son, how could he allow him to suffer such ignominy?"

Albert removed his glasses and cleaned them with his handkerchief. "Lenora, if you or Esmeralda . . . if one of you slapped me and I forgave you, it would mean that I would not hold you responsible for what you've done to me. But at the same time, I would have to suffer the insult of being slapped as well as suffer the smarting of my cheek." He folded his handkerchief, put it back in his pocket, and adjusted his glasses. "When we sin, we sin against God. We insult and injure him."

"Yes, I can see that."

"Well, Lenora, unlike the wrong we do to each other with finite results, sin against God is infinite. Nothing finite can make things right between ourselves and God. No finite redress is sufficient. It takes an infinite sacrifice to atone for sin."

That dear man leaned forward, his elbows on his knees, and said in the simplest, sweetest way ever a man spoke, "Lenora, Jesus, being eternal, is our infinite sacrifice for sin. By being executed, the Son of God bore the insult and the injury of all our sins against himself. Justice has been served; the righteous Judge can acquit us."

I just sat there with my mouth open. I had never heard it explained as good as that. Sitting there with the sun streaming through the windows, I knew I would never forget that morning in the parlor with Albert Ringstaff.

"Thank you, Albert," Lenora said and started collecting the cups. "I really must get back to work."

"And I as well," he said.

Can you guess the thought that came to me? Albert Ringstaff might well be the Bible teacher I'd been praying for.

18

In the next few weeks, things were working out very well. I had suggested to Ursula that we ask Mr. Ringstaff if he would be our Bible teacher, and she said we must get board approval before we asked him. Roger Elmwood, the president, true to his stuffed-shirt self, didn't think it was a good idea, especially since Ringstaff was a Presbyterian. I said, "Good heavens, what's that got to do with it? The man loves the Lord!"

Elmwood was a peacock who liked to show his feathers, and he was about as narrow-minded as they come. Like Splurgeon says, "He that is full of himself is very empty." So I suggested something to Ursula. "Dr. Elsie knows Mr. Ringstaff—he lives up there near her place. She's the board secretary, why don't you call and ask her what she thinks?"

Ursula jumped on the phone and asked Elmwood to put in a conference call to Dr. Elsie, who was still in Vermont.

Dr. Elsie must have give Elmwood an earful! Ursula

said she lit right in, telling him how during the Cold War Ringstaff got Bibles into the Soviet Union and how he took every opportunity to speak about the Lord to concert piano players and other famous people. But despite all that, Elmwood said, "Well, we'll take him on a trial basis and see how he does." When he said that, Dr. Elsie must have blew her stack! Ursula repeated what she said to him. "Esmeralda, Dr. Elsie told him, 'Roger Elmwood, it's no favor to Albert Ringstaff to ask him to teach for us. If he accepts the invitation it's you who should get down on your knees and thank him!'"

Ursula was so disgusted with Elmwood she said, "He must have fallen off a turnip truck!"

And I nearly fell out of my tree!

<hr />

Well, it was Ursula who did the asking, and Ringstaff said he would pray about it. I had no doubt in my mind but what it was the Lord's will that he come, so I made out a schedule that gave him prime time. While Ringstaff worked on the piano in the mornings, we would have Praise and Prayer, then do our chores, and after lunch, have the Bible class. Ursula thought one of us, either she or me, should sit in on his classes, and boy, that tickled me pink!

Was that man ever smart! He knew the Bible forward and backward. Linda must have sat up all night thinking of questions to ask him. It was plain to see she was out to shock him when she said she didn't believe "all that stuff about Mary being a virgin when Jesus was born." Well, Ringstaff was not ruffled in the least. He listened with both ears, then took pains to give her reasons for believing Jesus was born of a virgin.

I doubt Linda understood everything he said, but they talked back and forth until she ran out of comebacks.

It warmed my heart the way Ringstaff went through the Scriptures, explaining things like that. I asked him to tell the girls, the way he had told me, why Jesus had to die in order to forgive us. Hearing it the second time, I took notes, and that helped me get that down pat.

A few days later I wrote Beatrice in care of General Delivery, Albuquerque, New Mexico, and sent her copies of my notes. It was like I told her in that letter, Albert Ringstaff was a fine Christian and the sweetest, dearest man a body could ever meet. There was not a woman at Priscilla Home who didn't sit up and take notice when he was around. Especially Lenora. I believed that she was starting to live again. She fixed her hair, put on lipstick and a little blush. I told myself that the day she laughed, I'd know she was altogether alive.

Since Ringstaff always went on about my fried apple pies, I saw that he got a fresh one every morning when we served him coffee. I'd get up real early so I could make the pies before Brenda and Melba came down to do the cooking. Now, the kitchen window opened onto the front porch, and I'd open it first thing to get some fresh air. At that hour, everybody in the house was sound asleep, so I could sing to my heart's content. One morning I was singing "Power in the Blood." I love them words:

> There is power, power, wonder working power
> In the blood of the Lamb.

There is power, power, wonder working power
In the precious blood of the Lamb.

After I stopped singing, I heard somebody get up from a rocker on the porch and open the front door. *Uh-oh. Who can that be?* After wiping the flour off my hands, I turned to see Dora leaning against the doorframe of the kitchen. "Oh, so it's you, Dora?" I turned to slide the pies on the grill. "Guess you heard me and thought there was a screech owl let loose in here." I laughed. "Well, it wasn't no screech owl. It was me and what I call singing."

"I like hearin' you sing," she said and straddled the stool on the other side of the counter. "There's naught of music in Angela's singing, however high and sharp it be. Your singing comes from having heart. It comes from a bubbling spring in the heart of yon hills and streams down in falling water a-tumbling over rocks a-findin' its troublesome way—a-splashin' white water an' a-tossin' drops ever' whichaway to catch the sun."

I stood there with my mouth open. "Say that again?"

She ignored me and propped her elbows on the counter.

I poured us both a cup of coffee. "You're up early," I said.

"In my holler, a body who ain't up afore sunup is bound to be sick unto death, ready to be laid out."

I laughed. "Well, whether or not a body gets up before sunup, he's supposed to have three score years and ten before he leaves the planet."

I kept messing around in the kitchen, waiting to turn

235

over the pies. I figured Dora had something more she wanted to say. I figured she was putting her words together as she sat there with her hands around her mug of coffee. Once she was ready, she drank that hot coffee straight down. It would have scalded me!

"Miss E.," she said, "when I been a-readin' them words wrote by John, there's come a flicker or two of foxfire, but this morning, a-settin' in the day room a-readin', there come a big flash. It lit that stub of a candle inside o' me, an' it's a-flickerin' still. I set on the porch a spell, thinking about what was a-happenin', and I don't yet know. Maybe tomorrer there'll come a steady blaze to set my soul afire for good."

I knew exactly what Dora was talking about. Maybe that meant I was wicky-wacky, but I knew good and well she was telling me the Spirit was shedding light on her and bringing her closer to Jesus.

After that, whenever I came out of my room of a morning, I'd check the day room, and, sure enough, Dora was always in there reading her Bible. I knew better than to ask her if that "steady blaze" had set her soul on fire. We would all know when it did.

The Lord knew I needed encouragement, and letting me see how he was working in Dora was not the only way he blessed me. I was seeing a change in Ursula too. The girls told me that when it was her turn to sit in on Ringstaff's class, she sometimes asked a question, and they said in counseling sessions she was using the Bible more.

I even saw a change in Linda; she was actually learning the memory verses Ringstaff gave the class. I assigned her laundry duty so that while the clothes were in the dryer she could spend that time learning verses.

These encouragements was such good news, I couldn't wait for the Willing Workers to pay us a visit so they could hear all the good stuff going on at Priscilla Home. Clara had called and said that she, Thelma, and Mabel could come the middle of the week for two or three nights, if that would be convenient. Of course, it was convenient. Ursula said two of them could sleep in the guest room downstairs and one could sleep on the studio couch in her apartment.

During Praise and Prayer I told the girls that three of my friends from Live Oaks were coming to pay us a visit, and I got kind of carried away telling them how much the W.W.s had meant in my life. "I really want to show them a good time," I said. "You got any ideas?"

Well, of course, they did. They had been wanting to go to Grandfather Mountain, and having visitors was a good excuse for going. Sounded like a good idea to me.

After Praise and Prayer, Portia followed me upstairs. I was surprised. She was so cowed, so browbeat, I couldn't imagine her following me. At the top of the stairs I turned around, and she just stood there. "Portia, you not going outside with the others to smoke?"

She shook her head.

We walked on into the hallway. "No money for cigarettes?"

She shook her head again. "I quit."

I didn't know whether to believe her or not. I took a good look at her. Whatever was in her dark eyes that I had not seen before, I saw then, and it tore away at my heart. It was a hungry look.

"You did? You stopped smoking? How?"

She said one word. "Jesus."

I tell you, that sent a chill up my spine. The women tell me it's harder to quit smoking cigarettes than it is to quit heroin.

"Miss E.," she whispered, "would you go in the clothing room with me?"

"Sure," I said and handed her my Bible so I could look for the key on my ring. "You need something?"

"If company's coming—" She broke off in the middle of the sentence. "Do you think you could find me a turtleneck?"

"Sure. Let's look." *A turtleneck. She wants to hide that tattoo.*

We found three tops in her size. "Now could you use some pants?" I asked. She said she could, so we looked through the racks and finally found a couple that matched her tops. She thanked me, and with her arms full of clothes and my Bible on top of them, she peeked out the door, making sure no one would see her, and ran to her room.

As I was locking the door, I figured Portia was hiding those clothes so Linda wouldn't make a big to-do about them. *"She's got fear worms,"* Dora had said. *Well, Lord, let's see if we can't do something about deworming that poor child.* And I followed Portia to her room.

Sure enough, she had stuffed those clothes under her mattress and was smoothing out the covers. She jumped when she saw me, then quickly picked up the Bible and handed it to me.

I smiled. *She thinks I've come after my Bible.* "Portia, may I sit down?" I sat on the bed and patted the spread beside me. "Come, sit here." I waited and didn't watch as she eased onto the bed. I could actually feel her body trembling. *Dora's right,* I thought. *This girl is afraid of her own shadow.*

I had to set her mind at ease that I was not going to fuss at her. "Portia, I'm glad to see you like my Bible." I opened it on my knees. "I guess you like to read all these little things I keep filed in the pages?"

She nodded. I kept flipping through the pages and looking at slips of paper with sayings, poems, this and that. A yellowed page of a letter Bud wrote from Vietnam . . . a pressed flower from my mother's grave . . . a bookmark made of olive wood from the Holy Land. More than anything else were the poems and sayings. When I was satisfied that Portia understood I was not going to hurt her, I started to close the Bible, but Portia whispered, "And the verses."

"The verses?"

"The ones you marked."

"Oh yes," I said. There were scads of them highlighted or underlined with different-colored pens.

She timidly pointed her finger at something I had written in the margin. I held the Bible up close so I could read what it was. "Prayer is helplessness casting itself upon power." For the life of me, I couldn't remember who said that. "That's a good one, ain't it, Portia?" I said. "I don't remember when I scribbled that in there. I'm surprised you can read my writing."

She wanted to show me another place, so I handed her the Bible. A few pages over, she found it and I read it aloud. "Sunday is heaven once a week." I didn't feel too good about that one. It reminded me that since I'd been at Priscilla Home, I was too busy on Sundays to really enjoy the Lord's Day. "Portia, I use to keep Sunday better than I've been doing here lately. Seems there's always so much going on around here. But when I lived in Live Oaks, there was nothing like coming home from church, eating a good Sunday dinner, then putting up my feet and spending the rest of the day with the Lord."

We kept going through the Bible. On every page or two, there was a reference, a date, or something written in the margin that had meant something to me. I was amazed that my scribblings meant so much to Portia. That poor child was so pleased that I was enjoying this, she had stopped trembling and seemed excited. She turned some pages and pointed with a finger to what I had wrote: "My knowledge of the Maker will determine my expectations." Good heavens, it had been years since Pastor Osborne had said that in a sermon.

I didn't fully understand it then, but I'd pondered that one a whole lot since.

Portia asked me where she could find the Ten Commandments. "Emily wants me to read them to her."

I showed her Exodus 20 and waited while she read the chapter to herself. I was so caught up in what was going on with my old King James, I had almost forgot what I had come in there to take care of.

After she was finished reading that chapter, she put one of the bookmarks in the place and handed the Bible back to me.

"Portia, do you have a few minutes to spare?"

She nodded.

"Well, I want to tell you a story about a friend of mine. Her name is Beatrice, and we grew up together, went to school together, went to the same church, all the like of that. But sad to say, by the time we was in the eighth grade, Beatrice had lost all her family, and ever since then she depended on me a lot. To this day we are like sisters, and she really means a lot to me. But Portia, even though Beatrice was a Christian, she was so afraid of everything—high places, being alone, strangers—all the like of that. About ten years ago she had breast cancer, and after that you couldn't mention the word *cancer* without her going historical. I tell you, Portia, I use to talk myself blue in the face trying to make her see that she didn't have to have all them fears, but it didn't do a piece of good.

"Well, not long ago, all that changed. A nice Christian man came into her life. His name is Carl, and he saw how scared she was—scared of everybody and everything. He told Beatrice he knew what would help her. He said she should look up all the 'fear nots' in the Bible. You know, like, 'Fear thou not for I am with thee.' It must have took some time, but it worked. Today Beatrice is a different person. She can even say the word *cancer* and not mind it one bit."

When I was done, Portia didn't say anything, so I asked her, "Do you know why I told you that story?"

She nodded and looked so downcast I was sorry I asked.

With my finger under her chin, I lifted her small face and looked in her eyes. I asked the question I figured she wanted to ask. "How did Beatrice find all those 'fear nots'? I'll show you."

In the back of my Bible is a pretty good concordance. I turned to it and showed Portia how to look up "fear nots."

She wanted to start looking right away, so I patted her hand and smiled. "I'll leave my Bible with you, Portia. You have my permission to stay in your room as long as you like. When you're done, just leave the Bible outside my room door."

I stood up to leave. "I guess I better get busy planning for my friends' visit."

"Will Miss Beatrice be coming?"

"No. I wish she was though."

I left and gently closed the door behind me. As I made my way down the stairs, I still felt the way a body feels coming out of church when the Holy Spirit has been at work. That feeling stayed with me all morning as I was planning for the W.W.s' visit.

I made a list of things to do and planned menus I knew Clara and the other two would like. I'd get Wilma to go into town with me for the donuts. The rhododendron were in full bloom as well as cornflowers and daisies to fill all our vases. Evelyn and Lenora could pick some greenery to go with the flowers to give the house a good smell. Maybe by the time Clara and them came, the piano would be fixed and somebody would play it. But to be on the safe side, I called Nettie and invited the Valley Church trio to come for supper and sing for us afterward.

I tell you the truth, all of that happening in one day—well, all I got to say is it was one glad day. My cup was full and running over!

19

Whenever Albert Ringstaff came for supper, he would sit on the porch with us after we ate. For a while all the girls would be out there with us, listening as he told about his experiences. But in a little while they would leave, either to go to their rooms, watch a video in the day room, or play ping-pong. That left me, Ursula, and Lenora on the porch with Ringstaff. Sometimes Ursula had work to do, and then me and Lenora had him all to ourselves. For me, the best part of any day was when we could sit and talk with that fine man.

Of course, we invited him to come to supper the night we expected the W.W.s to arrive. He came early, wearing that tweed jacket and gray slacks I liked so much. I had never seen that man without a tie, except that one time he was fishing. In my book, he was old school through and through, and I liked that in a man. He pitched right in to help me rearrange tables and chairs so all the guests could sit at one table.

We had hardly done that when Wilma hollered, "Company's a-comin'!"

I saw Clara's car turning in the driveway, and rushed out on the lawn, waving and beckoning Thelma to drive around back. Then I ran around there to meet them at the back door. Oh, was I ever glad to see them! Clara was up front and Mabel was on the backseat. Getting out from behind the wheel, Thelma moved slow like all her joints were stiff, and was complaining about the Old Turnpike. I guessed the long ride was not easy for any of them.

Clara came around the car and hugged me. Mabel was practically buried under all the stuff they had piled in the backseat—jackets, sweaters and raincoats, a couple of bed pillows, packages galore, and a bushel basket of peaches.

Wilma, Nancy, and Evelyn were cleaning out the garage and stopped to help us unload. Ursula came down from the apartment, and I introduced everybody.

Thelma opened the trunk, and they started taking out suitcases. They must have had half a dozen! "We didn't have room to bring a lot," Clara said, "but we did manage to bring you some peaches, tomatoes, and boiled peanuts. Oh yes. Elijah remembered how you love Silver Queen corn, and he sent you what he had."

"Silver Queen corn? I can't believe it's come in already. And tomatoes? All we have on our bushes are blooms."

Mabel, hugging herself, shivered. "No wonder—it's so cold up here."

"If you think July is cold, you should have been here in

April," I told her. "Girls, take the produce to the kitchen, please, and come back for the baggage."

We sorted out the suitcases and sent Clara and Mabel's bags to the guest bedroom and Thelma's up to Ursula's apartment.

I had hardly got them settled when Nettie turned in the drive bringing the trio. I asked Ursula to give them a guided tour while I finished up in the kitchen, where I was making the biscuits.

It was one busy time, I tell you, but the house looked great—it was spic and span with flowers everywhere you looked. And I wanted that meal to be perfect. Melba made her special ham loaf; Brenda made corn pudding and was frying some green tomatoes. Martha made the dessert, blueberry cobbler, and to top it off, butter sauce. As soon as the biscuits were done, Brenda rang the bell.

I ran downstairs to the guest room to bring Clara and Mabel up to the dining room. Ursula brought Thelma. I seated the W.W.s, the trio, and Ursula at the table with me and Ringstaff. I asked him to ask the blessing.

I was anxious for the W.W.s to get to know Albert Ringstaff, and knowing how shy they were around new people, I got talking up a storm about him, telling them how I came to know him, about him fishing and all, and how he had traveled all over the world fixing pianos, meeting big shots, and how he's such a wonderful Bible teacher and all. I wanted to go on and on, but then I realized I was talking too much. I guess I was excited. Everybody else had finished eating before I even got half done. Lenora, who was one of the girls serving that night, was waiting for me to finish before she served the cobbler, even though I told her not to mind me, to go ahead with the dessert. I felt funny eating while everybody in the room was through and waiting for me to finish. Ringstaff helped take the attention off of me by asking Ursula some questions, but even so, I finally gave up on finishing my plate. Lenora took orders for the cobbler, offering a choice of butter sauce or ice cream. I resisted the temptation to have a little of both.

Everybody raved about that meal—even had the cooks, Brenda, Melba, and Martha, stand up, and we clapped for them.

After supper, the girls insisted that I go in the parlor with our guests and leave the kitchen to them. So I did. Here Ringstaff was surrounded by nothing but a bunch of women, but that did not seem to bother him. I never saw anything like the way he brought everybody into the conversation. First he asked the trio to tell him about their music. Nettie was a little nervous to start with, but once she got going she told us all about such things as shaped notes and how precentors used to travel the mountains teaching people to sing in parts. I didn't much have my mind on that, I was so anxious for everything to go off just right. I especially wanted the W.W.s to enjoy themselves.

Well, I think they did. Ringstaff got them talking about Live Oaks, and that's a subject right up Clara's alley. She can take a body back to the founding fathers and bring our history all the way up to Live Oaks' latest crime wave—boys busting watermelons in a field.

When the girls were finished in the kitchen, they gathered in the parlor for the singing. The trio started off with

"On the Jericho Road," which is lively, to say the least, and we were all clapping, keeping time. The next number was real pretty, "When They Ring Those Golden Bells." On the "glory, hallelujah, jubilee," those three women trilled like real bells. I can't remember everything they sang—oh, yes, they sang "The Old Gospel Ship" and "If I Could Hear My Mother Pray Again." They closed with "I'm Praying for You" but the girls wouldn't let them quit, so they sang "When I See the Blood."

It was 10:00 before everything was over. The trio and Ringstaff left and then I took the W.W.s to my room for a little visit before we went to bed.

Well, the news from Live Oaks was not good.

"Guess who's staying at Preacher Osborne's place?" Mabel asked me.

I couldn't guess, so she told me. "Percy Poteat and his new wife."

"What?" I had completely forgot about telling that deadbeat he could stay at my house a couple of days to show Live Oaks his new wife. At that time I'd had no idea I'd not be there—and that the Osbornes would be living in my house.

Clara was telling me, "They come riding up on a motorcycle early one morning looking for you. When you weren't there, Preacher Bob said they could stay anyway. So they did. Esmeralda, she is definitely not our kind." She looked at Mabel and Thelma for mutual agreement. "A bleached blonde wearing a leather jacket and boots is no lady! Esmeralda, do you reckon they're really married? Nowadays people like that think nothing of living in sin."

Thelma hooted. "Like as not it's one of those *relationships* the Lord calls adultery."

"They've been at Osborne's a couple of weeks," Mabel said, "and Percy keeps saying they're leaving but not yet."

I was so upset I was beside myself. "That's crazy! It's all my fault! I have to call Pastor Osborne and apologize."

"You don't need to do that," Clara said. "Preacher Bob is trying to lead Percy to the Lord, and he's got a long way to go yet."

"Oh, I'm gonna call him, and if I can get Percy Poteat on the phone, I'll tell him to hit the road in no uncertain terms. I've done it before and I can do it again!"

Mabel saw how upset I was. "Well, let me tell you some good news. Guess who's dating Boris Krantz?"

I thought it might be Clara's granddaughter, but one look at Clara's tight lips told me it wasn't.

"It's Lucy," Thelma blurted out.

Then I remembered how I'd sensed those two might be interested in each other. Well, they would make a fine couple.

"Lucy started helping Boris with his Spanish, and one thing led to another and now it looks like they might be getting serious," Mabel was saying.

Clara disagreed. "Why, it's nothing of the sort, Mabel. He wants to learn Spanish so he can help all the Mexicans coming into Live Oaks, and she's agreed to teach him. That's all there is to it, and you shouldn't be spreading rumors like that."

Mabel went right on talking. "By the way, Boris wants

to bring the young people up here on a mission trip. What do you think?"

"Well, we could use some help. We're cleaning out the garage to make a place for canning the vegetables when they come in. And the girls keep talking about wanting to build a gazebo."

Thelma got up from my chair still stiff and stretching. "Esmeralda, it's getting late. I better get over to the apartment before Miss Ursula goes to bed."

"Okay," I said. "Get a good night's rest, because tomorrow we're taking you to Grandfather Mountain."

Well, wouldn't you know it—the next morning it was raining cats and dogs. We had a good breakfast, though, with plenty of pastries from the donut shop. Then the W.W.s sat in on Praise and Prayer. Afterward, they wanted to know all about the different girls, especially Dora. I didn't tell them very much.

Ringstaff had come and was working on the piano, so I took the three of them in the kitchen while I fixed him his coffee and a fried apple pie. "Why don't you give him one of those cream horns?" Thelma asked. "They're real good."

"He likes my fried apple pies."

She raised her eyebrows. "Oh, he does, does he?"

I let her think whatever she wanted to. That morning I pulled a daisy from a vase and put it on his tray.

Most of the girls were in the craft room, so I told Clara they could go down there and see what the girls were making. After I served Ringstaff and visited with him a few minutes, I went down to join them.

Good heavens! The W.W.s had taken over! They were showing the girls how to make covers for Bibles, and the girls were scrounging through all those bins finding cloth and lace, stuff like that, to make them. The two sewing machines were going full speed ahead, and there was a lot of laughing and kidding around. Portia was in there making a frame for something.

Well, I was glad they were all having a good time. I went back upstairs to see about lunch. Melba and Brenda were in the kitchen washing the lettuce. We got talking, and I asked Brenda what would she think about putting a little rinse on my hair.

"You mean a little color?" She eyed my hair—had me turn around. "I think it would help a lot. If you really want to jazz it up, I'd go for the golden blond."

That didn't sound too good. "I don't want to jazz it up too much—nothing heavy, just a light ash blond might do the trick."

"Well, okay, if that's what you want. Ash blond will darken it some—give you a kinda slate color. You can find that in any drugstore, and I'll be glad to put it on for you."

"I'll get some the next time we go into town. . . . By the way, Brenda, how do you like Mr. Ringstaff's Bible lessons?"

"Miss E.," she said, "they're wonderful! I found out who I am."

"Oh," I said. "How's that?"

She stopped washing the lettuce and looked at me. "Miss E., I'm the woman at the well."

"The woman at the well?"

"Yes. I haven't had five husbands, but I've had twice as many men, and I'm just like her—I argue religion even though I'm a very tolerant person—you know, arguing with those people who come to the door with their literature. Miss E., I don't see how I could have sat in church all my life and never heard about that living water."

"You mean to tell me you never heard that before?"

"No, never. I been thirsting, all right. I was okay as long as I had Tommy, but after he left me, it was one man right after another. I had a steady diet of men and booze. Pills, too."

"You knew that was wrong, didn't you?"

"Oh, sure. I knew it was wrong, but all the time I was doing those things, I considered myself a Christian because I was baptized and a member of the church. I wasn't a Muslim or a Jehovah Witness or anything like that, I was a Christian."

Melba piped up, "A generic Christian—that's what you were."

"You're right, Melba. In a way, maybe it's a good thing I hit the bottle. At least it brought me here, where I learned I need Jesus."

"Well," I said, "if you're sure you understand—"

"Oh, I understand. It's clear as crystal—it's just that I love men and I love to drink."

"Then I'll tell you what I told somebody else: 'Choose your love and then love your choice.' It's a choice everybody has to make for herself. I made my choice when I was eleven years old. Because I loved the Lord when I was growing up, I've been spared a lot of grief. I never drank; oh, I tasted beer once, didn't like the taste. I never smoked except rabbit tobacco, and through all the trouble that has come my way, the Lord has give me grace, answered my prayers, and taught me a lot about himself. I'm far from perfect, Brenda, but I'm a lot better off than I would be without Jesus."

"So what you're saying is, I'm responsible for the mess I'm in."

"That's right. You chose to go with all those men, and every time you pop a can of beer or turn up a wine bottle, it's by your own choice. Brenda, as much as I care about you, I have to tell you the truth. 'The wages of sin is death.' It's like Splurgeon says, 'He shall have hell as a debt who will not have heaven as a gift.'"

Ursula was calling me at that moment. I hated to break off the conversation, but I went on into the office.

"Martha's husband just called," she told me. "He wants to bring their little girl for a visit. I told him we couldn't accommodate him here at the house because we have visitors. He's coming anyway. You might mention this to Martha."

"Okay," I said and went to look for her. I found her in the craft room, and we went in the day room to talk.

Martha looked disappointed. "He's ready for me to come home, Miss E."

"Well, are you ready to go?"

"I love this place. It's the nearest thing to heaven I've ever found, but, Miss E., my little girl needs me and he needs me."

"Do you think you'll be all right? Can you handle—"

"Miss E., you don't have to worry about me drinking. Like I told you the first night I came here, after seeing the Lord the way I did, I will never drink another drop so long as I live. I don't want it—I don't even *think* about drinking."

"I'm glad to hear that, Martha. I guess he'll be here tomorrow. Just remember, keep your eyes on the Lord. Read your Bible, find some Christian friends, and cast all your care on the Lord because he cares for you."

After lunch the W.W.s and I sat in on Ringstaff's class, and when it was over, Thelma wanted to know when they might get him to come to Apostolic for a Bible conference. Well, I didn't know about that. I told them Priscilla Home needed all the time he could spare, and they understood. Clara said, "I could sit and listen to that man all day long." I had never heard them rave about anybody the way they raved about Ringstaff. Well, who wouldn't?

The rain was still coming down but not as hard as before, so I figured we could take the W.W.s to that old country store on the Valley Road. There wouldn't be a crowd of tourists on a rainy day, and the W.W.s could find plenty of stuff to buy. The girls were excited about going somewhere, so we took the van. On the way I was the tour guide, telling them all about the old store—how they had candy cases like the kind we used to have in the Live Oaks variety store, how the floor smelled of creosote, and about the barrels of beans and coffee, the potbelly stove, and the checkerboard played with bottle caps. Linda piped up, "There's caskets on the second floor."

Well, that took care of that. I always enjoyed going to that store—made me think I was back in time. We spent the rest of the afternoon in there, and the W.W.s came out loaded with stuff. In the van they went through all their packages, showing what they had bought. I heard Mabel say, "You can't find a butter press anywhere nowadays. Look at this one I got."

I didn't know what she planned to do with a butter press—she'd never in her life churned butter—but if it made her happy, it was fine with me.

When we drove in the driveway, I was surprised to see Ringstaff's station wagon still there.

20

We piled off the van and came in the house. The mail had come, so the girls rushed up to the office, where Ursula was handing out letters. The W.W.s said they needed to go to their rooms and rest a few minutes before supper, which suited me fine. I went upstairs and looked for Ringstaff in the parlor, but he wasn't in there. *Now where do you suppose he is?*

Nancy came out of the office ripping open an envelope. As she read the letter her eyes filled up and tears began spilling down her cheeks. Crumpling up the letter, she went running to her room.

In a few minutes I decided I better see if I could help her.

She was pulling her suitcase out from under the bed when I got to her room. "Nancy—what in the world?"

"I'm leaving!"

"Why?"

"Look at this!" and she handed me the letter.

I had to smooth it out before I could read it. It was

from her State Medical Board; her nurse's license had been revoked.

"Oh, Nancy, I'm sorry. I'm so sorry, but why do you have to leave?"

She was furiously throwing things in the suitcase. "There's no need for me to stay here any longer."

"Oh?"

"It's unfair! It's all so unfair!" she sobbed, yanking things out of the closet. "The Board told me if I went through the program here and received a clean bill of health, they would review my case and make a decision at that time. But they've already made the decision!"

"Nancy, you're all upset. Don't you think you better wait awhile before you do something rash?" I sat in the desk chair waiting for her to get hold of herself.

I didn't think Nancy had yet gained the victory over her addiction, and that maybe after a few more weeks with Ringstaff teaching and the rest of us praying, she would. She was a good nurse. The night Martha was having such a fit, I don't think I could have handled it without Nancy. For her to leave like this would be a big mistake for her as well as a loss for me.

I needed to talk turkey. "Nancy," I said, "your only hope of getting your license back is to stay here until you graduate and then appeal their decision."

"It's over and done with, Miss E. They've ruled and they're just like Miss Ursula about rules—they'll never bend." Folding a blouse to pack, she wiped her eyes on a sleeve.

I reached and took the blouse out of her hands. "You

better let this dry," I said and put it back on a hanger. "Now, Nancy, sit down a minute."

I waited until she did. "Nancy, you love nursing, don't you?"

"Yes," she croaked.

"You're a good nurse, Nancy, and the world needs good nurses." She started to get up; I put my hand on her arm. "No, Nancy. Wait a minute . . ."

She sat there waiting.

"Nancy, isn't nursing your calling?"

"What difference does it make?"

"It makes a lot of difference. Haven't you always wanted to be a nurse?"

"Yes," she admitted, twisting the tissue to shreds. "I can't remember when I didn't want to be a nurse."

"See there! It's your calling! It's what you can do best for the Lord."

"The Lord?"

"Yes, the Lord."

"Miss E., it's just a lot of hard work, lots of headaches, lots of people sick and dying. Besides, I'll never ever get another job nursing."

"But, Nancy, nursing is your calling—that's what God wants you to do. Everybody's work is important to God—not just preachers' and missionaries' work."

I didn't know if she was listening or not. We just sat there a long time not saying anything. I wanted to tell her that one day she would meet the Lord and answer for the talents he had entrusted to her, but decided that was too strong for a person in her upset condition.

After a while, I took both her hands and made her

look at me. "Nancy, you need to stay here. Only Jesus can lick this problem you have got. Once you get over them pills, you can appeal that board's decision. The Lord can change their minds."

"It's no use," she mumbled.

"Well, do it for yourself."

"Miss E., you don't understand. I can't stay here any longer. I have got to get a job. My bills are piling up." Her face was puffed from all the crying, and she was in no shape to think straight. "Maybe I can get a waitress job or go to work in one of those fast food places." That brought on a fresh flood of tears.

I could see I wasn't making much headway. Then I thought of something. "Nancy, are you going to leave us way out here in the sticks where anything can happen—where one of these women can get deathly sick or break a bone or go wacko—and we have not anybody here trained for medical emergencies like that?"

She tried to wipe her eyes on a wadded up tissue. I had a fistful in my pocket and handed her a couple. "When Dr. Elsie is home, we can call on her, but she's in Vermont taking care of her sister. There's no telling when her sister will get better or die, one, so Dr. Elsie can come home. I know you got bills, but if you'll let me, I'll loan you the money you need until you graduate and can get back on your feet. We need you, Nancy—I need you. Won't you please stay on?"

She didn't answer but blew her nose and stopped crying. Finally, she said, "I'll think about it." As I was going out the door she said, "Thank you, Miss E."

Going back downstairs, I was pretty sure she was going to stay but I prayed to make sure.

I asked Ursula where Mr. Ringstaff was, and she said he and Lenora were taking a walk. "Oh," I said. Then I remembered—Lenora and Martha didn't go with us to the country store. "Is Mr. Ringstaff staying for supper?"

"Yes. He has a surprise for us. By the way, while you were gone, Martha's husband did come with their daughter, and Martha has gone home with them."

I was sorry I wasn't there to say good-bye, but things like that can't be helped when a body is going in all directions at the same time.

I went in my room to change clothes, but I couldn't decide what to wear. Finally, I put on the only decent Sunday dress I had, but as I looked in the mirror, I wasn't satisfied. I fished around in my jewelry box for some earrings Bud gave me. They probably cost him a fortune, and I was always so afraid of losing them I didn't wear them much. After I put them on I wondered if they looked right, so I stepped in the office and asked Ursula, "Do these earrings look all right with this dress?"

She said they did, but when I got back in the room I thought, *She's a poor one to ask.* I turned my head this way and that, looking in the mirror trying to decide. *Well, they are pretty, and they're the best I've got, so I'll wear them.* My hair was a mess and I didn't have time to use the curling iron, so I brushed it real good, scooped it up, twisted it in back, and fastened it in a kinda French twist with my rhinestone comb. Bud always liked when I wore it that way.

The bell rang for supper; I gave the ears a spray of Chanel Number Five, took one more look in the mirror, and let it go at that.

While I was waiting in the dining room for the W.W.s, lo and behold, I saw Lenora come in the parlor on Mr. Ringstaff's arm! I felt like telling her to cool it. They hung around the piano, tinkling the keys before they came in the dining room. Both of them were smiling like they shared some joke. Well, at least Lenora was finally smiling.

Then the W.W.s came in. They looked surprised when they saw me. "Aren't those the earrings Bud gave you?" Mabel asked.

"Well, yes, I believe he did give them to me."

Clara had to put in her two cents' worth. "And that dress—didn't you get that dress on sale last summer?"

"I might have," I said. They were embarrassing me.

How I got through that meal, I'll never know. When we finished eating, I asked Lenora in a nice way if she would mind helping in the kitchen while I entertained my guests in the parlor.

The W.W.s sat on the couch, and I gave Ringstaff the Morris chair. It was up to me to start the conversation. "Ursula tells me you have a surprise for us, Mr. Ringstaff."

He smiled. "Albert, the name is Albert, Esmeralda."

That was nice to hear, and it wasn't wasted on the

W.W.s. They looked at him and me and then rolled their eyes at each other.

I said, "Okay, Albert," pleased that it rolled off my tongue so easy. "What's the surprise?"

"Can you keep a secret?"

Thelma blurted out, "No, she can't! Esmeralda spills the beans every time." Then she laughed.

That's a Yankee for you, I thought.

Ringstaff laughed too. "Well, I've never found that to be the case with Esmeralda. The secret is, I've finished repairing the piano, but we'll wait until the ladies are finished in the kitchen before we play it."

We talked on, mostly about plans for turning the garage into a canning room. "We'll have to put in a sink," I said, "which shouldn't pose much of a problem since there are pipes in there that run up to the apartment. Lester Teague will know a good plumber. Then we'll need a stove, a fridge, and another freezer."

Once the girls were through in the kitchen, they scattered—mostly to the front porch to light up again. Lenora came in the parlor. "Albert, it's time you told them."

"I just did," he said. "We're waiting for the ladies."

"They won't be coming to the parlor," she said. "They'll be going to the day room or up to their rooms."

Good heavens, when did she get to be housemother?

"Well, I think I know how I can get them in here," he said. He got up, made his way across the room, and sat down on the piano bench. He lit right into playing, his fingers flying all over that keyboard. It was a rip-roaring piece I use to hear on the Lawrence Welk Show, and it was great!

"That's the 'Twelfth Street Rag,'" Lenora informed us.

"Yes, I know that one," I told her, as much as to say, *I didn't fall off a turnip truck, you know.*

Hearing that jazz, the girls came piling in from the porch. The only one I could see missing was Dora. She probably didn't cotton to piano music. The girls stood around the piano, leaning on it and getting a real bang out of watching him play.

Once he finished that number, he stood up and announced that now Lenora would play for us.

Well, she did. Without a sheet of music or hymn book or anything, she began playing soft music such as you hear on classic radio. "This is the 'Moonlight Sonata,'" he told us. I didn't care for it myself. I don't think the girls liked it either. I *know* the W.W.s were bored stiff.

Lenora looked up at Albert, her eyes all misty. "The *spielart* is perfect."

He smiled back at her. "I remembered the feel you like, Lenora, and I aligned all the moving parts to move freely yet with firmness to your touch so there'd be no side play."

If nobody else was enjoying the music, those two were. When Lenora ended that number, he asked her to play something from Liszt. I think that was the name. She began playing another smooth, slow number. "Ah, 'The Consolation,'" he said, all smiles. "No one can perform Liszt as well as you, Lenora. In a split second you change the mood and the phrasing."

The girls were polite, but with Lenora into the second number, one by one they were slipping out of the room.

Before Portia went upstairs, she came quietly over to where I was sitting and whispered in my ear. "Miss E., now that Martha's gone, will you let me move into her room?"

"I'll see what I can do," I whispered back.

I heard the screen door close and looked up to see Dora coming through the dining room into the parlor. She didn't stand near the piano or sit in a chair—she laid herself down on the carpet beside the piano, closed her eyes, and laid there like she was in some kind of other world.

The W.W.s looked at me as if to say, *What's wrong with her?* I didn't try to explain. A body has to be around Dora a while before you understand the way she is. In her case, lying on the floor listening to that slow music wasn't strange at all; she was probably hearing the wind and the rain in her holler, or seeing the moon rising, or whatever.

By the third or fourth long piece, the W.W.s and I had just about run out of politeness. They were shifting about on the couch as much as to say, *How long is this going on?* And I raised my eyebrows, which told them, *I don't have any idea.*

As for myself, I tuned out the music because I had other things to think about, especially Portia. I was glad she wanted to get away from Linda, but if Portia took Martha's place she'd be alone in that room. Chances were Linda would make her life miserable in there. *If Nancy stays, maybe I can get her to take Martha's place and let Portia room with Emily.* The more I thought about it, the more I liked that arrangement. After all, Portia and Emily were study partners, so it would make sense to have them room together.

As soon as Lenora finished playing the next piece, I thanked her for playing, then excused myself and said it was urgent that I talk to someone. The W.W.s saw their chance to escape and, saying they had a big day coming up and needed to get to bed, they said good night.

That left Lenora playing, Albert sitting beside her on the bench, and Dora lying on the floor, soaking her soul in that highbrow music. Well, to each his own, I always say.

I found Nancy in her room. She had put away the suitcase. "I'm glad you're staying, Nancy," I said and sat down on the bed. "I can rest easier with you here." But I could see she was still upset.

"I'll stay until Dr. Elsie gets back. After that, I can't promise anything."

"Okay," I said. "Nancy, I have a favor to ask of you. Portia wants to move out of her room."

"It's about time."

"About time?"

Nancy gave me a knowing look. "Don't you know?"

"Know what, Nancy?"

"If you don't know, sooner or later you'll find out."

I could see she didn't want to say anything more, so I asked her, "Since Portia and Emily are study partners, it would be nice if they roomed together, don't you think?"

"You want me to move, don't you?"

"Would you mind?"

"Don't ask me to move in with Linda."

"No, not Linda. Would you take Martha's room?"

She agreed to do that. "I'll pack my things."

I looked in on Portia to tell her what the deal was. Linda was in the room getting ready to take a shower. When she heard Portia was moving, she flew off the handle. "She's not leaving this room!" she yelled.

Portia stood up to her. "Yes, I am, Linda," she said and started taking her things out of the dresser.

"You do and I'll—"

I called her bluff. "What'll you do, Linda?"

"You'll see," she said and threw a brush across the room.

"We'll have none of that!" I told her. "Portia, Nancy's going to move in Martha's room so you can room with Emily. Since you and Emily are study partners I thought that would be nice. Why don't you ask Emily to help you move?"

"Okay," she said and left to find her.

I sat down on the bed to talk to Linda. "Now, what's this you're going to do to Portia?"

"You don't understand."

"Try me."

She was furious. "Miss E., I'm gay and proud of it! Portia's my girl. You think it's a sin to be gay, don't you? You probably never heard of gay pride."

"Oh, I've heard of gay pride and, yes, according to the Bible it's a sin for two women to live together like husband and wife."

"That's your interpretation. There's plenty of Christians who don't see it that way. In my case, I know it's not a sin because it's the way God made me. Being gay is as natural to me as—"

I shut the door so the others couldn't hear this conversation.

"You were saying?"

"I was born this way—it's the way God made me."

"Don't blame it on God. Blame it on Adam; he sinned and ever since, people have been born with all kinda handicaps. Maybe you were born that way and maybe you weren't. I'm no doctor. But Linda, how about the man who lusts after little children—he'd say he was born that way, too. And the—"

"How can it be wrong to love somebody?"

"Loving somebody doesn't mean you have to live with them. Linda, nobody *has* to have sex. Look at all the single people in the world who live alone and have a good life without sex. I've lived alone fourteen years, and before that my husband was sick and—"

"But you're old."

Somebody knocked on the door. Linda opened it, and Portia came in with Emily. "I'll get my things."

"You'll get what's coming to you," Linda growled and stormed out of the room to take her shower.

I stayed there while Portia carried all her stuff to the other room. After she was safely moved, I went on downstairs to bed.

Before I went in my room, though, I looked in the parlor—Lenora was still playing. I walked around the piano to see if Dora was still there. She was. I started to say good night, then realized the three of them weren't even aware I was in the room. I went on to bed.

21

Going up on the Grandfather was an all-day trip because there's animals behind fences to see, a museum, gift shops, picnic tables, and a swinging bridge. The girls didn't want to miss their Bible class, so we invited Albert to go along with us and have Bible class on the mountain. The W.W.s. were nervous about hairpin curves so I asked Albert to drive the van.

Albert was wearing one of those soft hats with a narrow brim and a little feather in the hatband. It matched his windbreaker. Even though Lenora was hanging on to him, Ursula was making it a threesome. I got a kick out of that.

When we visited the animal habitats, Albert supplied us with peanuts to throw to the bears and also explained all about the cougars we saw next. Some of the girls took pictures and included me with the W.W.s. Albert had brought a camera and he asked Evelyn to take a picture of me and him. We stood close; he put his arm around me. Of course, to be polite he turned right around and asked Evelyn to take one of him and Lenora.

I was determined that this picnic would outdo any spread put on by those TV chefs. I found picnic tables where the view was out of this world, and while the girls cooked hot dogs and hamburgers on the grill, Albert helped me unload the drinks and other stuff. Ursula and the W.W.s battled the wind to set out the paper plates and cups, buns, catsup, mustard, and pickles, while Albert and me set out the baked beans, tomatoes, lettuce, onions, slaw, pimento cheese sandwiches, deviled eggs, olives, grapes, and donuts—you name it, we had it!

But after all of that, Albert looked at me very disappointed. "Where's my fried apple pie?"

I laughed. "Albert, you'll get one tomorrow. Getting this picnic together this morning, there was no time to make pies."

That little exchange did not go unnoticed by the W.W.s, and I only wished Lenora had heard it. While waiting for the girls to finish cooking the meat, we sat down and tried to keep things from blowing off the table. I had brought my Bible along, and Albert asked if he could look at it. Of course, I let him, but he had a hard time keeping the wind from blowing away stuff I had in there. After he had looked as much as he could, he handed it back to me. "Ladies," he said, "this worn-out Bible explains a lot about our friend, Esmeralda, doesn't it?"

I was surprised when Ursula said, "Yes, it does."

Wilma hollered, "The meat's done!" And soon the girls came bearing trays of hamburgers and hot dogs. Albert asked the blessing, and we filed in behind the W.W.s to serve ourselves.

Mountain air makes a body hungry. Everybody kept saying how good the food was—that this was the best picnic they had ever went to. I ate so much I thought I would pop.

After we ate, cleaned the tables, and packed stuff back in the van, we gathered in close to hear Albert teach. In those beautiful surroundings, the blue mountains lying in waves as far as the eye could see, he chose Psalm 19, about the heavens declaring the glory of God. As long as I live I will never forget the beautiful message he gave. Even with the wind whipping the pages of my Bible, I managed to write his name and the date beside Psalm 19.

After the lesson we went to the museum, where we moseyed around looking at the exhibits. Then we went in the small theater they have got there and watched a movie about falcons and hang gliding. I got sleepy, and Mabel went sound to sleep. Once it was over and she saw the gift shop, she revived and couldn't get enough of poking around in there.

I thought we'd never get out of the gift shop. Between the girls and the W.W.s it looked like they were going to buy out the place. I bought a postcard to send to Beatrice then went outside and sat on a bench to wait.

It wasn't long before Albert came out—I knew he was looking for me. As soon as he saw me, he made a beeline to join me on the bench. "I bought you something," he said, reaching in a bag. He handed me a beautiful wood carving of a yellow finch.

"For me? Oh my, it's pretty. But why me?"

"Esmeralda, I see what you are doing for these ladies at Priscilla Home, and this is a little token of my appreciation."

"Well, *you're* the one! You're giving them the Word, and it's changing their lives."

"You think so?"

"I know so!"

He took off his hat, and the breeze did a number on his hair. I loved the way he ran those long fingers through it, trying to smooth it down. He put his hat back on.

"Well," he said, "I know there is one resident who has been brought to know the Lord." He crossed his legs and folded his arms across his chest. "It is all so providential, Esmeralda. Can you imagine Lenora and me finding each other the way we did? Years ago, after she left the concert stage and I learned about her problems, I never stopped praying for her—but I couldn't find where she was. That day on the rock, to find her like that—Esmeralda, it could only be the Lord's doing."

I fingered the little bird, turned it this way and that to see all sides, and agreed. "God works in mysterious ways."

"He certainly does," he said, turning around to look toward the gift store. Lenora and Ursula were coming. Quickly, he turned back to me. "Esmeralda, do you think we might drive into Rockville one evening, just the two of us?"

"Sure," I said. I couldn't believe my ears. Albert Ringstaff was asking me to go out with him!

"After your friends leave—say, Saturday evening?"

"That would be fine," I said as calmly as I could.

"I know a quiet little restaurant where we can have dinner and talk. I'll pick you up, say around 6:00?"

"That would be fine," I repeated, about as excited as a body can get and still stay in its skin.

❧

Albert drove us up to the swinging bridge, and everyone went out on it except the W.W.s and me. I felt like I had to keep those three company. In the building up there atop the mountain, there was another gift shop, so we went inside out of the wind, and they looked around while we were waiting. I was so excited, I must have showed it because Thelma said, "Well, you look happy. You look like the cat that swallowed the canary."

I didn't say anything, even though I was dying to tell them Albert had asked me out.

Wind on the bridge can be gale force, so I knew Albert would be cold. When the girls started straggling in off the bridge, I ordered a cup of hot coffee for him. It tickled him pink! Of course, Lenora came in with him and was snuggling up close to keep warm. He ordered a cup for her too.

❧

On the way home in the van, the girls were laughing and talking, eating boiled peanuts and throwing the shells out the window. I couldn't eat a thing I was so excited. Brenda was sitting across the aisle from me. I reached over and asked her when we might color my hair. "I want to get it done before Saturday," I told her.

"Any time," she said. "Whenever you get the rinse."

That night I could hardly sleep. I planned that as soon as the W.W.s left, I'd go into town and get that ash blond color.

The next morning I saw the three of them off after breakfast. They couldn't thank me enough for the wonderful time they'd had.

I thanked them for the peanuts, tomatoes, and peaches—told them we'd have cobblers and make peach pickle.

After hugging me, Clara held on to my hand. I'm not sure but what she had tears in her eyes. "Esmeralda, I just want to apologize for the way Mabel and me tried to keep you from coming up here. I speak for both of us—after we have seen this place and the wonderful work you're doing—we see how wrong we were. And the women you got here, for the most part, they could be our daughters or grandchildren—with few exceptions, they're no different from Live Oaks women, just down on their luck. We've been talking amongst ourselves and we see there's a lot we can do for Priscilla Home. We're going back home to tell everybody what a wonderful place this is and how the Lord is using you up here."

Oh, I told them there was no need to apologize, and I thanked them in advance for whatever they might do for us; especially asked them to pray for us. As I shut the car door, I motioned to Thelma to roll down the window. "Don't forget to thank Elijah for the corn he sent."

"We will," they all said.

I asked again if they were sure they had everything. They thought they had. "If you've left anything, we'll mail it to you. . . . Now, Thelma, you know the way back?" She said she did, so I was satisfied they would make it home okay.

I stood in the driveway waving and watching until the car pulled onto the Old Turnpike. As much as the W.W.s meant to me, I wasn't sorry to see them leave. I had to get my ducks in a row for Saturday night.

22

The garden was furnishing us with salad greens, green onions, squash, and some peas. Tomatoes were beginning to come in but were still green. Brenda had fried some twice. Soon an abundance of the beans would be coming in, and we would need to start canning them.

Dora and I decided to drive down to Lester's place to see about getting a plumber to put sinks in the garage. Along the way, I was surprised to see that flock of wild turkeys again, and we stopped to watch them. "Turkeys has got their regular range close by where they were borned," Dora told me. "They sleep in the same tree on the same limbs night after night, a-favorin' evergreens to bare branches. Won't light on the ground of a night afeared of bobcats and foxes. Lookee yonder at them two gobblers by that rotted fence."

I looked and saw only one, his head held high and erect. "I thought you said there were two."

"The one you're a-lookin' at be the lookout. The other 'un is a-bathin' hisself on the ground."

Then I spotted that one wallowing in the warm, dry sand, his feathers all fluffed out. He rose and shook himself, filling the air with dust and tiny feathers. After preening himself like a peacock, he took up the stand as watchman while his buddy took his dust bath.

I heard some gobbling, and Dora told me, "He's a-signalin' stray members of the flock." Suddenly, the whole flock took off and flew away from us.

I cranked the car, and we got back on the Turnpike. "People has not got the sense a turkey has got," Dora said.

"How's that?"

"A turkey a-guardin' a flock don't take nothin' for granted; for all that gobbler knew, we was turkey huntin'."

I didn't get the point. "What are you saying, Dora?"

"Miss E., Miss Ursula checks all them packages that come in our place, and after that she thinks you got no need to worry that somebody has snuck in some weed or pills. I could have brought in a load of my weed right under her nose and sold it at a good price."

"How could you do that?"

"In my pockets and underneath my clothes. But I'd not do a thang like that, beholdin' as I be to you. A body don't betray a trust an' live in peace with hisself."

We were turning in the lane to Lester's place. "Well, Dora, I had thought about that—that somebody could easy sneak in drugs—but there's a limit to what we can do to keep them from doing it. Priscilla Home is not a prison where they do body searches and the like." It was hard keeping the tires in the ruts. "You don't think any of the girls bring in stuff, do you?"

"Can't say," she said, and I knew that was all I could get out of her.

Lester was coming up from his garden as I parked the Chevy. I had brought him some leftovers and took them in the kitchen.

"Lester, you're looking good," I told him.

He had his hands full of ripe tomatoes and handed them to Dora. He came up on the porch. "I hear say the blight's bad this year."

"Your tomatoes look good."

"Blight won't touch my tomaters. It's store-bought plants brings in the blight." He set a folding chair for me. "Set down."

"We can't stay. Came to find out if you know a good plumber hereabouts. We're making a canning room out of the garage, and we've got to put a sink or two in there."

"You got little time to outfit a canning room. Yer garden must be coming in good now, and you ort to be fixed for canning."

"I know," I said. "We got to get a hold of a good plumber right away."

He looked off across the valley like he might be studying on that, but it was a long time before he said anything. "I done a little plumbin' in my day."

"You have?" I said. "We would pay you whatever you ask."

He didn't say anything, and I wondered if I had insulted him by bringing up the money business too quick. "When can you start? Could you go back with us today?"

It seemed like he wasn't paying any attention to my question because he said to Dora, "Fetch that milk pail out in the shed and pick what blueberries be ripe."

After she left, he just sat there looking off toward the river. I hoped he was studying on my question. I owed Lester some company, so I didn't leave the porch to help Dora.

Eventually, he started in talking about the weather and what we could expect in the months ahead—then he rambled on about the lumber company that once operated in the valley and the kind of logs they hauled down to the furniture markets—told me the river used to run through the middle of the valley not alongside like now. "Floods kept a-eatin' away at it," he said. "Changed its course."

I was beginning to think he had forgotten what I had asked him.

Finally, he said, "Oncet I see what fixings we'll need, you can take me into town and git most ever'thang at the Farmer's Hardware store."

I still didn't know if he was going home with us. As anxious as I was to get going, all I could do was wait for Dora to fill that bucket.

Finally, she came back to the porch, the bucket full of plump berries. "Good heavens, you picked all them? Lester, you sure you want us to have all of these berries?" He was sure, so I said, "Well, Dora, we best be going."

Without giving us leave, Lester got up, opened the screen door, and went inside the house. *Now what's he doing?* I wondered.

Dora put the berries in the car, and I stood on the

porch waiting. In a few minutes he came out again. He had torn off a scrap of a brown paper bag and had a stub of a pencil he was putting in his bib pocket. Lester had made up his mind; he was going with us. Dora got in the backseat and he crawled in the front seat.

Lester took his time making the measurements in the garage. When he finally finished, I took him into town, and he ordered everything he could buy in the Farmers Hardware. Then we went to the building supply store.

I was tied up with Lester all day, but I felt good about getting the canning room done. He would do a good job, and if nothing unforeseen happened, we'd be ready when the produce started coming in big time.

I was tired, but while in town I had got the color for my hair and Brenda said she'd do it after supper.

We went up on the third floor where they had a hair dryer, and she commenced putting that stuff on my hair. Portia was sitting on the couch watching, but she couldn't keep awake so I told her she better go on to bed.

I thought my hair turned out good. It was a light rinse, and Brenda said it gave a lift to my look, whatever that means. Anyway, I was satisfied we had done our best. I asked her if she could fix my hair Saturday afternoon, and she said she would.

The next morning, I was outside waiting for the building supply truck. It was almost lunchtime and still they hadn't come. Melba came to tell me Ursula wanted to see me, so I went up to the office. "It's Portia," Ursula said. "Emily can't get her awake."

"I'll go see about her."

Nancy was coming out of the bathroom. "Nancy, could you come with me a minute?"

Together we went in Portia's room. She was lying on the bed sound asleep, and Emily was standing against the wall looking scared as a jackrabbit. I leaned over the bed and called, "Portia?" Nothing happened. I asked Emily how long had she been asleep.

"Since early last night. Miss E., she never sleeps late—never!"

Nancy took a look, lifted Portia's eyelids. "Miss E., let's get her up and see if she can sit on the side of the bed." Together we tried, but Portia was as limp as a dishrag. Laying her back down, Nancy felt her forehead for fever, took her pulse, told Emily to bring her a wet washcloth.

After Emily left the room, Nancy told me, "Miss E., she's stoned."

My heart sank. "Stoned? On what? What's she taken?"

"My first guess would be sleeping pills. She must have taken a handful."

No, I told myself, *Portia wouldn't do that!* "Could she have had an overdose?"

"I don't think so. She's beginning to wake up; see her eyelids flutter. She'll be all right . . . Miss E., Portia has been coming along so well—really by leaps and bounds. It's hard to believe she would do a thing like this."

It's Linda, I know it's Linda! I was saying to myself.

I didn't realize Ursula had come in the room until she asked, "What is it, Nancy?"

Nancy didn't say anything. Ursula moved closer to look at Portia. "Are you trying to conceal the fact that she has ingested drugs? Is that it?"

"We can't be sure," Nancy answered.

Ursula turned on her heel. "I'll call her mother. Portia will be leaving as soon as arrangements can be made."

"Oh, now, wait, Ursula!" I said. "Let's not jump to conclusions. Maybe Portia is sick."

"Does she have a fever, Nancy?"

"No, I don't think so."

That's all Ursula needed to hear. She marched back to the office to make the call.

I could not believe what was happening. Nancy looked at me and without saying it, mouthed the name "Linda."

"Yes, Linda!" I said aloud. "Oh, Nancy, we can't let this happen. What can we do?"

Emily was back with the washcloth. Nancy took it and began bathing Portia's face and arms.

"Emily," I said, "would you go downstairs and run the vacuum in the day room? And, Emily, please don't say anything about this to anyone."

"I won't, Miss E., but some of the girls know already. Linda found out, and she's told everybody. Is Portia going to be all right?"

"Yes, she'll be all right," Nancy said.

I closed the door behind Emily. "Nancy, let's go through everything in here to see if we can find drugs. If there is no evidence in here, then maybe we can persuade Ursula to hold up on sending Portia home. At least until we can get to the bottom of this."

We searched dresser drawers and the closet and found nothing. Then I spotted Portia's jacket hanging on a hook on back of the closet door. Reaching in a pocket, I felt something and pulled out a handful of trash. Nancy leaned over my shoulder to help examine what was in there.

There were many small squares of stiff paper, silver on white, with plastic bubbles popped open and empty. Nancy fingered them carefully, counting.

"Nancy, what do you make of this?"

She looked like she hated to tell me, but I already knew. "This is the way they package sleeping pills?" I asked.

She nodded. "You can buy these over the counter, and it would be easy to smuggle them in here in your underwear."

Nancy was thinking the same thing I was thinking. "Miss E., if I was to guess, I'd say Linda did this—bought the pills, dropped them in something Portia ate or drank, then planted the wrappers in her jacket pocket."

"How can we prove that?"

"Maybe when Portia wakes up, she'll be able to tell us what happened."

I laid my hand on that sleeping form and closed my eyes. *Lord, help this poor girl wake up. Make Ursula change her mind.*

Portia did wake up, slowly at first, and was very groggy. Nancy asked her if she knew how or why this happened to her. She shook her head and closed her eyes.

"Portia," Nancy said, "look at these wrappers."

Without opening her eyes, Portia murmured, "Linda."

"Portia, how did she do this to you?"

"I don't know," she mumbled.

I looked at Nancy, and she shook her head. "We'll never know, Miss E. All we can do is pray."

I brushed my hand across Portia's hair. "We're going to try to prove you weren't responsible for this, Portia." But even as I said it, I had no faith that we would.

❧

Ursula was dead set on sending Portia home. I tried reasoning with her. "Ursula, you're making a mistake. Linda is back of this. She said she would get even with Portia for moving out of her room, and she's done it. Don't you see? This was an easy way for her to get even—just slip the pills in Portia's food or drink."

Looking in the phone book for a number, Ursula muttered, "Hearsay, hearsay." She found the number. "Esmeralda, you dislike Linda. You have disliked her from the beginning. From what she tells me, you have done irreparable harm to her self-image, and here you are trying to blame her for Portia's ingesting drugs." She punched in the number. "I have called her mother, who will wire the money for a plane ticket today. I'm calling the airline now to see if I can make a reservation for tomorrow. They'll keep me on hold, so you can run along."

"Can't you hold off until we get to the bottom of this?"

"We have gotten to the bottom of this, Esmeralda.

Hearsay is not worthy of consideration; we have the facts. Portia was found unconscious. She could have died from such an overdose. If she had, there would no doubt be litigation against Priscilla Home, and the media would ruin our reputation. We cannot tolerate such blatant violation of house rules. And you, Esmeralda, would be well advised to cease these irresponsible accusations."

I was on my way out the door when she called me back. "You dropped something." Before I could get to it, she had come around the desk and picked it up. It was one of the little silver wrappers. "What's this?"

I didn't answer. She looked at me hard. "Where did you find this?"

I still didn't answer.

"This is something that held a pill, isn't it? Now tell me, did you find this in Portia's room?"

"I'd rather not say."

Convinced she had the evidence in hand, she smugly went back around the desk and sat down. "Insubordination does not become you, Esmeralda."

I couldn't have cared less.

🐦

For the rest of the day I kept to myself. There was no way in the world to keep the lid on things, and I didn't want to be bombarded with questions. Nancy told me all the girls thought Linda was in back of Portia's ordeal, and they were making efforts to prove it. But so far they had come up with nothing.

Once Portia was up and about, she tried to avoid Linda, but Nancy said that when the girls were doing crafts,

Linda held up three fingers in Portia's face, tormenting her. Seeing that, Wilma waited until Linda was outside, got her in back of the garage, and punched out her lights until Linda got loose and ran.

"Don't give me details," I said. "I don't need to know anything about that."

"Oh, Linda won't say anything. She's afraid of Wilma."

All day I wracked my brain trying to think of a way to prove Linda's guilt. Albert was coming after supper for a hymn sing. I was going to tell him the whole story. Maybe he could help.

By suppertime Ursula had everything settled. She had picked up the money from Western Union and made a reservation for Portia on the 12:30 flight out of Greensboro. I offered to drive Portia to the airport, but Ursula said she was taking her. "I want to make sure this young lady goes straight home to her mother. She may have in mind doing what she's done before—cash in the ticket and use the money for more drugs."

"More drugs?"

"Yes. That's what I said."

"But Portia doesn't even smoke cigarettes anymore!"

At the supper table there was deathly silence. There was such a lump in my throat I couldn't eat, and before the meal was over, I shoved my plate away and sat waiting for the rest of them to finish. When Portia, her chin trembling, smiled at me, I had to excuse myself and leave the table.

After supper, most of the girls were in Portia's room, helping her pack, when Albert came. He sat on the piano bench, and I drew up a chair beside him. Ursula was across the room on the couch, shuffling papers. I had just about finished telling him the situation when Ursula interrupted me. "Mr. Ringstaff, I am sure you understand the gravity of this matter. As you can see, if I do not dismiss Portia, my authority as director will be greatly diminished."

Ursula thought Albert would be on her side, but she was dead wrong. He shook his head and was about to say something when she started in again. "If I am to maintain the integrity of Priscilla Home, this resident must be dismissed." But seeing he was not agreeing with her, she went on, "This is a staff matter, Mr. Ringstaff, and is none of your affair."

But Albert would not be put off. "Ursula, any injustice is everyone's affair. Esmeralda believes Portia was framed, that another resident is responsible."

"Mere hearsay."

"Hold on, Ursula. Esmeralda is not given to wild speculation. Neither is she alone in her point of view. I talked with Nancy on the porch, and she said the consensus among the ladies is that Linda has something to do with this. I just think the matter should be looked into before you make a decision."

"I've already made my decision. Do you not agree that it is incumbent upon any leader to adhere strictly to rules and regulations?"

He looked her in the eye. "Ursula, 'A foolish consistency is the hobgoblin of little minds.'"

"Emerson!" she snapped and, mad as a wet hen, marched into her office.

That night I could not sleep. I cried and I prayed, and by morning I was a wreck. Before I could get dressed, I heard a timid little knock on my door. I knew it was Portia. I opened the door, and there she stood like some poor little lamb.

"I made something for you," she said and handed me a small package wrapped in tissue paper she had found somewhere. When I opened it, I could have cried. Portia had framed that poem from my Bible:

> Only one life, 'twill soon be past;
> Only what's done for Christ will last.

"Do you like it?" she asked.

"I love it! I've always wanted to have that little poem framed." I wanted to tell her why. "Sit down, Portia, right there on the bed." And I told her how the Lord used that poem as one of the ways of leading me to Priscilla Home.

"Portia, I wish I had something to give you."

"Miss E., you've given me everything I need."

"I never gave you anything. What did I ever give you?"

"Jesus."

That was more than I could take. I was so full I couldn't say a word.

Portia picked up my Bible from off the table but didn't open it; she just held it in both hands, hugging it to her chest. I could hardly control myself. "Portia, would you like to have my Bible?"

She looked up at me like she couldn't believe what she had heard.

"I mean it. I want you to have it. Just let me take out a few things I've stuck in there."

She handed it to me, and her hands were trembling. There were only two things in there I knew wouldn't mean anything to her—the pressed flower and Bud's letter.

"Miss E., I can't take your Bible—"

"Portia, you're not taking it, I'm giving it to you. I want you to have it."

Ursula was blowing the horn. As we hugged each other, I squeezed back the tears. I held on to her until Ursula was blowing again. Portia, with the Bible in her arms, opened the door then looked back at me with tears in her eyes. I took her in my arms and held her again. Ursula was sitting on that horn; I had to let Portia go.

23

After Portia left, steam was rising from all the angry feelings toward Linda. I knew it wouldn't take much for tempers to boil over. Linda knew it and was sticking to me like a leech. The next day, we were in the garage with Dora and Wilma, trying to decide where to build the shelves. "They're ganging up on me, Miss E.," Linda told me.

"Why?" I asked as if I was blind as a bat to what was going on.

Wilma let her have it. "It's because you're a rat fink, Linda. You're low-down, mean, stinking, trashy, and common!"

"Miss E., are you going to let her talk to me that way?"

"Yes," I said. It popped out before I even thought about it, but I didn't care. At least it shut her up.

Of course, as soon as Ursula got back from the airport, Linda went running to the office to complain. So, after lunch before Albert arrived for Bible study, the girls gathered in the parlor and Ursula took to the lectern.

"Miss Esmeralda, what do you know about this beating Wilma gave Linda in back of the garage?"

I gave her tit for tat. "Nothing but hearsay," I said.

The sarcasm was not lost on her. Hearsay didn't count in Portia's case, so Ursula could hardly use it against Wilma.

"Hearsay?"

"That's right. Nothing but hearsay," I said, sticking by my guns. The girls were snickering over the way I was getting Ursula's goat. Ursula must have realized there was no use asking the women about the fight. She opened her Bible and started looking for something.

I heard Albert's station wagon as he was driving around back. Ursula looked flustered and kept turning the pages. Whatever she was looking for, she didn't find it, and she closed the Bible.

In a few minutes Albert slipped in the parlor, and I nodded to him. Seeing the tense situation, he sat on the piano bench and kept quiet.

Ursula cleared her throat and began again. "Whatever your perceived grievances are against Linda, it is incumbent upon you to forgive her. The Bible teaches that we are to forgive one another as Christ has forgiven us." Nervous, she turned to Albert. "Isn't that correct, Mr. Ringstaff?"

"Well, now," he said, "even Jesus does not forgive the sinner until he asks."

Linda bellowed out, "I haven't done anything wrong!"

"You have nothing to repent of?" he asked, smiling.

"No!"

"Then we have a stalemate." He stood up, ready to begin class. Ursula picked up her Bible and stormed back in the office.

Naturally, the discussion about forgiveness spilled over into the Bible class. "In our hearts we must always forgive every wrong done to us," Albert said, "and we are not to keep a record of those wrongs. After all, we pray that our Father will forgive us as we forgive others. But in cases like this one before us, we are seeking reconciliation. In such cases, Jesus said, 'As often as he *repents,'* forgive him openly. Linda says she has nothing to repent of."

"That's a lie," Wilma snapped.

Albert was as cool as a cucumber. "Be that as it may, whatever your conflict, reconciliation is a two-way street. When we are wronged, we must have a readiness to publicly forgive the moment we are asked to forgive. But to grant forgiveness without repentance destroys all hope for reconciliation."

Linda didn't like what she was hearing. "That's not what a preacher told my mom. Every time my dad beat the stuffin' out of her, the preacher said she must forgive him, and she did. I don't care what anybody says, you gotta forgive everybody if you believe the Bible like you say you do."

Albert did not argue with her. "Sometimes it is hard to love a person who has wronged us, but Christ loved us when we were still sinners and doing him wrong every day. Loving isn't easy. It means we keep no record of the wrongs. Only Christ can give us his kind of love—Calvary love. It always helps to remember that Jesus died for the person who does us wrong, as well as for us. Let us ask the Lord to give us that kind of love."

I had heard that same explanation of forgiveness from Pastor Osborne, but not the *Calvary love* part. As Albert was praying, I asked the Lord to give me Calvary love for Linda and for Ursula.

Well, I didn't feel much different after we prayed. I sat there thinking about how I had thought Ursula was beginning to change, but then I'd seen her at her worst. This business with Portia had set back any love I had for her a hundred years.

After the class was over, Albert waited until everyone had left the room before he asked me, "Are we still on for tonight?"

"Oh yes."

I went back to work in the garage. Albert's lesson had lowered the steam somewhat, but Linda was still sticking close to me. Portia was on my mind. *She must be nearly home by now.*

It was the middle of the afternoon when Ursula sent for me. As I went up to the office, Linda dogged my heels. "It's Portia's mother," Ursula said as she handed me the phone.

That poor woman could hardly talk for crying, she was so happy. She kept thanking me and thanking the Lord that Portia was back home safely. I didn't get to speak to Portia, though, since her mother was calling from work.

Well, that helped me, but it still stuck in my craw that Linda was getting away with this. Linda had really pulled the wool over Ursula's eyes, and she would keep on causing trouble. When I left to go back outside, Linda stayed in the office with Ursula. I just knew they'd rehash everything Albert had taught and do their best to pick it apart.

After I had left the office, Brenda asked if it wasn't time to do my hair. "Melba and I will have to start supper before long." They all knew I was going out, but how they knew, I'll never know. There must be a Priscilla Home satellite that beams information straight to their ears. I looked at my watch and figured it wouldn't hurt to get my hair done and over with so I could take my time getting ready. "I'll go up and take a shower, then I'll meet you on the third floor."

Passing the office door, I saw Linda was still in there with Ursula. They were drinking coffee, and I overheard Linda say, "She's got a date with Mr. Ringstaff."

Well, I didn't care that she knew. In fact, I was glad.

While in the shower I could hear Lenora playing the piano in the parlor. I shampooed my hair and was toweling it dry as I went upstairs. All the girls had gathered around to watch. "Good heavens, don't you have anything better to do than look after me?"

"No, we got nothing better to do than to see to it you look like the Queen of Sheba when you walk out our door," Melba said. "I'm gonna do your nails."

"My nails? I have never in my life went to a beauty parlor for a nail job. What's your charge?"

"A blow by blow report when you come home."

I laughed. "I can't promise that."

Those girls sat around on the third floor eating potato chips and kidding around while my hair was getting blow-dried, teased, styled, and sprayed. Brenda handed me a mirror to look at her handiwork and, believe me, whatever she did made me look like one of them "Golden Girls" on TV.

Next I was in for the nail job. "Good grief, Miss E., you got the hands of a scrub woman," Melba told me. "I'm gonna put your hands in this dish detergent to soak while we pick out the polish. What are you gonna wear?"

"Oh, I don't know. Maybe something blue."

They were making such a fuss over me it made me nervous, but I went along with whatever they wanted to do because I did need to look my best.

When Melba was finally done, I did my thank-yous and started downstairs, but the whole crowd came with me. I knew Ursula wouldn't like them gathering in my room, but I didn't care. They flopped all over the bed and floor. Angela picked up my little yellow bird and asked if Mr. Ringstaff gave it to me. I laughed. "That's for me to know and for you to find out!"

"I know he did. I saw him buying it in the gift shop."

I changed the subject. "Now, what do you think I should wear?"

That's all they needed—Evelyn and Nancy started pawing through the clothes in my closet. They picked one outfit after another, holding them up for approval. Finally they all settled on a bright blue suit and sporty looking blouse. Once they decided, I went in the bathroom and dressed.

When I came back, I asked, "Well, how do I look?"

There was not a word, just a murmur going around the room. "The outfit is all right," Melba said, "but you got to wear it right. See here, Miss E., let me pull that collar up in back and fix it in front." She unbuttoned the top button on my blouse, fixed the collar, and said, "There. Now that's smart looking."

Approval was not forthcoming. Brenda, looking me over, said, "Something's not right."

"It's her shoulder pads," somebody said, so Brenda reached inside my blouse and straightened them. "Now let's see about that belt. You've got it too loose, Miss E." She pulled it in two full notches. "Now you've got a waistline."

"Her pantyhose don't match that blue suit," somebody said. "You got some lighter ones?"

I fished in my stocking drawer to find a pair but couldn't find any. Before I realized she had left the room, Nancy was back with a pair of her own. "Try these, Miss E."

I put them on, and I could see they made a big difference. Then those angels of mercy lit in to making up my face. They gave me the works—a moisturizer, then a foundation, blush, eyebrow pencil, even an eye-liner. I felt silly letting them do all that—even putting my lipstick on for me.

"Now for your joools," Wilma said. "She's got nice earrings—see what else she's got." The girls searched my jewelry box, tried several necklaces and pins to go with the earrings. Once they were satisfied, they told me to look in my full-length mirror. I felt real silly, but when I looked, I hardly recognized myself I looked so good!

By the time I was all turned out, the girls had to get ready for their supper, so I went downstairs in the day room to wait for Albert. Lenora finished playing whatever it was she was playing, and I guess she went upstairs to get ready for supper.

Albert came early, and he looked like a million dollars. "Esmeralda," he said, "you look lovely."

"Thank you," I said. I did begin to feel like the Queen of Sheba the way he offered me his arm and escorted me to the car. There's something about the feel of a man's suit coat that's nice. I can't explain it. I guess I noticed it because I had not been in the company of any man in this way since before Bud went to war.

Driving down the Old Turnpike with his kind of music playing softly on the radio was as good as it gets. I was so used to sitting in the driver's seat, I enjoyed sitting back and letting him drive. The way he handled the car on that winding road—his hands firm on the wheel—well, it made me feel good.

"We're going to that nice little French restaurant beside the river. Have you been there?"

"No," I said. To tell the truth, I'd never heard of it.

"It's quiet and the cuisine—the food—is especially good. This restaurant isn't crowded at this hour, and I've reserved a table in the corner where we can be alone and talk freely."

I don't know what made me think about the W.W.s, but something did. *Wait until they hear this! It's enough to knock the socks off all of them. And Beatrice—she'll be so happy for me.*

"Esmeralda, I've been wanting to talk to you for some time."

He has the nicest voice. I bet he sings.

"What I have to say is very important to me, and I need answers that only you can give."

Good heavens, this can't be what I'm thinking—can it?

We pulled up in the parking lot. I had to remind myself not to go hopping out the car but wait for him to come around and open the door for me.

The restaurant was really nice—none of that loud noise you get in the diner, just soft light and palm plants. A man in a tux met us and led us to our table—held my chair for me to sit down then pushed me forward. There were linen tablecloths and napkins folded fancy, lots of heavy silverware, fresh flowers, candles on every table, and soft music playing. Picture windows overlooked a garden of old-fashioned flowers, delphinium, foxglove, and the like, and beyond the garden it was still light enough to see the river and the mountains. I was thinking, *Anybody who don't get romantic in this place must be on life supports!*

The menu was in French, and Albert offered to order for me. He would read off things and ask me what I liked. When he read, "Trout Marguery," I heard the word "trout," so I said I'd take that.

The first thing served was onion soup. The waiter stood over me ready to dump something in my bowl. That frustrated me, so I said no before I realized it was cheese. He kept coming with one thing after another to add, and I said no to all of them. Then he whipped out a big pepper shaker and without asking started grinding pepper over my soup and telling me, "I see, Madam, you do not know the onion soup."

I felt my neck getting warm. Nobody ever called me a madam!

Albert had ordered what he called "Trout Marguery," but when it came I couldn't find the fish under all that sauce they had on it. I don't eat nothing that's not in plain sight. The plate was full of shrimp, mushrooms, and a kinda round thing I never saw before. I forked it and held it up for Albert to see.

"What's this?"

"Truffles," he said and smiled. "A subterranean edible fungi of tuber."

"You sound like Ursula."

He laughed.

I put the thing back on the edge of my plate. *Fungus? I'm not eating that.*

Albert hardly touched his food. "Esmeralda, I can't keep this to myself any longer. What I have to say may come as a shock to you."

My fork was halfway to my mouth, and my heart was going pitty-patty. I set the fork down and managed to smile at him. He only sighed and looked away. "Well, Albert," I said. "Try me. I'm not easy to shock."

He looked back at me and still wasn't smiling. "Esmeralda, ever since that day on the rock, I have come to realize how lonely I have been since my wife died. During these days since, when I have had the privilege of coming to Priscilla Home to teach the Bible, a certain Scripture has been repeatedly impressed on my mind."

"What's that, Albert?"

"God said, 'It is not good for man to dwell alone.' . . . Increasingly, I have come to realize that, at least in my case, this is true." He was looking straight at me with those warm, dark eyes melting me to mush. "Esmeralda, sometime I want to take you to my little cottage up there on the hill. It's a nice place, but without someone to share it with me, it feels as empty as a tomb."

The dinner was going to waste—neither one of us was eating. "I'd like that," I said, trying to keep calm.

He turned in his chair to face the window. "I just don't know if this is the Lord's will." He fell silent.

I couldn't stand the suspense. "If what is the Lord's will, Albert?"

He turned back and was looking in my eyes like he wasn't really seeing me, just thinking. Finally, he took a deep breath, then, seeing me for sure, said, "Esmeralda, I'm afraid I'm in love."

I thought my heart would jump out of my throat! "Afraid?" I asked, and almost laughed.

"Yes, afraid."

"Why?"

"I'm afraid for several reasons. I'm afraid Lenora won't have me."

Lenora? What? Am I hearing right?

"Oh, I wouldn't blame her if she turned me down. She's younger than I am. But I'm also afraid because she has hardly had time to truly overcome her addiction. How much longer should she stay at Priscilla Home? That takes a while, doesn't it?"

I could hardly get the words out. "For most it does." I took a drink of water, and my hand was shaking.

"You're the only person I can talk to about this, Esmeralda. Lenora and I have had some long walks together, and on one of those walks, she made a commitment to Christ. Since then I can see a definite change in her. Do you?"

I had to nod my head.

"From what I have heard, it was a great step forward when she began playing the piano again. What do you think?"

"I hardly know what to say."

"You have seen other changes in her, haven't you?"

"I haven't been with her very much." I could only think that if this man knew how hard this was for me, he'd not be putting me through it. "Well, she's a good piano player," I added feebly.

"How long do you think it takes a person to know for sure they have overcome their addiction?"

"Maybe a year." I was so choked up I hardly knew what I was saying.

"Now, that's what I needed to know. A year, you say?"

"If they go home and don't relapse for a year—"

"You're not saying Lenora should go back to New York?"

I wished he wouldn't ask me all those questions. "If a grad can live the Christian life at home, she can live it anywhere."

"Oh, but the New York supper club is anything but an abstinence environment. What Lenora needs is someone to take care of her—someone who loves her the way I do."

I couldn't bear to sit there and listen to all that. "If a body can't live the Christian life in the place they came from, they can't live it anywhere."

He was taken aback by that. "I see," he said and pushed his plate aside. "Then you're saying I should wait a year to propose to Lenora?"

"I'm not telling you what to do, Albert. You asked my advice, and all I know is what I told you."

His face clouded over. "Well, she probably won't have me anyway."

"There's only one way to find out; ask her."

There was not a doubt in my mind but what any woman would jump at the chance to marry him, but I didn't tell him that. I just wanted to get this thing over with.

"I guess you're right . . ." He toyed with his glass. A smile began to spread across his face. "Do you know that overlook on the Parkway, the one with the view that stretches for miles around? That's the place I've picked to propose to her. On the first clear day, when there's no haze, nothing to cloud the view, we'll drive up there in the late afternoon. That's when the sun is setting, the light is soft on the slopes, and the after-glow is showing in the sky. Lenora will love it, don't you think?"

"Yes." I was ready to leave that fancy restaurant. "Could we go now?"

"Dessert?"

I shook my head.

"Coffee?"

When I said no, he called the waiter, paid the check, and we left.

On the way home he did all the talking. Albert Ringstaff was a happy man.

24

All the girls were waiting for me in the day room, gorging on snacks and excited to hear my report. Before anyone could ask, I closed the door behind me and told them, "Girls, if you don't mind, I need to be alone for a while."

They stopped eating and stared at me.

"Cool it, girls," somebody said. "Give Miss E. some space, she needs some space."

I thanked them and went up the stairs. Lenora was in the parlor playing the piano.

Inside my room, I leaned my back against the door, closed my eyes, and wished I could just crawl in a hole and stay there for the rest of my life. I felt numb. *What a fool I've made of myself! How could I ever get it in my fool head that Albert Ringstaff would take a second look at me, much less propose marriage?*

I slid down, sat flat on the floor, and pulled off my earrings. Holding them in my hand, I thought of Bud.

Whatever in the world would he think of me if he knew what a fool I've been?

That little yellow bird was looking at me from the dresser. I sat looking back at it for some time. Then I got up, picked up the bird, and shut it away in a drawer. As I was standing there, I saw myself in the mirror. The face looking back at me wasn't mine. It belonged to some old fool that didn't have the sense God promised a billy goat.

I took off the necklace, turned the collar down like it was supposed to be, and started unbuttoning my jacket. I didn't feel like taking another shower—I'd just wash off all that makeup. Numb as I was, I went through the motions of getting ready for bed but knew I wouldn't sleep, so I sat in the chair. Out of force of habit, I reached for my Bible, then remembered I'd given it to Portia.

The longer I sat there, the harder it was to hold it all in. Tears rolled down my cheeks, my nose ran, and then—well, then, it all busted loose and I was bawling so hard my whole body shook.

They say you have to get something like this all out of your system before you can think straight. That may be, but it don't do much for the ache in the heart. I was hearing the clock ticking for an hour or so before I started coming to my senses.

After all, I told myself, *I don't have nothing in common with Albert Ringstaff except love for the Lord . . . Live Oaks is a long way off from New York City and all the places he's lived and traveled to.*

Of course, I knew that all along but, being a fool, I had just shut it out of my mind. *I have played the fool, haven't I, Lord? Maybe those two were made for each other—her and him. . . . They have lived most of their lives in that world of highbrow music—traveled all over the world and met all kinds of stylish people. I wouldn't fit in with all of that. Now that he's alone, he really needs somebody, and she needs somebody, too.*

I didn't need a husband. I had my work to do, and a man would just be in the way. Well, maybe not in the way . . .

Somebody was knocking on my door. *Now, who can that be?*

I went to open the door. It was Ursula, and she had been crying.

"What's the matter, Ursula?"

"It's Linda, Esmeralda. I caught her with her hand in the petty cash."

"Oh, I'm sorry. Here, sit down."

She sat on the other chair and was sniffling. She could hardly talk. "Esmeralda, I don't know how I could have been so stupid as to trust her. . . . It's just that she has so many problems and I was confident I was making progress with her. . . . Now I must dismiss her, send her home no better than when she came."

I put my hand over hers. "Well, Ursula, you must remember, when a person hardens their heart, there's nothing a body can do. The Lord don't go against nobody's will, but he cries over them same as you. You ever read that verse in Isaiah where God says about hard-headed people, 'All day long I have stretched out my hands unto

305

a disobedient and a gainsaying people'? Now, that's what he's saying about Linda."

"I know," she said, "but I feel so foolish. Why couldn't I see that she was playing games with me? She deceived me, Esmeralda!"

"Well, Ursula, don't feel bad. Sooner or later everybody in this kind of work gets conned."

"It's not only that, Esmeralda. What grieves me most is taking her word against yours about Portia. That was unconscionable. I should have listened to you and investigated thoroughly before making my decision."

"We all make mistakes, Ursula."

"Not like me. Priscilla Home is a different place since you came here. Morale has never been this good. They love you, Esmeralda, and I love you, too." She came over and put her arms around me and was just sobbing. "I guess it's . . . it's just my nature to be nasty." I held on to her, stroking her hair and trying to make her feel better. She really was a pitiful case—probably never had no mothering, no normal kind of life.

I held Ursula in my arms like that for a long time. When she got hold of herself, she got up and, still sniffling, talked some more. "I know you will forgive me, but I doubt the ladies will." She blew her nose and walked toward the door. "Tomorrow, I'm going to call them all together, confess how wrong I was about Portia, and beg their forgiveness."

"They'll forgive you," I said.

Standing with her hand on the knob, her shoulders drooping, she looked back at me. "Esmeralda . . . thank you."

"You go along to bed, Ursula. Get a good night's sleep. You'll feel better in the morning."

Long after she was back in her apartment, I sat there thinking about the whole situation. I was feeling even more guilty than Ursula. As much as I hated to see Portia leave Priscilla Home, I hated all the more to see Linda go. After all, Portia took the Lord with her, but Linda was yet a far cry from being a believer. I had failed that girl miserably. Failed to love her, failed to say the things I might have said. I felt so bad I couldn't ask the Lord to forgive me, I just asked him to have mercy on me.

The temptation to resign was mighty strong. Life would be so much easier back there in Live Oaks where there were no life-and-death problems—where I could live out my days without a care in the world and forget all about Albert Ringstaff.

I tell you, I mulled that over for some time before I got up to get in bed. I was about to turn out the lamp when I noticed the poem Portia had framed for me hanging on the wall above the TV. "Only one life . . ."

It came to me all at once. *There'll be other Lindas.* It made me think maybe the Lord was telling me something. It was true, there would be other Lindas, other Portias, and Evelyns, and Nancys.

I turned out the lamp and rolled over, satisfied that the Lord had laid claim on me for the rest of my life.

The next morning I was up by 4:30 and in the kitchen making Albert's fried apple pies, and I was singing:

> What a Friend we have in Jesus,
> All our sins and griefs to bear!
> What a privilege to carry
> Everything to God in prayer!

I looked up. There she was leaning against the door-frame. "Good morning, Dora."

Epilogue

Dear Beatrice,

Since you and Carl faithfully support this work, you deserve to hear how the Lord has worked here. I came to Priscilla Home four years ago, and the women who were the first ones I knew have now had time to prove themselves one way or another. As you know, Lenora married Albert Ringstaff, and they seem happy. She doesn't know much about making a home for him, but they have their music. He asked me to teach his wife how to make fried apple pies, but she never got the hang of it, so I still make them for him. For my birthday they gave me a leather-bound King James Bible.

Portia is still using my old Bible. She works at a fish cannery, and she asks me to pray for the workers she's trying to win to the Lord. Every time she gets paid she sends us five dollars.

I don't know much about Linda. She talks to Ursula, tells her she's collecting money to buy us a tractor. So far she hasn't sent us anything.

When Boris Krantz and Lucy brought the youth group up here on a mission trip, Angela started flirting with Boris. Poor Lucy, she was no match for that blue-eyed blonde with the cute figure. Angela packed up and went back with the group to Live Oaks. She and Boris got married, and now they have a baby. Clara tells me it's a rocky marriage.

The board hired Nancy to be on staff as my assistant, and she's doing a good job. Martha comes back for a visit every summer and brings her little girl. Samantha is in the third grade now.

Melba went back to her old job as a beauty supply salesman. Before she left, she told us she had done some modeling. Her hands are the ones you see on packages of press-on nails, and her legs are pictured on a hair-removal product. The good thing is, because Emily has such pretty red hair, Melba persuaded her to try out as a model for hair color products. Well, Emily was hired, and with the money she got modeling, she's opened her own aerobics studio. Her sister handles the book work, and their business is getting off the ground. The last time I talked to her, she said she had not only kicked heroin, but she had also quit smoking.

It hurts me to think about Evelyn. While she was here she had a serious crisis—she was bleeding so bad we had to rush her to the hospital. Ursula called her parents, and they came that night. Ursula had a conference with them and told them the major cause of Evelyn's disorder was due to their controlling her. Evelyn's daddy got so mad he yanked Evelyn out of Priscilla Home and took her home. We never heard another word about her until some months later when Wilma saw her obituary in the newspaper and called us. Albert led a memorial service for her in the parlor, and the Valley Church trio sang.

Before Wilma left P.H., she told me she needed a job that gave her more time at home to be with her thirteen-year-old daughter. She had never taken the child to church, and because she was a long distance truck driver, there was no way she could. But she said she couldn't afford to quit, that trucking paid more than other jobs she could get.

Well, a funny thing happened. Wilma had a delivery to make in New York City. She made a wrong turn and wound up going the wrong way on a one-way street! That blocked traffic for some time and cost her company a big fine, so they fired her. Wilma was out of work for a year, except for driving a school bus. But now she's got a good job delivering the mail. She and her daughter never miss a service at church.

You remember Brenda is a hairdresser. Well, a preacher come in the shop to have his hair cut. That's when it all started. She went back to the Methodist church where he preached, they courted, and when the bishop moved him to Virginia, they got married. She lives up there now.

Now let me tell you about Dora. When she graduated,

Albert gave her a harmonica that he ordered out of New York and told her it had all the notes she would need to play anything she wanted. I didn't think much of that. Dora could have used the money a lot better. Albert had given P.H. a recorder and a lot of tapes with high-class music, and since Dora was the only one who ever listened to them, I told her to take them home with her.

Before she left, we had a good talk about how she was going to pay those medical bills now that she wasn't going to grow pot. She had it all planned. Said she had beehives and would sell sourwood honey and that there was "wind-throwed" trees on her property that she was going to saw into firewood and sell by the truckload. And there was still ginseng growing up on a slope and some other herbs she could sell.

It wasn't everything, but maybe it would bring in enough to keep paying along on those bills.

Well, it didn't work out so good. She wrote that by the time she got home, a bear had robbed the hives. The next thing we heard, somebody had sneaked onto her property and harvested all the "sang," as she called it. Still, that winter she managed by selling firewood. That is, until her truck broke down.

For more than a year we didn't hear one word from Dora. Then one day here come a money order from her for five hundred dollars! As glad as we were to get the money, it worried me a little. In a few weeks here come another money order for one thousand dollars! My worst fears had to be true—Dora was growing pot again!

As time went on, we continued getting money from Dora. Finally, Ursula and I agreed this had to be drug money, and she decided to ask the board if we should accept it.

Then one day I was in the garden when Ursula flung open the window of the apartment and yelled for me to come up there immediately. I dropped the hoe and went flying up the steps. Ursula was standing wide-eyed before the TV. "It's Dora! Dora's on TV!"

Lo and behold, it was—our Dora standing on stage, still wearing that old hunting coat!

"That's Carnegie Hall," Ursula told me. "It's some kind of festival. Shhh, they're introducing her."

I was so excited I don't remember all that the announcer said, but it was about her being a recording artist. Then the orchestra started playing, and Dora put that mouth organ to her lips, closed her eyes, and laid into making music such as you won't get no other place but heaven. It was strong music, and in my mind's eye I could see that old chimney standing against a gale; I heard the roar of the falls and felt the wet cold of that day. And then the music changed. It was gentle and sweet, warm as the little candle flickering inside of her.

When her playing ended, people jumped to their feet clapping and hollering—whistling through their teeth. The man in a tuxedo came out and stopped Dora from going off stage. He held her there waiting for the applause to die down. They just kept on clapping!

Finally the man got them quiet, and they sat down to hear what he had to say. By then Ursula had out her clipboard to write down what he said. "Ladies and gentlemen, this young lady has given us the rare gift of musical genius." More applause. "Since Miss Dora's first recording was released, musical critics have been mesmerized by her astounding interpretive rendition of the classics. PBS is offering her a contract for a solo concert next season, but she has not decided whether or not to sign." A ripple of laughter went through the audience. "She may not! In fact, it took considerable coaxing to persuade this artist to leave her home in Tennessee to come to this city and perform in this historic hall." He turned to Dora. "Miss Dora, it is you who have made history here tonight. Never again will the harmonica be relegated to hobo camps, prisons, and cowboy campfires."

The people stood up, cheering and still clapping when the camera turned to a commercial.

Well, Beatrice, it's almost time for Praise and Prayer, so I'll sign off. Tell Carl not to take no wooden nickels.

Yours very truly,

Esmeralda

Acknowledgments

I am indebted to Franz Mohr, author of *My Life with the Great Pianists,* for technical information on the Steinway piano, with apologies to Elizabeth, his wife, for modeling a character after her husband!

Jennie Free and Elizabeth Dagley, my sisters, and two friends, Alvera Mickelsen and Jean Abrahamsen, read the manuscript and offered significant insights. Without my agent, Joyce Hart, who put me in touch with Baker/Revell and facilitated the business between us, this novel would never have been published.

No matter how good a book may be, without the expertise of acquisition people, editors, copyeditors, artists, publicists, production personnel, and sales representatives, it would not be successful. I am indebted to the gifted Baker/Revell staff who have worked hard to give *Good Heavens* such a splendid send-off: Karen Steele, Karen Campbell, Lonnie Hull Dupont, Twila Bennett, Sheila Ingram, Kristin Kornoelje, Cheryl Van Andel, Ruth Waybrant, Marilyn Gordon, and Chris Tobias (the artist who created the eye-catching cover).

Margaret Graham is the author of seven nonfiction books, one juvenile work of fiction, and three novels, including *Mercy Me*. She conveys her deep love of the Scriptures as a speaker, Bible teacher, and newspaper columnist. Graham resides in Sumter, South Carolina.